TITHE

A MODERN FAERIE TALE

HOLLY BLACK

SIMON &
SCHUSTER

SIMON &
SCHUSTER

First published in Great Britain by Simon & Schuster UK Ltd, 2003
A Viacom company

Originally published in 2002 by Simon & Schuster Inc. New York.
Copyright © Holly Black, 2002

Book design by Paul Zakris
The text for this book is set in Meridien

1 3 5 7 9 10 8 6 4 2

Simon & Schuster UK Ltd
Africa House
64-78 Kingsway
London WC2B 6AH

A CIP catalogue record for this book is available from the British Library

ISBN 0689837070

Printed and bound in Finland by WS Bookwell

TITHE

For my little sister Heidi

I am grateful to my kind editor, Kevin Lewis, for his patience; to my dear friends Steve Berman, Dianna Muzaurieta, and Frank Burkhead for their brutal and inventive comments; to Katja Byrne for telling me it was a YA novel in the first place; to Tony DiTerlizzi and Angela DeFrancis for hand-holding above and beyond the call of duty; and to Theo for enduring the misery along the way. In addition, I am indebted to my first readers: Caitlin, Ed, Gram, Jay, Jenni, Judy, Joe, Jon, Katherine, and Mike.

"And pleasant is the faerie land
But an eerie tale to tell,
Ay at the end of seven years
We pay a tithe to Hell;
I am sae fair and fu o flesh,
I'm feard it be mysel."

— "YOUNG TAM LIN"

Prologue

*"And malt does more than Milton can
To justify God's ways to man."*

— A. E. HOUSMAN,
"Terence, This Is Stupid Stuff"

Kaye took another drag on her cigarette and dropped it into her mother's beer bottle. She figured that would be a good test for how drunk Ellen was – see if she would swallow a butt whole.

They were up on stage still, Ellen and Lloyd and the rest of Stepping Razor. It had been a bad set and watching them break down the equipment, she could see that they knew it. It didn't really matter, the sound system was loud and scratchy and everyone had kept drinking and smoking and shouting so she doubted the manager minded. There had even been a little dancing.

The bartender leered at her again and offered her a drink "on the house."

"Milk," Kaye smirked, brushing back her

ragged, blonde hair and pocketing a couple of matchbooks when his back was turned.

Then her mother was next to her, taking a deep swallow of the beer before spitting it all over the counter.

Kaye couldn't help the wicked laughter that escaped her lips before she thought better of it. Her mother looked at her in disbelief.

"Go help load up the car," Ellen said, voice hoarse from singing. She was smoothing damp hair back from her face. Her lipstick was rubbed off the inside of her lips but still clung to the edges of her mouth, smudged a little. She looked tired.

Kaye slid off the counter and leapt up onto the stage in one easy move. Lloyd glared at her as she started to pick up the stuff randomly, so she stuck to what was her mother's. His eyes were glazed. "Hey kid, got any money on you?"

Kaye shrugged and took out a ten-dollar bill. She had more, and he probably knew it – she'd come straight from Chow Fat's. Delivering Chinese takeaways might pay crap, but it still paid better than being in a band.

He took the money and ambled off to the bar, probably to get some beer to go.

Kaye picked up Ellen's stuff and started hauling it through the crowd. People mostly got out of her way. The cool autumn air outside the bar was a welcome relief, even stinking as it was with iron and exhaust fumes and the subways. The city always smelled like metal to Kaye.

It only took her a few minutes to get the car loaded up. She went back inside, intent on getting her mother in the car before someone smashed the window and stole the equipment. You couldn't leave anything in a car in Philly. The last time Ellen's car had been broken into, they'd done it for a secondhand coat and a bag of towels.

The girl checking IDs at the door took a long look at her this time but didn't say anything. It was late anyway, almost last call. Ellen was still at the bar, smoking a cigarette and drinking something stronger than beer. Lloyd was talking to a guy with long, dark hair. The man looked out of place in the bar, too well dressed or something, but Lloyd had an arm slung over the man's shoulder. She caught a flash of the man's eyes. Cat-yellow, reflecting in the dark bar. Kaye shivered.

But then, Kaye saw odd things sometimes. She'd learned to ignore them.

"Car's loaded," Kaye told her mother.

Ellen nodded, barely listening. "Can I have a cigarette, honey?"

Kaye fished the pack out of her army-surplus satchel and took out two, handing one to her mother and lighting the other.

Her mother bent close, the smell of whiskey

and beer and sweat as familiar as any perfume to Kaye. "Cigarette kiss," her mother said in that goofy way that was embarrassing and sweet at the same time, touching the tip of her cigarette to the red tip of Kaye's and breathing in deeply. Two sucks of smoke and it flared to life.

"Ready to go home?" Lloyd asked, and Kaye almost jumped. It wasn't that she hadn't known he was there; it was the sound of his voice. It sounded velvety, a shade off of sleazy. Not normal asshole Lloyd voice. Not at all.

Ellen didn't seem to notice anything. She swallowed what was left of her drink. "Sure."

A moment later, Lloyd lifted his arm as though he were going to punch Ellen in the back. Kaye reacted without thinking, shoving him. It was only his drunkenness that made her slight weight enough to push him off balance. She saw the knife as it clattered to the floor.

Lloyd's face was completely blank, empty of any emotion at all. His eyes were wide and his pupils dilated.

Frank, Stepping Razor's drummer, grabbed Lloyd's arm. Lloyd had just enough time to punch Frank in the face before other patrons tackled him and somebody called the police.

By the time the police got there, Lloyd couldn't remember anything. He was mad as hell, though, cursing Ellen at the top of his lungs. The police drove Kaye and her mother to Lloyd's apartment and waited while Kaye packed their clothes and stuff into plastic rubbish bags. Ellen was on the phone, trying to find a place for them to crash.

"Honey," Ellen said finally, "we're going to have to go to Grandma's."

"Did you call her?" Kaye asked, stacking her Grace Slick vinyl albums into an empty orange crate. They hadn't so much as visited once in the six years that they'd been gone from New Jersey. Ellen barely even spoke to her mother at Christmas before passing the phone to Kaye.

"Yeah, I just woke her up." Kaye couldn't remember the last time her mother had sounded quite so tired. "It'll just be a little while. You can visit that friend of yours."

"Janet," Kaye said. She hoped that was who Ellen meant. She hoped her mother wasn't teasing her about that faerie bullshit again. If she had to hear another story about Kaye and her cute imaginary friends . . .

"The one you e-mail from the library. Get me another cigarette, okay, hon?" Ellen tossed a bunch of CDs into the crate.

Kaye picked up a leather jacket of Lloyd's she'd always liked and lit a cigarette for her mother off the gas ring. No sense in wasting matches.

1

"Coercive as coma, frail as bloom
innuendoes of your inverse dawn
suffuse the self;
our every corpuscle become an elf."

— MINA LOY,
"Moreover, the Moon,"
The Lost Lunar Baedeker

Kaye spun down the worn, grey planks of the boardwalk. The air was heavy and stank of drying mussels and the crust of salt on the jetties. Waves tossed themselves against the shore, dragging grit and sand between their nails as they were slowly pulled back out to sea.

The moon was high and pale in the sky, but the sun was just going down.

It was so good to be able to *breathe*, Kaye thought. She loved the serene brutality of the ocean, loved the electric power she felt with each breath of wet, briny air. She spun again, dizzily, not caring that her skirt was flying up over the tops of her black thigh-high stockings.

"Come on," Janet called. She stepped over the overflowing, leaf-choked gutter along the street

HOLLY BLACK

parallel to the boardwalk, wobbling slightly on fat-heeled platform shoes. Her glitter makeup sparkled under the street lamps. Janet exhaled ghosts of blue smoke and took another drag on her cigarette. "You're going to fall."

Kaye and her mother had been staying at her grandmother's a week already, and even though Ellen kept saying they'd be leaving soon, Kaye knew they really had nowhere to go. Kaye was glad. She loved the big old house caked with dust and mothballs. She liked the sea being so close and the air not stinging in her throat.

The cheap hotels they passed were long closed and boarded up, their pools drained and cracked. Even the arcades were shut down, prizes in the claw machines still visible through the cloudy glass windows. Rust marks above an abandoned shopfront outlined the words CANDY FLOSS.

Janet dug through her tiny bag and pulled out a wand of strawberry lipgloss. Kaye spun up to her, fake leopard coat flying open, a ladder already in her stocking. Her boots had sand stuck to them.

"Let's go swimming," Kaye said. She was giddy with night air, burning like the white-hot moon. Everything smelled wet and feral like it did before a thunderstorm, and she wanted to run, swift and eager, beyond the edge of what she could see.

"The water's freezing," Janet said, sighing, "and your hair is fucked up. Kaye, when we get there, you have to be cool. Don't seem so weird. Guys don't like weird."

Kaye paused and seemed to be listening intently, her upturned, kohl-rimmed eyes watching Janet as warily as a cat's. "What should I be like?"

"It's not that I want you to be a certain way – don't you want a boyfriend?"

"Why bother with that? Let's find incubi."

"Incubi?"

"Demons. Plural. Like octopi. And we're much more likely to find them" – her voice dropped conspiratorially – "while swimming naked in the Atlantic a week before Halloween than practically anywhere else I can think of."

Janet rolled her eyes.

"You know what the sun looks like?" Kaye asked. There was only a little more than a slice of red where the sea met the sky.

"No, what?" Janet said, holding the lipgloss out to Kaye.

"Like he slit his wrists in a bathtub and the blood is all over the water."

"That's gross, Kaye."

"And the moon is just watching. She's just watching him die. She must have driven him to it."

"Kaye . . ."

Kaye spun again, laughing.

"Why are you always making shit up? That's what I mean by weird." Janet was speaking loudly, but Kaye could barely hear her over the wind and the sound of her own laughter.

"C'mon, Kaye. Remember the faeries you used to tell stories about? What was his name?"

"Which one? Spike or Gristle?"

"Exactly. You made them up!" Janet said. "You always make things up."

Kaye stopped spinning, cocking her head to one side, fingers sliding into her pockets. "I didn't say I didn't."

The old merry-go-round building had been semi-abandoned for years. Angelic lead faces, surrounded by rays of hair, divided the broken panes. The entire front of it was windowed, revealing the dirt floor, glass glittering against the refuse. Inside, a crude plywood skateboarding ramp was the only remains of an attempt to use the building commercially in the last decade.

Kaye could hear voices echoing in the still air all the way out to the street. Janet dropped her cigarette into the gutter. It hissed and was quickly carried away, sitting on the water like a spider.

Kaye hoisted herself up onto the outside ledge and swung her legs over. The window had been long gone, but her leg scraped against the residue as she slid in, fraying her stockings further.

Layers of paint thickly covered the once-intricate mouldings inside the carousel building. The ramp in the centre of the room was tagged by local spray-paint artists and covered with band stickers and ballpoint pen scrawlings. And there were the boys.

"Kaye Fierch, you remember me, right?" Doughboy chuckled. He was short and thin, despite his name.

"I think you threw a bottle at my head when we were eleven."

He laughed again. "Right. Right. I forgot that. You're not still mad?"

"No," she said, but her blithe mood was gone, leaving her drained and anxious. Janet climbed on top of the skateboard ramp to where Kenny was sitting, a king in his silver flight jacket, watching the proceedings. Handsome, with dark hair and darker eyes. He held up a nearly full bottle of tequila in greeting.

Marcus handed Kaye the bottle he was drinking from, making a mock throwing motion as he did so. A little splashed on the sleeve of his flannel shirt. "Bourbon. Expensive shit."

She forced a smile as she took it. Marcus resumed gutting a cigar. Even hunched over, he was a big guy. The brown skin on his head gleamed, and she could see where he must have nicked himself shaving it.

"I brought you some sweets," Janet said to Kenny. She had candy corn and peanut chews.

"I brought you some sweets," Doughboy mocked in a high, squeaky voice, jumping up on the ramp. "Give it here," he said.

Kaye walked around the round room. It was magnificent, old and decayed and fine. The slow burn of bourbon in her throat was perfect for this place, the sort of thing a man in a summer suit who always wore a hat might drink.

"What flavour of Oriental are you?" Marcus asked. He had filled the cigar with weed and was chomping down on one end. The thick, sweet smell almost choked her.

She took another swallow from the bottle and tried to ignore him.

"Kaye! You hear me?"

"I'm half Japanese." Kaye touched her hair, blonde as her mother's. It was the hair that baffled people.

"Man, you ever see the cartoons there? They have them little, little girls with these pigtails and shit in these short school uniforms. We should have uniforms like that here, man. You ever wear one of those, huh?"

"Shut up, dickhead," Janet said, laughing. "She went to grade school with Doughboy and me."

Kenny looped one finger through the belt rings of Janet's jeans and pulled her over to kiss her.

"Yeah, well, damn." Marcus laughed. "Won't you hold up your hair in those pigtails for a second or something? Come on."

Kaye shook her head. No, she wouldn't.

Marcus and Doughboy started to play football with an empty beer bottle. It didn't break as they kicked it boot to boot, but it made a hollow sound. She took another long sip of bourbon. Her head was already buzzing pleasantly, humming in time with imagined merry-go-round music. She moved farther back into the dim room, to where old placards announced popcorn and peanuts for five cents apiece.

Against the far wall was a black, weathered door. It opened jerkily when she pushed it. Moonlight from the windows in the main room revealed only an office with an old desk and a corkboard with yellowed menus still pinned to it. She stepped inside, even though the light switch didn't work. Feeling in the blackness, she found a knob. This door led to a stairwell with only a little light drifting down from the top. She felt her way up the stairs. Dust covered the palms of her hand as she slid them along the railings. She sneezed loudly, then sneezed again.

At the top was a small window lit brightly by the murderess moon, ripe and huge in the sky. Interesting boxes were stacked in the corners. Then her eyes fell on the horse, and she forgot all the rest. He was magnificent –

HOLLY BLACK

gleaming pearl white and covered with tiny pieces of glued-down mirror. His face was painted with red and purple and gold, and he even had a bar of white teeth and a painted pink tongue with enough space to tuck a sugar cube. It was obvious why he'd been left behind – his legs on all four sides and part of his tail had been shattered. Splinters hung down from where his legs used to be.

Gristle would have loved this. She had thought that many times since she had left the Shore, six years past. *My imaginary friends would have loved this.* She'd thought it the first time that she'd seen the city, lit up like never-ending Christmas. But they never came when she was in Philadelphia. And now she was sixteen and felt like she had no imagination left.

She tried to set the horse up as if he were standing on his ruined stumps. It wobbled unsteadily but didn't fall. Kaye pulled off her coat and dropped it on the dusty floor, setting the bourbon next to it. She swung one leg over the beast and dropped onto its saddle, using her feet to keep it from falling. She ran her hands down its mane, which was carved in golden ringlets. She touched the painted black eyes and the chipped ears.

The white horse rose on unsteady legs in her mind. The long curls of the gold mane were cool in her hands, and the great bulk of the animal was real and warm beneath her. She wove her hands in the mane and gripped hard, slightly aware of a prickling feeling all through her limbs. The horse whinnied softly beneath her, ready to leap out into the cold, black water. She threw back her head.

"Kaye?" A soft voice snapped her out of her daydream. Kenny was standing near the stairs, regarding her blankly. For a moment, though, she was still fierce. Then she felt her cheeks burning.

Caught in the half-light, she could see him better than she had downstairs. Two heavy silver hoops shone in the lobes of his ears. His short, cinnamon hair was mussed and had a slight wave to it, matching the beginnings of a goatee on his chin. Under the flight jacket, his too-tight white T-shirt showed the easy muscles of someone who was born with them.

He moved towards her, reaching his hand out and then looking at it oddly, as though he didn't remember deciding to do that. Instead he petted the head of the horse, slowly, almost hypnotically.

"I saw you," he said. "I saw what you did."

"Where's Janet?" Kaye wasn't sure what he meant. She would have thought he was teasing her except for his serious face, his slow way of speaking.

He was stroking the animal's mane now. "She was worried about you." His hand fascinated her despite herself. It seemed like he was tangling it in imaginary hair. "How did you make it do that?"

"Do what?" She was afraid now, afraid and flattered both. There was no mocking or teasing in his face. He was watching her so intensely that he seemed drained of expression.

"I saw it stand up." His voice was so low she could almost pretend that she didn't hear him right. His hand dropped to her thigh and slid upward to the cotton crotch of her knickers.

Even through she had seen the slow progression of his hand, the touch startled her. She was paralysed for a moment before she sprang up, letting the horse fall as she did. It crashed down, knocking the bottle of bourbon over, dark spirits pouring over her coat and soaking the bottoms of the dusty boxes like the tide coming in at night.

He grabbed for her before she could think, his hand catching hold of the neck of her shirt. She stepped back, off-balance, and fell, her shirt ripping open over her bra even as he let go of it.

Shoes pounded up the stairs.

"What the fuck?" Marcus was at the top of the stairwell with Doughboy, trying to shove his way in for a look.

Kenny shook his head and looked around numbly while Kaye scrambled for her bourbon-soaked coat.

The boys moved out of the way, and Janet was there, too, staring.

"What happened?" Janet asked, looking between them in confusion. Kaye pushed past her, shoving her hand through an armhole of the coat as she threw it over her back.

"Kaye!" Janet called after her.

Kaye ignored her, taking the stairs two at a time in the dark. There was nothing she could say that would explain what had happened.

She could hear Janet shouting. "What did you do to her? What the fuck did you do?"

Kaye ran across the carousel hall and swung her leg over the sill. The glass she had carefully avoided earlier slashed a thin line on the outside of her thigh as she dropped among the sandy soil and weeds.

The cold wind felt good against her hot face.

Cornelius Stone picked up the new box of computer crap and hauled it into his bedroom to drop next to the others. Each time his mother came home from the flea market with a cracked monitor, sticky keyboard, or just loads of wires, she had that hopeful look that made Corny want to hit her. She just couldn't comprehend the difference between a 286 and a quantum computer. She couldn't understand that the age of guerilla engineering was at a close, that being a motherfucking genius wasn't enough. You needed to be a rich motherfucking genius.

He dropped the box, kicked it hard three times, picked up his denim jacket with the devil's head on the back, and made for the door.

"Can you use that stuff, honey?" His mother was in Janet's room, folding a new pair of secondhand jeans. She held up a T-shirt with rhinestone cats on it. "Think your sister will like it?"

"Thanks, Mum," he said through gritted teeth. "I've got to get to work." He walked past The Husband, who was stooped over, getting a beer from the case under the kitchen table. The white cat was waddling along the countertop, its belly dragging with another pregnancy, screaming for tinned food or pickles and ice cream or something. He petted its head grudgingly, but before it began rubbing against his hand in earnest, he opened the screen door and went outside.

The cool October air was a relief from the recirculated cigarette smoke.

Corny loved his car. It was a primer-coloured Chevy blooming with rust spots and an inner lining that hung like baggy skin from the roof. He knew what he looked like. Beaky. Skinny and tall with bad hair and worse skin. He lived up to his name. Cornelius. Corny. Corn-dog. But not in his car. Inside, he was anonymous.

Every day for the last three weeks he had

left a little earlier for work. He would go to the convenience store and buy some food. Then he would drive around, cruise past all the local rutting joints, imagining he had a semiautomatic rifle in the car and counting how many he could have got. "Pow," he'd say, softly, to rolled-up windows as a brown-haired boy with broad shoulders and a backwards baseball cap ran up to the giggling girls behind the window of a red truck. "Pow. Pow."

Tonight, he bought a cup of coffee and a package of black liquorice. He lingered over a paperback with an embossed metallic dragon on the cover, reading the first few sentences, hoping something would interest him. The game was becoming boring. Worse than boring, it made him feel more pathetic than before. Nearly a week before Hallowe'en and all, this was the point when a real maniac would go and get a gun. He sipped at the coffee and almost spat it out. Too sweet. He sipped at it some more, steeling himself to the taste. Disgusting.

Corny got out of his car and chucked the full coffee into the car park. It splashed satisfactorily on the asphalt. He went inside and poured himself another cup. From behind the counter, a matronly woman with frizzy red hair looked him over and pointed to his jacket. "Who are you supposed to be, the devil?"

"I wish," Corny said, dropping a dollar twenty-five on the counter. "I wish."

2

"The stones were sharp,
The wind came at my back;
Walking along the highway,
Mincing like a cat."

— THEODORE ROETHKE, "Praise to the
End!"

The wind whipped tiny pebbles of rain across Kaye's face. The droplets froze her hands, making her shiver as they slid down her wet hair and under the collar of her coat. She walked, head down, kicking the scattered rubbish that had eddied up on the grassy shores along the highway. A flattened drinks can skittered into a sodden chrysanthemum-covered foam heart, staked there to mark the site of a car crash. There were no houses on this side of the road, just a long stretch of wet woods leading up to a petrol station. She was over halfway home.

Cars hissed over the asphalt. The sound was comforting, like a long sigh.

I saw you. I saw what you did.

Awfulness twisted in her stomach, awfulness and anger. She wanted to smash something, hit someone.

How could she have done anything? When she tried to make a magazine page turn on its own or a penny land on heads, it never worked. How could she have made Kenny see a broken-legged carousel horse move?

Never mind that she might as well assume that Spike and Lutie and Gristle *had* been imaginary. She'd been home for two weeks, and there was no sign of them, no matter how many times she had called them, no matter how many bowls of milk she left out, no matter how many times she went down to the old creek.

She took a deep breath, snorting rain up her nose. It reminded her of crying.

The trees seemed like flat lead panels missing the stained glass to fit between their branches. She knew what her grandmother was going to say when she got back, stinking of alcohol with a torn shirt. True things.

The same things that Janet would say tomorrow. There was no way to explain what had happened without admitting to something. His hand on her leg was what Janet would really care about – that, and that she had let it rest there, even if only for a moment. And she could imagine what he was telling Janet now –

flushed, angry, and drunk – but even a badly managed lie would sound better than the truth.

I saw it stand up.

But even if he didn't go that far, who would believe that he touched her crotch on purpose, but ripped her shirt by accident? No, he must have told an entirely different story. So what was Kaye supposed to say when Janet asked what happened? Janet thought she was a liar already.

She could still feel the heat of Kenny's hand, a stroke of fire along her thigh in contrast to her otherwise rain-soaked skin.

Another gust of rain stung her cheeks, this one bringing a shout with it from the direction of the woods. The noise was brief, but eloquent with pain. Kaye stopped abruptly. There was no sound except the rain, hissing like radio static.

Then, just as a truck sped past, kicking up a cloud of drizzle, she heard another sound. Softer, this one, maybe a moan bitten off at the end. It was just inside the copse of trees.

Kaye moved down the slight slope, off the short grass and into the woods. She ducked under the dripping branches of an elm, stepping on tufts of short ferns and looping briars. Weeds brushed across her calves, leaving strokes of rain. The storm-bright sky lit the woods with silver. An earthy, sweet odour of rot bloomed where she disturbed the carpet of leaves.

There was no one there.

She half turned towards the highway. She could still see the road from where she was standing. What was she doing? The sound must have carried over from the houses beyond the thin river that ran along the back of the woods. No one else would be dumb enough to go trooping through wet, dripping woods in the middle of the night.

Kaye walked back up to the road, picking her way through spots that looked somewhat drier than others. Burrs had collected along her stockings, and she bent down to pull them off.

"Stay where you are." She jumped at the voice. The accent was rich and strange, though the words were pronounced precisely.

A man was sprawled in the mud only a few steps from her, clutching a curved sword in one hand. It shone like a sliver of moonlight in the hazy dark. Long pewter hair, plastered wetly to his neck, framed a face that was long and full of sharp angles. Rivulets of rain ran over the jointed black armour he wore. His other hand was at his heart, clutching a branch that jutted from his chest. The rain there was tinted pink with blood.

"Was it you, girl?" He was breathing raggedly.

Kaye wasn't sure what he meant, but she shook her head. He didn't look much older than she was. Certainly not old enough to call her "girl."

"So you haven't come to finish me off?"

She shook her head again. He was long-limbed – he would be tall if he were standing. Taller than most people, taller than any faerie she had ever seen – still, she had no doubt that was what he was, if for no other reason than the pointed tops of his ears knifing through his wet hair – and that he was beautiful in a way that made her breath catch.

He licked his lips. There was blood on them. "Pity," he said quietly.

She took a step towards him, and he twisted into a defensive crouch. Wounded as he was, he still moved swiftly. Hair fell forward across his face, but his eyes, shining like mercury, studied her intently.

"You're a faerie, aren't you?" she said soothingly, holding her hands where he could see them. She had heard stories of the court fey – the Gentry – from Lutie-loo, but she had never seen one. Maybe that was what he was.

He stayed still, and she took another half step towards him, holding out one hand to coax him as if he were some fascinating, dangerous animal. "Let me help you."

His body was trembling with concentration. His eyes never flickered from her face. He held the hilt of his sword in a white-knuckled grip.

She did not dare take another step. "You're going to bleed to death."

They stayed like that a few more minutes

before he slumped down to one knee in the mud. He bent forward, fingers clutching the leaves, and spat red. The wet lashes over his half-closed eyes were as silver as a safety pin.

She took two steps and knelt down next to him, bracing herself with shaking hands. This close, she could see that his armour was stiff leather sculpted to look like feathers.

"I cannot draw the arrow myself," he said softly. "They are waiting for me to bleed a little more before they come against my blade."

"Who is waiting?" It was hard to understand that someone had shot him with a tree branch, but that seemed to be what he was saying.

"If you would help me, draw this arrow." His eyes narrowed, and he shook his head. "If not, then push it in as deep as you can and hope that it kills me."

"It will bleed more," Kaye said.

He laughed at that, a bitter sound. "Either way, no doubt."

She could see the despair in his face. He obviously believed her to be part of some plan to kill him. Still, he slid his body back until he could lean against the trunk of an oak. He was braced, waiting to see what she would do.

She thought of the faeries she had known when she was a child – impish, quick things – no mention of wars or magical arrows or enemies, certainly no lies, no deception. The man bleeding in the dirt beside her told her how wrong her perceptions of *Faery* had been.

Her fingers flinched away from the wound in his chest. Her lungs turned to ice as she looked at the grisly wound. "I can't do it."

His voice stayed soft. "What do they call you?"

"Kaye," she said. There was silence for a moment as she noticed the cold cloud of her breath rise up with the word.

"I'm Roiben." Faeries didn't give their names easily, even part of their names, although she had no idea why. He was trying to show her that he trusted her, maybe trying to make up for the assumptions he had made about her. "Give me your hand."

She let him take her hand in his and guide it to the branch. His hand closed over hers, both of them chilled and wet, his fingers inhumanly long and rough with calluses. "Just close your hand on it and let me pull," he said. "You don't even have to look. As long as I'm not touching it, I might be able to draw it out."

That shamed her. She had told him that she wanted to help him, he was in a whole lot of pain, and it was no time for her to be squeamish. "I'll do it," she said.

Roiben let go of her hand, and she gave a sharp tug. Although his face constricted with pain, the branch only pulled out a short way.

Were there really other faerie folk in the

trees, waiting for him to be weak enough to defeat? Kaye thought that if so, now was a great time for them to come down and have a go at it.

"Again, Kaye."

She took note of the angle of the armour this time, changing her position so that the branch couldn't catch on one of the plates. She raised herself to one knee, braced, and then stood, pulling upwards as hard as she could.

Roiben gave a harsh cry as the branch slid free of his chest, its iron tip black with blood. His fingers touched the wound and he raised them, slick with blood, as if suddenly disbelieving that he had been shot.

"Very brave," he said, touching his wet fingers to her leg.

Kaye tossed the stick away from her. She was shuddering, and she could taste the ghost of blood in her mouth. "We have to stop the bleeding. How does your armour come off?"

He seemed not to understand her at first. He just looked at her with a kind of incredulity. Then he leaned forward with a groan. "Straps," he managed.

She came and sat behind him, feeling over the smooth armour for buckles.

A sudden wind shook the branches above, raining an extra shower of heavy droplets down on them, and Kaye wondered again about faeries in the trees. Her fingers fumbled in her haste. If those faeries were still afraid of Roiben, they didn't have to worry for much longer – she was betting that it would be only a few more minutes before he passed out entirely.

To get off his breastplate, she not only had to detach it from the backplate at his shoulders and sides – there were also straps that connected it to the shoulderplates and to his legplates. Finally, she managed to peel it off his chest. Underneath, the bare skin was mottled with blood.

He tipped back his head and closed his eyes. "Let the rain clean it."

She pulled off her coat and hung it on one of the branches of the tree. Her shirt was ripped already, she reminded herself as she took it off. She tore it into long strips and began winding them around Roiben's chest and arms. He opened his eyes when she touched him. His eyes narrowed, then widened. Their colour was mesmerising.

He straightened up, horrified. "I didn't even hear you rip the cloth."

"You have to try to stay awake." Kaye's cheeks felt so warm that the cold rain actually felt good against them. "Is there somewhere you can go?"

He shook his head. Fumbling near him, he picked up a leaf and wiped it against the underside of the leather breastplate. It came away shining red. "Drop this in the stream. I – there is a kelpie there – it is no sure thing that I will be able to control her in this weather, but it is something."

Kaye nodded quickly, although she had no idea what a kelpie was, and made to take the leaf.

He did not let it go immediately. "I am in your debt. I mislike not knowing how I must repay it."

"I have questions . . ."

He let her take the leaf. "I will answer three, as full and well as is within my power."

She nodded. Like a faerie tale. Fine; it wasn't as if she had wanted anything from him anyway.

"When you drop the leaf in the water, say Roiben of the Unseelie Court asks for your aid."

"Say to what?"

"Just say it aloud."

She nodded again and ran in the direction of the water. The steep bank of the stream was choked with vegetation and broken glass. Roots, swept bare of the mud that should have surrounded them, sat above the bank like over-turned baskets or ran along the ground like the pale arms of half-buried corpses. She forbade herself to think of that again.

She squatted down and set the leaf, blood side down, into the water. It floated there, spinning a little. She wondered if it was too close to the bank, and tried to blow it farther out.

"Roiben of the Unseelie Court asks for your help," she said, hoping that she had got it right. Nothing happened. She said it again, louder, feeling foolish and frightened at the same time. "Roiben of the Unseelie Court needs your help."

A frog surfaced and began to swim in her direction. Would that have something to do with a kelpie? What kind of help were they supposed to get from a shallow, polluted stream?

But then she saw that she had been mistaken. What she had taken for the eyes of a frog were actually hollow pits that quavered as *something* swam through the water towards her. She wanted to run, but fascination combined with obligation to root her to the spot. Hollow pits formed into flaring nostrils on the snout of a black horse that rose up from the black water as if created from it. Moss and mud slid from its dripping flanks as the thing turned its head to regard Kaye with luminous white eyes.

She could not move. How many minutes passed as she stared at those mottled grey flanks, smooth as sealskin, and stared into the impossible glow of those eyes? The creature inclined its neck.

Kaye took a half step backwards and tried to speak. No words came.

The horse-thing snuffled closer to her, its hooves sinking in the mud, snapping twigs. It smelled of brackish water. She took another careful step backwards and stumbled.

She had to say something. "This way," she managed finally, pointing through the trees. "He's this way."

The horse moved in the direction she pointed, speeding up to a trot, and she was left to follow it, nearly shaking with relief. When she got to the clearing, Roiben was already straddling the creature's back. His breastplate had been haphazardly strapped on. She let out a breath she hadn't known she was holding.

He saw her emerge from under the canopy of branches and smiled. His eyes seemed darker in the moonlight. "Were I you, I would stay clear of the Folk in the future. We are a capricious people, with little regard for mortals."

She looked at him again. There were scratches on his armour that she didn't remember. Could he have been attacked? He could barely lift his head before – it was impossible to believe that he could have fought with someone. "Did something happen?"

His smile deepened, wiping the weariness from his face. His eyes glittered. "Don't waste your questions." Then the horse rode, moving like no living thing, darting between trees with unearthly speed and grace. Leaves flurried from kicks of its hooves. Moonlight glowed along its flanks.

Before she could think, she was alone in

the wood. Alone and shivering and proud of herself. She moved to retrieve her coat, and a glimmer of light caught her eye. The arrow.

She knelt and picked up the branch with its iron tip. Her finger ran up the rough bark and touched the too-warm metal. A shudder went through her, and she dropped it back in the mud. The woods were suddenly menacing, and she walked as quickly as she could back towards the road. If she started running, she didn't think she'd be able to stop.

Kaye dug her feet into the muddy slope that marked the edge of her grandmother's lawn and heaved herself up. She slid past the overflowing rubbish bin, the broken-down Pinto, the rusted coffee tins wired together as a fence for a wilted herb garden.

All the lights in the house seemed to be on, highlighting the grubby curtains. Blue lights flickered in the living room where the TV was.

She opened the backdoor and walked into the kitchen. Pots and pans, crusted with food, were piled in the sink. She was supposed to have washed them. Instead, she went to the cupboard and took out a bowl, filled it with milk, then put a piece of stale white bread on top of it. It would have to do, she thought as she carefully opened the door and set it on the step – after all, the only things likely to come for it any more were neighbourhood cats.

Kaye crept into the living room.

On the other side of the staircase, Ellen was sitting in front of the television, eating one of the miniature Snickers Grandma had bought for the trick-or-treaters. "Leave me the fuck alone," she muttered to the drink in front of her.

"You think I don't know anything. Okay, you're the smart one, right?" Kaye's grandmother said in that too-sweet voice that pissed off Kaye so much. "If you're so smart, then how come you're all alone? How come all these men just use you and leave you? How come the only one to take you in is your old, stupid mother?"

"I heard you the first million fucking times you said it."

"Well, you're going to hear it again," Kaye's grandmother said. "Where is your daughter tonight? It's almost one in the morning! Do you even care that she's out gallivanting around who knows where, trying her damnedest to turn out just like – "

"Don't you start in on my daughter!" Kaye's mother said with surprising vehemence. "She's just fine. You leave her out of your bitching."

Kaye bent her head down and tried to walk up the stairs as quickly and quietly as she could.

She caught her own reflection in the hallway mirror, mascara and glitter eyeshadow smeared across her cheeks and under her eyes, running in crusted and glittering streaks that looked like they were made by tears. Her lipstick was smudged and dull, arching across her left cheek where she must have wiped it.

Kaye turned to take a furtive look into the living room. Her mother caught her glance, rolled her eyes, and motioned her up the stairs with a furtive hand movement.

"While she's in this house she's going to live by the same rules that you lived by. I don't care that she's spent the last six years in a rat-infested apartment with whatever hoodlums you took up with. From now on that girl's going to be raised decent."

Kaye crept the rest of the way up the stairs and into her room. She closed the door as quietly as she could.

The tiny white chest of drawers and tooshort bed seemed to belong to someone else. Her rats, Isaac and Armageddon, rustled in their fish tank on top of the old toy box.

Kaye stripped off her clothes and, not caring about the wet or the mud or anything, climbed into the small bed, wrapped a blanket around herself, and folded her legs so that she fitted. Kaye knew what obsession was like – she saw how her mother craved fame, pined over men who treated her like shit. She didn't want to want someone she would never have.

But just for tonight, she allowed herself to

think of him, to think of the solemn, formal way he had spoken to her, so unlike anyone else. She let herself think of his flashing eyes and crooked smile.

Kaye slid down into sleep like water closing over her head.

3

"A cigarette is the perfect type of perfect
pleasure. It is exquisite, and it leaves one
unsatisfied. What more can one want?"
    — OSCAR WILDE, *The Picture of Dorian Gray*

Kaye was standing in a little stream clutching a Barbie doll by its blonde hair, the cool water tickling her toes. Heat beat down on her back, and she could smell green things and the rich mud of summer. She was nine.

It made perfect dream sense, even though she knew that it hadn't happened quite this way. The warm green memory was younger than nine. But in this patchwork dream, Spike sat on the carpet of moss that ran along the bank. He was sewing a doll's dress and bag out of leaves. Lutie straddled the waist of a sitting Ken doll, her iridescent butterfly wings fluttering slightly while she sang bawdy songs that made nine-year-old Kaye giggle and blush at the same time.

"I could pretend that he could bend,
But I'm bound to be sad when he is
    unclad.
A smooth plastic chest doesn't make
    up for the rest;
Even a boy-doll has to try to make a
    girl-doll sigh."

Gristle stood silently beside Kaye. Laughing, she turned to him, and he made to speak, but the only thing that dropped from his mouth was a single white stone. It splashed into the stream, settling along the bottom along with the other rocks, shining with a strange light.

"A shiny plastic boy's not a proper toy.
Each and every girl's got a pearl."

A squawk made Kaye look up suddenly. A crow had settled in the tree, black feathers shimmering with colour, like petrol floating on the surface of water. When the crow cocked its head down at her, its eyes were as pale as the stone.

"Never mind that you can't find
The thing – he can't even find his
    ding!"

The crow shifted its claws along the branch, then dropped into the air. A moment later she felt the scrape of claws along her wrist and the bite of its beak on her hand as her doll was pulled into the air.

Kaye screamed with a shrill, childish hysteria and reached down to throw something at the bird. Her hand closed on a stone, and she hurled it without thinking.

The crow spiralled into the cushion of trees, and Kaye ran towards it. The forest around her blurred, and she was suddenly looking down at the black shape. It was still, feathers ruffling slightly in the breeze. Her doll was there too, lying apart from the dead bird, and between them was a smooth white stone. The stone that Gristle had spoken.

And then she woke up.

Kaye's mother was standing in the doorway of the bedroom holding a cordless phone. "I've been calling and calling you from downstairs. Janet's on the phone."

"What?" Kaye blinked through eyes crusty with day-old makeup. She stretched her legs out, and her feet kicked the footboard of the tiny bed.

The sun was alive again, glowing with fury at the night's trickery at the hands of Mistress Moon. Flares of lemony light threatened her with a headache if she opened her eyes.

"Rough night?" Kaye's mother leaned against the doorframe and took a drag on her cigarette.

Kaye rubbed her eyes. Her knuckles came away black and glittery.

"Janet's on the phone." Kaye's mother sounded both annoyed and amused at having to repeat herself. "You want me to tell her you'll call her back?"

Kaye shook her head and took the phone. "Hullo?" Her voice was rough, thick with phlegm.

Ellen left the doorway, and Kaye heard her thump down the stairs.

"What happened last night?" It took Kaye a few moments to understand what Janet was asking.

"Oh. Nothing. Kenny tried to catch me, and my shirt ripped."

"Kaye! How come you ran out like that? I thought he'd done something terrible to you! We were fighting all night about it."

"I didn't think you'd believe me," Kaye said flatly.

That must have sounded enough like best-friend contrition, because Janet's tone softened. "Come on, Kaye. Of course I believe you."

Kaye struggled for what to say to the unexpected reprieve. "Are you okay?" Janet asked.

"I met someone on the way home last night." Kaye sat up in bed, realising that she'd gone to bed with her bra, skirt, and stockings still on. No wonder she felt uncomfortable.

"You did?" Janet sounded surprised and almost sceptical. "A boy?"

"Yeah," Kaye said. She wanted to say it aloud, to hold on to it. Already her recollection of Roiben was blanched by the sun, the way a dream fades when you don't write it down. "He had grey eyes and long hair."

"Like a metal head?"

"Longer," Kaye said. She wrapped the puke-pink duvet more tightly around her. Like everything else in her bedroom, it was slightly too small.

"Weird. What's his name?"

"Robin," Kaye said, a little smile on her face. She was glad Janet couldn't see her right now – she was sure she looked idiotically happy.

"Like Robin Hood? Are you for real? Did he hit on you?"

"We just talked," Kaye said.

Janet sighed. "You didn't meet anyone, did you? You're making this up."

"He's real," Kaye said. He *was* real, the most real person she had met in a long time. Hyper real.

"The party sucked anyway," Janet said. "I almost kicked this girl's ass. Dough kept telling me to chill, but I was too wasted and upset. Well, come over and I'll tell you the rest."

"Sure, okay. I've got to get dressed."

"Okay, 'bye." The phone clicked as Janet

hung up. Kaye turned it off and dropped it on the duvet.

Kaye looked around her bedroom. Her clothes lay in drifts on the floor, most still in the black rubbish bags. All the furniture was the same as it had been when she was four, child-size white furniture, pink walls, and a reproachful, glass-eyed army of dolls arranged in the bookshelves.

I have to find Gristle and Spike. She hadn't ever needed to call them before. They'd always been around when she had needed them. But that was when she had been little, when she had believed in everything, before her legs stuck out over the end of the bed and she had to bend over to see her face in the mirror. Kaye sighed. She guessed that she wasn't really unicorn-pure anymore. Maybe that kind of thing mattered.

Kaye stripped out of her clothes and found a worn pair of jeans and a blue G-Force T-shirt. In the bathroom, as she splashed cold water on her face and rubbed off last night's makeup, she inspected herself. The purple dye she'd combed into her hair was already faded. She stared at her upturned eyes and thin cheeks. For the first time, she wondered where they had really come from. She hadn't seen Roiben well in the moonlight, but his upturned eyes could have got him mistaken for Oriental if he hadn't had such an angular nose.

She sighed again and pulled her hair up into ragged pigtails. Hey, if she looked ten again, maybe kid-loving faeries would come and talk to her.

Her leopard coat was too soggy to wear. Kaye pulled on Lloyd's leather jacket and checked the pockets. A couple of crumpled receipts, a faux-tortoiseshell guitar pick, loose change. Kaye pulled her hand out as though she'd been stung.

There, sticking out of the pad of her finger, was a slim, brown thorn. It just figured that Lloyd would have something annoying in his pocket. She pulled it out and sucked the tiny red dot on her finger. Then, dropping the thorn on the chest of drawers, she went downstairs.

Kaye's mother was sitting at the kitchen table, flipping through a magazine. A slug of gin was sitting uncapped on the table, and a cigarette had almost burned itself to ash on a plate beside her.

"You going to Janet's?" Ellen asked.

"Yeah."

"You want some coffee before you go, honey? You don't look so awake."

"I'm okay. Grandma's gonna freak when she sees that plate." Kaye didn't even bother to mention the gin.

Kaye's mother leaned back in the wooden chair. "Don't try to mother your mother," Ellen said. It was only then that Kaye heard the slur in her voice.

"Heard from asshole Lloyd?"

Ellen shook her head. "Nah. I called a couple of old friends from Sweet Pussy, but they've all gone respectable."

Kaye laughed. She remembered Liz jumping around the stage in her amazing purple plastic catsuit like a glam-rock Julie Newmar. It was hard to picture what respectable would look like on her. "You going to get together?"

"Maybe," Ellen said airily. "Sue and Liz have some little hole-in-the-wall CD store in Red Bank."

"That's great."

Ellen sighed. "Whatever. I wonder when was the last time either one of them picked up a fucking instrument."

Kaye shook her head. It was kind of stupid to think that her mother would just give up on going back to the city, but she couldn't help hoping. "Tell Grandma I won't be home late."

"You come home when you want. I'm your mother."

"Thanks, Mum," Kaye said, and walked out the door.

The wind was blowing gusts of vivid, lipstick-coloured leaves across the lawn. Kaye took a deep breath of cold air.

"Lutie-loo," she whispered into the wind. "Spike, Gristle . . . please come back. I need you."

I'll just walk over to Janet's. I'll just go over to Janet's like I said and then I'll figure out a plan.

Janet lived in a trailer park along the main road at the back of the petrol station her brother had worked at since Kaye left for Philadelphia in the first place. She waved to him as she cut through the lot.

Corny smiled grudgingly. His hair was a longish brown mop, cut too short in the front and too long in the back. He was wearing a denim jacket and dirty jeans. His skin was red in patches. He was exactly like she remembered him, only taller.

Kaye walked back behind the little office and bathroom area of the petrol station and cut through the overgrown shrubs to the trailer park. The trailers were vehicles in name only – none of them had wheels, and most of them had fences and porches anchoring them with steel and cement to the firmament. She walked up a pebble road towards the trailer.

A brown-haired girl about Kaye's age was hanging out some washing. Behind her, an opulently fat man lounged in a hammock; flesh oozed through the crisscrossed strings. A trio of dachshunds barked madly as they chased each other along a chain-link fence.

Kaye came to the screen door and banged on it.

"Come on in," Janet called. Kaye could see her feet through the screen, flung over the edge of the grungy blue couch, toes dark with polish. Janet's toes had wads of toilet paper stuffed between them so they couldn't quite touch.

The door squeaked hideously as she opened it. Rust had stiffened the hinges where the white enamel was chipped off. The main room of the trailer was dark, the windows covered by curtains. Light flickered from three sources: the door, the dim amber kitchen light, and the television. On the screen, two women were screaming at one another in front of a studio audience. One of the women had rhinestone eyebrows.

"Want to do your nails?" Janet asked. "I have a cool blue."

Kaye shook her head, although Janet probably didn't see her do it. "Can I make some coffee?"

"Sure, make me some too." Janet stretched, pointing her shiny maroon toes as she arched her back. She was wearing a boy's sleeveless undershirt and daisy-print cotton knickers. "I am totally hungover."

"Where's everybody?"

"Mum and The Husband are at the flea market. Corny'll be back from work anytime now. You'll never believe what she got me the last time she was out – a half shirt with rhinestone cats on it! I mean – where would you even find something like that?"

Kaye laughed. Janet's mother collected all kinds of kitschy stuff, but especially all things Star Trek. The trailer walls were covered with collectable plates, framed fan art, and shadow-boxed phasers and tricorders. A collection of Spock-related needlepoint throw pillows competed with Janet for couch space. "I saw Corny when I walked over. I don't think he recognised me."

"He's an asshole. All he does is sit in his room and jerk off. He's probably gone near-sighted."

Kaye took two mugs down from the shelf and filled them with water from the tap. "Maybe I just don't look the way I used to." Kaye punched the keypad of the microwave and put the cups in. They spun on the greasy glass tray.

"I guess." Janet flipped through the channels and stopped on VH1.

"So what happened last night?" Kaye knew that it would please Janet if she asked.

Janet did, in fact, pull herself into a sitting position, and she turned down the sound on the TV. "Well, when we got to Fatima's place, Aimee was, like, playing with Kenny's hair, rubbing her hands all over it and saying how soft it was. She must have known we were fighting."

"I'm sorry."

"It's cool." Janet pressed a Live-Long-and-

Prosper pillow to her chest. "So anyway I go up to her and start rubbing my hands through her hair and telling her how nice it felt, really going to town, and Marcus starts laughing. You know that weird, rumbling Buddha-belly laugh he has. So fucking loud."

"What did Kenny do?" Kaye wondered if Kenny hit on every girl he met. She was embarrassed that she'd let him touch her – sometimes she wondered if there wasn't some sick part of her that actually wanted popular boys to like her. He had surprisingly gentle hands.

"Nothing; he loves girls to fight over him." Janet shook her head as if she were talking about an incorrigible child. "So she starts calling me psycho and dyke, not backing down at all, saying that she was just talking."

Kaye nodded. "Did you hit her?" The microwave beeped, and Kaye stirred instant-coffee "crystals" into both cups. A thin white foam formed on the surface.

Janet nodded. "I totally went after her, but Dough stopped me and Kenny stopped her and Fatima came over and started saying how it was a big misunderstanding and all that, even though she didn't see what happened. She just didn't want her house to get fucked up."

Looking down into the cup, she saw the dark, still water of the stream. Her heart was suddenly beating triple-time even though nothing at all was happening. Roiben – the most cool, amazing, dangerous storybook guy ever – said he was going to see her again. Glee made Kaye's chest hurt.

"Are you listening to me?" Janet asked.

"Here's your coffee," Kaye said, stirring sugar and powdered milk into Janet's before handing it to her. "I'm listening."

"Well, have you ever seen an uncircumcised dick?"

Kaye shook her head.

"Me neither. So I say sure, we'll give you a dollar apiece if you show us. And he says, 'That's only ten bucks.'"

Kaye smiled and nodded as Janet spoke, but she still saw Roiben in her mind's eye, drenched with rain and blood, shot nearly through the heart with a gnarled arrow.

The hinges screamed their protest as Corny opened the door and stomped into the trailer. He glared at both of them, stalked to the refrigerator, opened it, and then swigged Mountain Dew out of the bottle.

"What's up your ass?" Janet said.

A white cat, her belly swollen with kittens, had slunk in when Corny opened the door. Kaye dropped her hand to pet the little head.

"Motherfucker didn't show up this morning. I've been at work since midnight." Kaye could see that the patch on the back of his jacket was a devil's head. In his back pocket, the outline of his wallet was connected to a chain that ran to his front belt loop.

"Mum hates it when you drink out of the bottle," Janet said.

"So what?" Corny said. He took another deliberate swig. "You going to tell her about that? How about I tell her how you need your own Roman vomitorium, you fucking bulimic."

"Shut up, fuckfist." Janet picked up the phone in the kitchen and started punching in numbers. She walked towards her bedroom as she dialled.

Corny glanced at Kaye. She looked away from him and pulled the heavy, soft cat onto her lap. It purred like a hive of hornets.

"You're that girl that believes in faeries, right?" Corny said.

Kaye shrugged. "I'm Kaye."

"Want a drink? I didn't backwash into it." He wiped the side of his sleeve against his mouth.

Kaye shook her head. Something – like a small stone – bounced off her knee.

The windows were closed. Kaye looked at the ceiling, but there were no small parts hanging off the overhead light. Maybe something from a shelf. When she looked down at the floor near her feet, the only object she saw was an acorn. They were abundant outside this time of year, scattering from the nearby tree all over the lawn. She picked it up and looked towards the window again. Maybe it was open after all. The acorn was light in her hand, and she noticed a tiny strip of white sticking out from under the cap.

Corny was dampening a towel and wiping off his face. She didn't think he'd thrown the acorn – she'd been talking to him when she'd felt it hit.

Kaye pulled lightly on the acorn cap, and it came loose. Inside the nutshell, all the meat was gone, leaving an empty space where a slip of paper was coiled. Kaye removed it carefully and read the message written in a pinkish red ink: "Do not talk to the black knight any more. tell no one your name. everything is danger. Gristle is gone. We need your help. meet you tomorrow night. LL&S"

What did it mean, Gristle is gone? Gone where? And the black knight? Could that be Roiben? She hadn't been talking to anyone else that fitted that description. What did it mean, that everything was danger?

"Kaye," Janet said, leaning out of her bedroom, "you want to go to the mall?"

Kaye fumbled to tuck the acorn into one of her pockets.

"I suppose that you are expecting me to take you," Corny said. "Y'know, most people that go shopping actually have money."

"Shut up, geek," Janet said, and ushered Kaye into her bedroom.

Kaye sat down on Janet's bed. Janet's room was full of mismatched furniture: a wooden chest of drawers with glass knobs, a white dressing table, and a dented black metal daybed. The room was as messy as Kaye's, with clothes hanging out of open drawers and littering the floor, but the disarray seemed glamorous here. While Kaye's clothes were all T-shirts and retro attic finds, Janet had red skirts with feather fringe, and shirts that shimmered blue and gold like fish scales. Pots of eyeshadow, glittery barrettes, body sprays, and tubes of hair goo covered her dressing table and the top of her chest of drawers. On the walls, posters of bands competed with messages written in multicoloured markers on the white walls. JANET & KENNY TLF was written in glitter on the back of Janet's door. She wasn't sure, but she thought she saw traces of some other name underneath Kenny's.

"What should I wear?" Janet held up a pink, fuzzy half-of-a-half sweater that came to just under her breasts. "Will I freeze?"

"You need a poodle miniskirt." Kaye sat on the bed and leaned back against the pillows. In the pocket of her jacket, the acorn still lay against the hot flesh of her palm, the tiny point indenting her thumb.

"What are you going to wear?"

"This." Kaye indicated her faded T-shirt and jeans with a sweep of her hand.

Janet sighed and made a face. "Do you know how many girls would die to be Oriental and blonde?"

Kaye shook her head morosely. What boys liked about Asian girls was weird. It was all mail-order brides and kung fu at the same time.

"How about you wear this?" Janet held up a shiny black shirt that had no back at all. It tied around the neck and waist like a bikini.

"No way," Kaye said.

This time Janet just laughed.

They walked into the mall through the cinema entrance. Boys and girls were gathered in packs on the steps, waiting for rides or having a cigarette before their film started. Janet walked past them like a goddess, not looking at anybody, perfectly curled hair and glistening lipstick looking as though it was effortless for her. It made Kaye wonder where she'd learned this skill with beauty – as a kid Janet had had a perpetually woolly perm and unlaced trainers.

Kaye caught her own reflection in a window and grimaced. Her T-shirt was a bit of thin, faded cloth that even sported a couple of holes from launderette abuse. Her jeans were hand-me-downs from her mother, and they hung low on her hipbones, forcing her to hitch them up occasionally when she felt like they were going to fall all the way off.

"Okay," Janet said. "Want to show me those skills you bragged about?"

Kaye grinned. One thing that they'd e-mailed about for a while was the audacity of the things they'd shoplifted. Kaye's all-time greatest heist had been her two rats. They might not have been expensive, but pocketing a squirming animal and then keeping it in your pocket was harder than it sounded.

She nodded. "Here are Kaye's Principles of Thieving, okay?"

Janet folded her arms. "Kidding, right?"

"Listen. No independent stores. Just chains or megastores – they can afford it, and the people who work there don't give a shit. Oh, and no places where the employees are actually nice."

"I can't believe you have rules."

Kaye nodded solemnly. "Minimising my karmic damage."

A few hours later they were sitting on the kerb outside the Wiz divvying up their loot. It wasn't, strictly speaking, far enough from the mall to be entirely safe, but they were feeling untouchable. Kaye was trying a new, heavy stick of smoky eyeliner, smearing it thickly under her eyes. Janet was drinking a raspberry smoothie.

Kaye dug through her jeans for matches and lit a cigarette. Taking a deep breath of smoke, she leaned back and exhaled, letting the smoke whorl up and away. She reached up lazily to change the pattern. It shifted at the touch of her fingers, and she could see figures dancing in it – no, they weren't dancing, they were fighting. Swordsmen duelling in the rising smoke.

"How long are you going to be in town?" Janet asked.

Kaye dropped her hand. She'd forgotten where she was. "I figure at least a couple of months."

"It's weird, you know. Us being friends after all this time and you being so far away and all. I've been thinking about last night."

"Yeah?" Kaye asked warily.

"He was hitting on you, wasn't he?"

Kaye shrugged. There was no way to explain what really happened. She certainly couldn't have explained why she'd let him run his hand up her thigh, why she hadn't minded in the least until she'd suddenly remembered who they were and what was really happening. "A little, I guess. But I honestly fell. I guess I drank too much or something."

"How come you were up there in the first place?"

Kaye grinned easily now. "Just exploring.

There was the most outrageously cool old carousel horse. Did you see it? The legs were gone but the rest of it was perfect – the paint wasn't even badly faded." She sighed wistfully. "Even if I had some way to bring that thing home, there is no way I could drag it from apartment to apartment."

Janet sighed. It was obvious this was the sort of reason she could easily believe.

Kaye took another drag on her cigarette, wondering why that made her angry. This time the tendrils of smoke reminded her of Roiben's hair, raw silver silk. Thinking about that made her feel even more restless and frustrated. She had to see him again.

"Earth to Kaye," Janet said. "What were you thinking about?"

"Robin," Kaye said. That was also something she imagined Janet would easily believe.

"He's for real? Honest?" Janet sucked hard on her smoothie, trying to draw out a chunk of frozen raspberry that was clogging the straw.

"Don't be a bitch," Kaye said without real heat.

"Sorry. It's just that it's so unlikely – meeting a guy in a rainstorm while you're walking home. I mean, what was he doing out there? I wouldn't have even talked to him."

"I guess he easily fits into the 'stranger' category," Kaye said, smiling.

Janet frowned disapprovingly. "Doesn't he even have a car?"

"Look, I'm only going to be in town for a couple of months, at most. The only thing that matters is that he is cross-my-heart-and-hope-to-die beautiful." Kaye waggled her eyebrows suggestively.

That at least brought a scandalised gasp. "You *slut*," Janet crooned. "Do you even know if he likes you?"

Kaye ground out the stub of her cigarette on the rough cement, smearing ash in a roughly circular line. She didn't want to go over the list of things to recommend her to a faery knight; there wasn't a single thing she could think of to put on such a list.

"He'll like me," she said, hoping that the charm of speaking words aloud would make those words come true.

That night Kaye let Isaac and Armageddon run all over the bed while the CD player blasted Grace Slick singing "White Rabbit" over and over again. A grown-up, fucked-up Alice suited her. Then she put on Hole and listened to Courtney Love grate out, "I want to be the girl with the most cake . . . someday you will ache like I ache."

She cracked the window and lit a cigarette, careful to blow the smoke out onto the lawn.

The row of dolls watched her impassively from the bookshelf, their tea party propriety almost certainly offended. She caught both rats and put them up there with the dolls, to get to know one another. Then she turned back to the bed.

Pushing it up against the wall, she dragged the mattress onto the floor. It took up most of the space in the room, but at least her feet would be able to hang comfortably over the edge. And if she covered the boxspring with one of her mother's batik throws, it could almost be a couch.

Putting out her cigarette and lying back down, she watched the rats crawl over the laps of the dolls – heedless of velvet riding coats or gold lace princess gowns – to snuffle plastic hair, and nibble at delicate, porcelain fingers. Finally her eyes closed, and she drifted softly down into sleep.

4

"All day and all night
my desire for you
unwinds like a poisonous snake."

— SAMAR SEN, "LOVE"

That Monday morning, Kaye woke up early, got dressed, and pretended to go to school.

She had been pretending for the better part of a week now, ever since her grandma had insisted she was going to march down to the school and find out what was taking them so long to enrol her. There was no way to tell her that the transcripts were never coming, so Kaye packed a peanut-butter-and-honey sandwich and an orange and went out to kill time.

When they had first moved to Philadelphia, she had transferred easily to a new school. But then they'd started moving around, living for six months in University City and another four in South Philly and then a couple of weeks in the Museum District. Each time, she either had to find a way to get to her old school or transfer to the new school. About a year back, the confusion had gotten the better of her, and she'd started working full-time at Chow Fat's instead. They needed the money and, aside from that, they needed the free food.

Kaye kicked a flattened drinks can down the street ahead of her. Even she could see that she was going in no good direction, and not just literally. Her grandmother was right about her – she was turning into her mother – no, worse, because she didn't even have an ambition. Her only talents were shoplifting and a couple of cigarette-lighting tricks you needed a Zippo to perform.

She considered going to Red Bank and trying to find Sue and Liz's store. She had some money, but she still might be able to sneak on the train for the couple of stops. Her biggest problem was that Ellen hadn't said what they'd called the place.

It occurred to her that maybe Corny would know. He probably had another hour before the graveyard shift ended and the morning guy came in. If she bought him coffee, he might not mind her hanging around too much.

The Quick Check was mostly empty when she went in and filled two large paper cups with hazelnut coffee. She made hers with cinnamon and skimmed milk, but she didn't know how he liked his, so she pocketed little packets of sugar and several creamers. The yawning woman didn't even look at Kaye as she rang her up.

Corny was sitting on the bonnet of his car, playing chess on a small, magnetic board.

"Hey," Kaye called. He looked up with a not-so-friendly expression on his face. She held out the coffee, and he just looked confused.

"Aren't you supposed to be in school?" he asked finally.

"Dropped out," she said. "I'm going to get my GED."

He raised his eyebrows.

"Do you want the coffee or not?"

A car pulled up in front of one of the pumps. He sighed, sliding off the bonnet of the car. "Put it by the board."

She pulled herself onto his car and carefully set down her cup, searching her pockets for the sugar and creamers. Then she uncapped hers and took a deep sip. The warmth of the liquid braced her against the cold, wet autumn morning.

Corny came back a few minutes later, settling onto the hood. After a considering look, he started pouring sugar into his coffee, stirring it with a filthy pen from his pocket.

"Which you are you playing against?" Kaye asked, drawing up her knees.

He looked up at her with a snort. "Did you come here to fuck with me? Coffee is cheap."

"Geez, I'm just talking. Who's winning?"

Corny smirked. "He is, for now. Come on, what are you really doing here? People do not visit me. Being social to me is, like, tempting the Apocalypse or something."

"How come?"

Corny hopped down again with a groan as another car pulled up in front of the petrol pump. She watched him sell a carton of cigarettes and fill the tank. She wondered if the owner would hire a sixteen-year-old girl – her last paypacket wasn't going to stretch much further. Corny had worked here when he was younger than she was now.

"Corny," she said when he came back, "do you know of any small CD stores in Red Bank?"

"Trying to bribe me for a ride?"

She sighed. "Paranoid. I just want to know what it's called."

He shrugged, playing out a few more moves without editorial comment. "My comic book store is next to some CD store, but I don't know the name."

"What comics do you read?"

"Are you saying that you read comics?" Corny looked defensive, like maybe she was leading him into some verbal trap.

"Sure. *Batman. Lenore. Too Much Coffee Man.* Used to read *Sandman,* of course."

Corny regarded her speculatively for a moment, then finally relented. "I used to read X-

everything, but I read a lot of Japanese stuff now."

"Like *Akira*?"

He shook his head. "Nah. Girl comics – the ones with the pretty boys and girls. Hey, do you know what *shonen-ai* is?" His expression was dubious.

"I wish I could speak some Japanese," Kaye said, shaking her head.

Corny smirked. "I thought you *were* Japanese."

She shrugged. "So says my mum. My dad was part of some local glam-goth band my mother worshipped in high school. Very new wave. I never met him. It was a groupie thing."

"Wild."

"I guess."

A car pulled into the station, but instead of parking in front of the pumps, it stopped next to Corny's car. A dark-skinned kid got out.

"Nice of you to show up today," Corny said, tossing him a set of the keys.

"I said I was sorry, man," the kid said.

Turning to Kaye, Corny said, "Where you going now?"

Kaye shrugged.

"You want to come too? You could hang out and wait for Janet to get home."

She nodded. "Sure."

They walked over to the trailer together.

He switched on the TV and walked back to his room. "I'm going to check my mail."

Kaye nodded and sat down on the couch, only then feeling a little awkward. It was weird to be in Janet's house without Janet. She flipped through the channels, settling on Cartoon Network.

After a few minutes, when he didn't return, she went back to his room. Corny's room was as unlike Janet's as a room could be. There were bookshelves on all the walls, filled to overflowing with paperbacks and comics. Corny was sitting at a desk that looked like it could barely hold up the equipment piled on it. Another box of wires and what looked like computer innards was next to his feet.

He was tapping on his keyboard and grunted as she came in. "Almost done."

Kaye sat down on the edge of his bed the way she would have if she was in Janet's room and picked up the nearest comic. It was all in Japanese. Blond hero and heroine – she always thought it was weird there were so many blonds in anime – bad guy with really, really long black hair and a cool headpiece. A cute, fat ball with bat wings fluttering around as a sidekick. She flipped a little further. Hero naked and lashed in the bad guy's bed. She stopped flipping and stared at the picture. The blond's head was thrown back in either ecstasy or terror as the villain licked one of his nipples.

She looked up at Corny and held out the book. "Let me guess . . . this is *shonen-ai*?"

HOLLY BLACK

He shot a glance at her from the computer, but she couldn't miss the smug expression. "Yeah."

Kaye wasn't sure what to say to that, which was probably the point. "You like boys?"

"There's a technical term for it," Corny said. "Faggot. Although those are mighty pretty boys."

"Does Janet know?" She couldn't understand why he would tell *her* if Janet didn't know, but certainly Janet would have said something. Janet's E-mails were summaries of her whole day, boring and full of gossip about people Kaye had never met.

"Yeah, the whole family knows. It's no big deal. One night at dinner I said, 'Mum, you know the forbidden love that Spock has for Kirk? Well, me too.' It was easier for her to understand that way." He sounded like he was daring Kaye to say something.

"I hope you aren't expecting some kind of reaction," Kaye said finally. "Because the only thing that I can think of is that is the weirdest coming-out story I have ever heard."

His face relaxed. Then she started to laugh and both of them were laughing and looking at the comic and laughing some more.

By the time Janet got back from school, Corny was sleeping and Kaye was reading a huge pile of kinky comics.

"Hey," Janet said, looking surprised to see

her sofa occupied.

Kaye yawned and took a sip from a half-full glass of cherry cola. "Oh, hi. I was hanging out with your brother and then I figured I'd just wait for you to come home."

Janet made a face, dumping her armful of books onto the chair. "You make *school* look fun. If you're going to drop out, you might as well . . . I don't know."

"Do something seedy?"

"Totally. Look, I'm gonna go out . . . I gotta meet the guys. You want to come?"

Kaye stretched and got up. "Sure."

The Blue Snapper diner was open twenty-four hours, and they didn't care how long you sat in the mirror-lined booths or how little you ordered. Kenny and Doughboy sat at a table with a girl Kaye didn't know. She had short black hair, red nails, and thin, drawn-on eyebrows. Doughboy was wearing a short-sleeved team shirt over a long-sleeved black undershirt; the laces of his hiking boots spilled out from under the table. He'd cut his hair since she'd seen him last, and it was shaved along the back and sides. Kenny was wearing his silver jacket over a black T-shirt and looked exactly the same: scruffy, cute, and totally off-limits.

"Sorry I freaked the other night," Kaye said, shoving her hands in the pockets of her jeans and hoping no one wanted to talk about it too much.

HOLLY BLACK

"What happened?" the girl asked. Something made a clicking sound as she spoke, and Kaye realised that it was the girl's tongue-stud tapping against her teeth.

Doughboy opened his mouth to make some comment, and Kenny cut him off. "'S cool," he said with a jerk of his chin, "C'mon and slide in, ladies."

"Kaye," Janet said, sliding into the booth next to the girl, "this is Fatima – I e-mailed you about her. Kaye's my friend from Philly."

"Right. Sure. Hi." It was Fatima's party she'd missed two nights ago, and she had no idea what had been said after she left. Kenny was barely glancing in her direction, but Doughboy was watching her like she might do something weird or funny. Kaye wished she'd stayed in the trailer. This was too awkward.

"You're the girl with the mum who's in a band," Fatima said.

"Not any more," Kaye said.

"Is it true that she fucked Lou Zampolis? Janet said she sang backup for Chainsuck."

Kaye grimaced. She wondered if all her E-mails had been relayed like this. "Unfortunately."

"Does that freak you out – I mean does she, like, screw your boyfriends and shit?"

Kaye raised her eyebrows. "I don't date guys in bands." She tried to imagine what Ellen would think of Kenny. It was impossible to picture Ellen meeting Roiben.

"I have this friend, right," Fatima said, "and her mother and her sister both slept with the guy that got her knocked up. I mean, how Jerry Springer is that?"

"Erin, right?" Janet said. "She's in rehab."

The waitress stopped by their table. She was wearing a brown uniform that looked too small on her, and her name tag read RITA. "Can I get you guys anything?"

"Diet whatever," Janet said.

"Coffee," Kaye chimed in.

"I want . . . can I have some Disco Fries, Rita?" Doughboy said.

"I'll be back with refills in a minute," the waitress said, smiling guardedly at Dough for using her name.

Kenny turned to get his cigarettes and lighter out of the pocket of his coat, and Kaye saw a tattoo on the back of his neck. It was a tribal design of what looked like a scarab. It made her wonder what other tattoos he might have snaking down areas covered by his shirt. Janet would know.

"Anyone want?" he asked, offering up the pack.

"I do," Kaye said.

"Whatever you want, you get," he tossed back, giving her a cigarette with a smirk that made the heat rise to her face.

Janet was talking to Fatima about Erin's baby, not paying attention to either of them at

HOLLY BLACK

the moment. Doughboy was picking at the cheese-and-gravy-covered fries the waitress had plunked down in front of him.

"Want to see a trick?" Kaye asked, suddenly not wanting to back down from the implied challenge in Kenny's voice. "Let me see your lighter."

It was silver with an enamel eight-ball medallion soldered to the front of it. He handed it over.

Kaye had learned this trick from Liz back in her mother's Sweet Pussy days. Liz had offered to teach it to her, claiming that was a sure way to impress the boys. Kaye had had no idea why Liz would want to impress anyone since she already had Sue, but she'd learned the trick and it had impressed bartenders, at least.

Kaye held the metal body of the lighter between the first two fingers of her left hand; then she flipped it first over and then under each finger so that the metal shimmered like a minnow. Faster and faster, she made the lighter hurdle her fingers. Then she stopped, flicked the lid open, and lit it, all with her right hand resting on the table. She leaned over and generously offered the flame to Kenny's cigarette.

Once Kaye found the record store, she would have to tell Liz that she had been right. Both the boys looked impressed.

Kenny's lopsided grin was an invitation to

mischief.

"Cool," Doughboy said. "Want to show me how to do that?"

"Sure," Kaye said, lighting her own cigarette and taking a deep breath of bitter smoke. She showed him, doing the trick in slow motion so that he could see how it was done, then letting him try it.

"I gotta get out of the booth for a minute," Kenny said, and she and Doughboy scooted out.

Before she could get back in, Kenny nudged her arm and jerked his head towards the bathrooms.

"Be right back," Kaye told Janet, dropping her cigarette into the ashtray. "Bathroom."

Janet must not have noticed anything since she just nodded.

Kaye walked behind Kenny to the small hallway. Even though she had no idea what he wanted, her cheeks were already warm, and a strange thrill was coiling in her belly.

Once they were in the hallway, Kenny turned to her and draped his lean body against the wall.

"What did you do to me?" Kenny asked, taking a quick drag from his cigarette and rubbing the stubble along his cheekbone with the back of one hand.

Kaye shook her head. "Nothing. What do you mean?"

He lowered his voice, speaking with a quiet intensity. "The other night. The horse. What did you do?" He paused and looked the other way before continuing. "I can't stop thinking about you."

Kaye was stunned. "I . . . honestly . . . I didn't *do* anything."

"Well, undo it," he said, scowling.

She struggled for an explanation. "Sometimes when I daydream . . . things happen. I was just thinking about riding the horse. I didn't even hear you come in." Her cheeks felt even hotter when she remembered a theory Sue had once explained about why all young girls want their own ponies.

He looked at her as intensely as he had in the attic of the carousel building, bringing his cigarette to his lips again. "This is fucked," he said a little desperately. "I mean it; I can't get you out of my head. You're all I think about, all day long."

Kaye had no idea what to say to that.

He took a step closer to her without seeming to notice. "You have to do something."

She took a step back, but the wall halted her. She could feel the cool tile against her spine. The pay phone to her right blocked her view of the register. "I'm sorry," she said.

He took another step, until his chest was against hers. "I want you," he said urgently. His knee moved between her legs.

"We're in a diner," Kaye said, grabbing him by the shoulders so that he had to look at her face. He was pale except for a touch of hectic pink in the cheeks. His eyes looked glazed.

"I want to stop wanting you," he said and moved to kiss her. Kaye turned her head so that he got a mouthful of hair, but it didn't seem to bother him. He kissed his way down her throat, biting the skin punishingly, licking the bites with his tongue. One of his hands ran up from her waist to cup her breast while the other threaded through her hair.

Her hands were still clenched on his shoulders as she wavered in indecision. She could shove him off. She should shove him off. But her traitorous body was urging her to wait a little longer, clasp him a little closer and see what might happen.

"Guys, I was . . . what the hell?"

Kenny pushed back from Kaye at the sound of Janet's voice. Several strands of long blonde hair were still caught on his hand, shimmering like spiderwebs.

He drew himself up. "Don't give me more of your insecure girlfriend bullshit."

Janet had tears in her eyes. "You were kissing her!"

"Calm the fuck down!"

Kaye fled to the toilets, locking herself in a cubicle and sliding into a sitting position on the dirty floor.

Her heart was beating so fast, she thought it might beat its way out of her chest. The space was too small for pacing, but she wanted to pace, wanted to do something that would work answers out of her tangled mind. Magic, if there was such a thing, should not work like this. She should not be able to enchant someone she barely knew without even deciding to do it.

The delight was the worst part, the part of her that could overlook the guilt and see the poetic justice in making Kenny unable to stop thinking about her freaky self. It would be easy to like him, she thought, cute and cool and wanting her. And unlike an unattainable faerie knight, he was someone she could really have.

Taking a deep breath, she left the stall. She went to the sinks and splashed her face with water from the tap. Looking up, she saw her own reflection in the mirror, faded red Chow Fat T-shirt spattered with dark droplets of water, eye makeup smudgy and indistinct, blonde hair hanging in tangled strands.

Something caught her eye as she turned away, though. Approaching the mirror, she looked at her face again, closely. She looked the same as ever. Kaye shook her head and walked to the door. For a moment, she had thought that the face she saw in the mirror was green.

More coffees were on the table when she got back, and she sipped at the one in front of where she had been sitting. Her cigarette had burned down to ash in the glass tray. Doughboy was telling Kenny about the new car he was restoring, and Janet was glaring at Kaye.

"Your pardon, Kaye," said a voice that was both familiar and strange.

There was a moment when Kaye just froze. Her mind was screaming that this was impossible. It was against the rules. They never did this. It was one thing to believe in faeries; it was totally another thing if you weren't allowed to even have a choice about it. If they could just walk into your normal life, then they were a part of normal life, and she could no longer separate the two in her head.

But Roiben was indeed standing beside their booth. His hair was white as salt under the fluorescent lights and was pulled back in a ponytail. He was wearing a long black wool coat that hid whatever he was wearing underneath all the way down to his thoroughly modern leather boots. There was so little colour in his face that he seemed to be entirely monochromatic, a picture shot in black-and-white film.

"Who's the goth?" Kaye heard Doughboy say.

"Robin, I think his name is," Janet replied glumly.

Roiben raised an eyebrow when he heard that, but he went on. "May I speak with you a moment?"

She felt incapable of doing more than nodding her head. Getting up from the booth, she walked with him to an empty table. Neither one sat down.

"I came to give you this." Roiben reached into his coat and took out a lump of black cloth from some well-hidden pocket. And smiled, the same smile she remembered from the forest, the one that was just for her. "It's your shirt, back from the dead."

"Like you," she said.

He nodded slightly. "Indeed."

"My friends told me not to talk to you." She hadn't known she was going to say that till it came out of her mouth. The words felt like thorns falling from her tongue.

He looked down and took a breath. "Your friends? Not, I assume, those friends." His eyes flickered towards the booth, and she shook her head.

"Lutie and Spike," she said.

His eyes were dark when he looked at her again, and the smile was gone. "I killed a friend of theirs. Perhaps a friend of yours."

Around her, people were eating and laughing and talking, but those normal sounds felt as far away and out of place as a laugh track. "You killed Gristle."

He nodded.

She stared at him, as though things might somehow reshuffle to make sense. "How? Why? Why are you telling me this?"

Roiben didn't meet her gaze as he spoke. "Is there some excuse that I could give you that would make it better? Some explanation that you would find acceptable?"

"That's your answer? Don't you even care?"

"You have the shirt. I have done what I came here to do."

She grabbed his arm and moved around to face him. "You owe me three questions."

He stiffened, but his face remained blank. "Very well."

Anger surged up in her, a bitter helpless feeling. "Why did you kill Gristle?"

"My mistress bade me do so. I have little choice in my obedience." Roiben tucked his long fingers into the pockets of the coat. He spoke matter-of-factly, as though he was bored by his own answers.

"Right," Kaye said. "So if she told you to jump off a bridge . . . ?"

"Exactly." There was no irony in his tone. "Shall I consider that your second question?"

Kaye stopped and took a breath, her face filling with heat. She was so angry that she was shaking.

"Why don't you . . . ," she began, and stopped herself. She had to think. Anger was making her careless and stupid. She had one more question, and she was determined that she would use it to piss him off, if nothing else. She thought about the note she'd got in the acorn and the warning she'd been given. "What's your full name?"

He looked like he would choke on the air he breathed. "What?"

"That's my third question: What is your full name?" She didn't know what she had done, not really. She only knew that she was forcing him to do something he didn't want to do, and that suited her fine.

Roiben's eyes darkened with fury. "Rath Roiben Rye, much may the knowledge please you."

Her eyes narrowed. "It's a nice name."

"You are too clever by half. Too clever for your own good, I think."

"Kiss my ass, Rath Roiben Rye."

He grabbed her by the arm before she even saw him move. She raised her hand to ward off the coming blow. He threw her forward. She shrieked. Her hand and knee connected hard with the stone floor. She looked up, half expecting to see the gleam of a sword, but instead he pulled her jeans hard at the waistband and pressed his mouth against the exposed swell of her hip.

Time seemed to slow as she slipped on the slick floor, as he rose easily to his feet, as diner patrons stared, as Kenny struggled out from the booth.

Roiben stood over her. He spoke tone-lessly. "That is the nature of servitude, Kaye. It is literal-minded and not at all clever. Be careful with your epithets."

"Who the fuck do you think you are?" Kenny said, finally there, bending down to help Kaye up.

"Ask her," Roiben said, indicating Kaye with his chin. "Now she knows exactly who I am." He turned and walked out of the diner.

Tears welled up in Kaye's eyes.

"Come on," Fatima was saying, although Kaye was barely paying attention. "Let's take her outside. Just us girls."

Fatima and Janet led her outside and sat down on the bonnet of one of the parked cars. Kaye dimly hoped it belonged to one of them as she sat down, wiping tears from her cheeks. Already she'd stopped crying; the tears were more from shock than anything else.

Fatima lit a cigarette and handed it to Kaye. She took a deep drag, but her throat felt thick and the smoke just made her cough.

"I had a boyfriend like that once. Used to beat the shit out of me." Fatima sat next to Kaye and patted her back.

"Maybe he saw you with Kenny," Janet said without looking at her. She was leaning against a headlight, staring out across the high-way at the military base opposite the diner.

"I'm sorry," Kaye said miserably.

"Give her a break," Fatima said. "It's not like you didn't do the same thing to me."

Janet turned to look at Kaye then. "You're not going to get him, you know. He might want to fuck you, but he'd never go out with you."

Kaye just nodded, bringing the cigarette to her mouth with trembling hands. It would have been a better idea, she decided, if she had sworn off boys entirely.

"Is that Robin guy going to come after you?" Fatima asked. Kaye almost wanted to laugh at her concern. If he did, no one could do anything to stop him. He'd moved faster than Kaye could even see. She'd been very stupid not to be afraid of him.

"I don't think so," she said finally.

Kenny and Doughboy walked out of the diner, swaggering in tandem towards the girls.

"Everything okay?" Kenny asked.

"Just a couple of bruises," Kaye said. "No big deal."

"Damn," Doughboy said. "Between the other night and tonight, you're going to be too paranoid to hang out with us."

Kaye tried to smile, but she couldn't help wondering how double-edged those words were.

"Want me to drive you home?" Kenny asked.

Kaye looked up, about to thank him, when

Fatima interrupted. "Why don't you take Janet home, and I'll drop off Dough and Kaye."

Kenny looked down at the scuffed tops of his Doc Martens and sighed. "Right."

Fatima drove Kaye home in relative silence, and she was grateful. The radio was on, and she just sat in the passenger seat and pretended to listen. When Fatima pulled up in front of Kaye's grandmother's house, she cut the lights.

"I don't know what happened with you and Kenny," Fatima began.

"Me neither," Kaye said with a short laugh.

The other girl smiled and bit one of her manicured nails. "Look, I don't know about Robin and you or anything, but if you are just looking for some way to piss off your boyfriend, don't do it. Janet really loves Kenny, y'know? She's devoted."

Kaye opened the door and got out of the car. "Thanks for the ride."

"No problem." Fatima flicked the car lights back on.

Kaye slammed the door of the blue Honda and went inside.

When Kaye walked into the kitchen, her mother was on the phone, sitting at the kitchen table with a spiral notebook in front of her. When she saw Kaye come in, she gestured towards the cooker. There was a pot of cold spaghetti and sausages. Kaye took a fork and picked at some of the spaghetti.

"So you think you can get Charlotte?" her mother said into the phone as she doodled band names on the pad.

"All right, call me when you know. Absolutely. 'Bye, chickadee."

Ellen hung up the phone, and Kaye looked over at her expectantly.

Her mother smiled and took a sip from a mug on the table. "We're going to New York!"

Kaye just stared. "What?"

"Well, it's not totally definite, but Rhonda wants me to front her new all-girl group, Meow Factory, and she thinks she can get Charlotte Charlie. I said that if they can get her, I'm in. There are so many more clubs in New York."

"I don't want to move," Kaye said.

"We can crash with Rhonda until we can find another place to live. You'll love New York."

"I love it here."

"We can't impose on my mother forever," Ellen said. "Besides, she's a pain in your ass as much as mine."

"I applied for a job today. Grandma will be a lot happier once I'm bringing home money. You could join a band around here."

"Nothing's set in stone," Ellen said, "but I think you should really get used to the idea of New York, honey. If I'd wanted to stay in Jersey, I would have done it years ago."

* * *

A hundred matchbooks, from a hundred bars that her mother played one gig in, or from restaurants that they got a meal in, or from men that they lived with. A hundred matchbooks, all on fire.

She was on fire too, aflame in a way she was not sure she understood. Adrenalin turned her fingers to ice, drawing her heat inwards to dance in her head, anger and a strange sense of *possibility* thrumming through her veins.

Kaye looked around her dark bedroom, lit only by the flickering orange light. The glassy eyes of the dolls danced with flames. The rats curled up on one another in the far corner of the cage. Kaye breathed in the sharp smell of sulphur as she struck another matchbook, watching the flame catch across the rows of white match heads, the cardboard covering exploding into fire. She turned the paper in her hands, watching it burn.

5

"I ate the mythology & dreamt."
— Yusef Komunyakaa, "Blackberries"

Kaye awoke to a scratching at the window. The room was dark and the house was silent.

Something peered in at her. Tiny black eyes blinked beneath heavy eyebrows, and long ears rose up from either side of a bare head.

"Spike?" Kaye whispered, crawling up off the mattress on the floor where she had been sleeping. The covers tangled with her legs.

He tapped again, eyebrows furrowing. He was smaller than she remembered him and clad only in a thin bark that ran over his waist and down part of his legs. At his elbows, points extended into the shape of thorns.

Behind him, she could make out Lutie-loo's thin form, incandescent against the dark tiles of the roof. Her wings were so translucent as to be nearly invisible.

Kaye pushed on the window, but it took several tries to get it unstuck from the old, swollen sill. Two white moths fluttered in.

"Spike!" Kaye said. "Lutie! Where have you been? I've been back for days and days. I left milk out for you, but I think one of the cats got it."

The little man cocked one eye towards her, like a sparrow. "The Thistlewitch is waiting," Spike said. "Hurry."

His tone of voice was odd, urgent and strangely unfriendly. He had never talked to her that way before. Still, she obeyed out of familiarity: same old room, same little friends coming in the middle of the night to take her to catch fireflies or pick sour cherries. She pulled a black jumper on over the white old-lady nightdress her grandmother had loaned her to sleep in and kicked on her boots. Then she scanned the room for her coat, but it was just another black, soft pile in the dark, and she left it. The jumper was warm enough.

Kaye climbed out onto the roof. "Why does she want to see me?" Kaye had always thought of the Thistlewitch as a crotchety aunt, someone who didn't like to play and who you could get in trouble with.

"There's something she needs to tell you."

"Can't you tell me?" Kaye said. She swung her legs off the edge of the roof while Spike scuttled down over the bark and Lutie glided down on iridescent wings.

"Come on," Spike said.

Kaye pushed herself off the edge and dropped. The dry branches of a rhododendron bush scratched her legs as she landed, spry as a cat, on her two feet.

They ran towards the street, Lutie-loo dancing half in the air around Kaye whispering, "I missed you, I missed you."

"This way," Spike said, needlessly. Kaye remembered the way.

"I missed you too," Kaye said to Lutie, reaching out her hand to brush the light body. Lutie felt slick as water, smooth as smoke.

The Glass Swamp, so called because of the abundance of broken bottles choking the little stream, ran beneath the road a half a mile down the street. They climbed down the steep bank, Kaye's boots slipping in the mud. Beer bottles sat on rocks, some already smashed into big pieces. The thin rivulets of water shimmered with multicolour hues like a church window.

"What's happening? What's the matter?" she called as quietly as she could and still have Spike hear her. Something was definitely wrong – he was hurrying along like he couldn't look her in the face. But then, maybe she was too old to be fun any more.

He didn't answer.

Lutie darted up to her, hair whipping the air like a banner of cream. "We have to hurry.

Don't worry. It's good news – good news."

"Hush," Spike said.

The heavy growth close to the stream forced her to pick her way near the water's edge. Kaye stepped carefully along the bank, darkness making it hard to see whether the next step would plunge her boot into cold water. They walked in silence while Kaye tried to make out her path by the dim light of Lutie's glow.

A flash of white caught her eye – cracked eggshells bobbed in the narrow stream. Kaye stopped to watch the armada of shells, some small and spotted, others gleaming supermarket white. In the centre of one, a spider scuttled from side to side, an unwilling captain. In another, a black pin anchored the centre as the shell spun dizzily.

Kaye heard a chuckle.

"Much can be divined from an eggshell," the Thistlewitch said. Large black eyes peered out from the braided weeds and briars that covered her head like hair. She was sitting on the opposite side of the riverbank, her squat body covered in layers of drab cloth.

"They have even caught us," the Thistlewitch went on, "with the brewing of eggshells. Pride makes braggarts of even the wisest of the folk, so it is said."

Kaye had always been a little afraid of her, but this time she felt nothing but relief. The

Thistlewitch had kind eyes, and her scratchy voice was sweetly familiar. She was as unlike Roiben and his demon-horse as anything could be.

"Hullo," Kaye said, not sure how to address her. When she was a child, most of the times she had spoken to the faerie had involved a splinter or a skinned knee or an apology for dragging one of her friends Ironside for a prank. "Spike said you had something to tell me."

The Thistlewitch regarded her for a long moment, as if taking her measure.

"So much focus on the egg – it is life, it is food, it is answer to a hundred riddles – but look at its shell. The secrets are writ on its walls. Secrets lie in the entrails of things, in the dregs." The Thistlewitch poked a pin into either side of a tiny blue egg and put it to her lips. Her cheeks puffed out with air, and a trickle of clear, thick snotlike liquid drizzled into a copper bowl in her lap.

Kaye looked at the eggshells, still bobbing down the stream. She didn't understand. What secrets did they hold, except a spider and a pin?

The Thistlewitch tapped the damp earth beside her. "Would you see what I see, Kaye? Sit beside me."

Kaye looked for a dry patch and crossed the stream with an easy leap.

A tiny being wearing a moleskin coat

slithered onto the Thistlewitch's lap and poked its head inquisitively into the bowl.

"Once, there were two courts, the bright and the dark, the Seelie and the Unseelie, the folk of the air and the folk of the earth. They fought like a serpent devouring its own tail, but we kept from their affairs, kept to our hidden groves and underground streams, and they forgot us. Now they have made truce and remembered that rulers must have subjects. There is such a habit of service among us." The Thistlewitch stroked the gleaming fur of the little faerie's coat absently as she spoke. "They have brought back the Tithe, the sacrifice of a beautiful and talented mortal. In the Seelie Court they may steal away a poet to join their company, but the Unseelie Court requires blood. In exchange, those who dwell in Unseelie lands must bind themselves into service. Their service is hard, Kaye, and their amusements are cruel. And now you have drawn their notice."

"Because of Roiben?"

"Oh do speak his name again," Spike hissed. "Shall we invite the whole Unseelie Court to afternoon tea while we're being daft?"

"Hush," the Thistlewitch soothed. Spike stomped his foot and looked away.

"You mustn't even use their speaking names aloud," the Thistlewitch told Kaye. "The Unseelie Court is terrible, terrible and dangerous. And of the Unseelie Court, no knight is as feared as . . . the one you spoke with. When the truce was made, each of the Queens exchanged their best knights – he was the offering from the Seelie Court. The Queen sends him on the worst of her errands."

"He is so unpredictable that even his Queen cannot trust him. He's as likely to be kind as to kill you," Spike put in. "He killed Gristle."

"I know," Kaye said. "He told me."

Spike looked at the Thistlewitch in surprise. "That's exactly what I mean! What perverse ovation of friendship is that?"

"How . . . how did he do it?" Kaye asked, half of her dreading the answer, but needing to know nonetheless. "How did Gristle die?"

Lutie flitted to hover in front of her, tiny face mournful. "He was with me. We went to the knowe – the faerie hill. There was cowslip wine, and Gristle wanted me to help him filch a bottle. He was going to trade it for a pair of pretty boots from one of his hob friends.

"It was easy to find the way inside. There's a patch of grass that's all brown and that's the door. We got the bottle, easy-peasy, and were on our way out when we saw the cakes."

"Cakes?" Kaye was baffled.

"Beautiful white honey cakes, heaped on a plate for the taking. Eat 'em and you get wiser, you know."

"I don't think it works that way," Kaye said.

"Of course it does," Lutie-loo scolded. "How else would it work?"

Continuing, the tiny faerie gripped onto a thin twig and hung from a low bush as she spoke. "He swallowed five before they caught him."

Kaye didn't point out that if these cakes were supposed to make him wiser, it should have occurred to him to stop after one. It didn't make his death any less horrifying.

"They probably would have let him go, but *she* needed a fox for her hunt. Since he stole the cakes, she said he was the perfect fox. Oh, Kaye it was awful. They had these dogs and horses, and they just rode him down. Roiben was the one that got him."

"What is it with you fools and saying his name?" Spike growled.

Kaye shook her head. Roiben had killed Gristle for fun? Because he stole some food? And she'd helped the bastard. It made her skin crawl to think of the easy way she'd spoken with Roiben, the ways she had thought of him. She wondered what exactly could be done with a name, what sort of revenge she could really have.

The Thistlewitch held out the little egg. "Come, Kaye, blow out the insides of the egg and then break it open. There is a secret for you."

Kaye took the little blue egg. It was so light

that she was afraid it would break from the slight pressure of her hand.

She knelt over the Thistlewitch's bowl and blew lightly into the pinhole of the egg. A viscous stream of albumen and yolk slithered from the other side, dropping into the bowl.

"Now break it."

Kaye pressed her thumb against the egg and the whole side of it collapsed, held together by a thin membrane.

Spike and Lutie looked surprised, but the Thistlewitch just nodded.

"I did it wrong," Kaye said, and brushed the eggshells into the stream. Unlike the little boats, this egg was a shower of confetti on the water.

"Let me just speak another secret then, child, since this one eludes you. If you think on it, I'm sure that you'll admit there's something passing strange about you. A strangeness, not just of manner, but of something else. The scent of it, the spoor of it, warns Ironsiders off, makes them wary and draws them in all the same."

Kaye shook her head, not sure where this was going.

"Tell her a different secret," Spike warned. "This one will only make things harder."

"You are one of us," the Thistlewitch said to Kaye, black eyes glittering like jewels.

"What?" She'd heard what was said, she

understood, she was just stalling for time for her brain to start working again. She could not seem to get a breath of air into her lungs. There were grades to impossible, levels, at least, of unreality. And each time Kaye thought she was at the lowest level, the ground seemed to open up beneath her.

"Mortal girls are stupid and slow," Lutie said. "You don't have to pretend any more."

She was shaking her head, but even as she did it, she knew it was true. It felt true, unbalancing and rebalancing her world so neatly that she wondered how she didn't think of it before now. After all, why would only she be visited by faeries? Why would only she have magic she couldn't control?

"Why didn't you tell me?" Kaye demanded.

"Too chancy," Spike said.

"So why are you telling me now?"

"Because it is you who will be chosen for the Tithe." The Thistlewitch crossed her lanky arms serenely. "And because it is your right to know."

Spike snorted.

"What? But you said I'm not . . ." She stopped herself. Not one single intelligent comment had come out of her mouth all night, and she doubted that was likely to change.

"They figure you're human," Spike said. "And that's a good thing."

"Some crazy faeries want to kill me and you

think it's a good thing? Hey, I thought we were friends."

Spike didn't even have the grace to smile at the weak joke. He was entirely wrapped up in his planning. "There is a knight from the Seelie Court. He can pull the glamour off you. It will look like the Unseelie Queen wanted to sacrifice one of our own – the sort of jest many would well believe of her." Spike took a breath. "We need your help."

Kaye bit her upper lip, running her teeth over it in deep concentration. "I'm really confused right now – you guys know that, right?"

"If you help us, we'll be freeeeee," Lutie said. "Seven years of free!"

"So what's the difference between the Seelie Court and the Unseelie Court?"

"There are many, many courts, Seelie and Unseelie alike. But it is nearly always true that the Unseelie Courts are worse and that the gentry of either court enjoy their rule over the commoners and still more over the solitary fey. We, without ties to any courts, are at the mercy of whoever rules the lands to which we are tied."

"So why don't you just leave?"

"Some of us cannot, the tree people, for instance. But for the others, where would we go? Another court might be harder than this one."

"Why do the solitary fey trade their freedom for a human sacrifice?"

"Some do it for the blood, others for protection. The human sacrifice is a show of power. Power that could force our obedience."

"But won't they just take you back by force, then?"

"No. They must obey the agreement as we do. They are bound by its constraints. If the sacrifice is voided, then we are free for seven years. None may command us."

"Look, you guys, you know I'll help you. I'd help you do anything."

The huge smile on Spike's face chased away all her former concern over his gruffness. He must have just been worried she'd say no. Lutie flew around her happily, lifting up strands of her hair and either tangling or braiding them; Kaye couldn't be sure.

Kaye took a deep breath and, ignoring Lutie's ministrations, turned to the Thistlewitch. "How did this happen? If I'm like you, how come I live with my . . . with Ellen?"

The Thistlewitch looked into the river, her gaze following the wobbling egg-boats. "Do you know what a changeling is? In ancient times, we usually left stock – bits of wood or dying fey – enchanted to look like a stolen babe and left in the cradle. It is rarely that we leave one of our own behind, but when we do, the child's fey nature becomes harder and harder to conceal as it grows. In the end, they all return to Faery."

"But why – not why do they return, but why me? Why leave me?"

Spike shook his head. "We don't know the answer to that any more than we know why we were told to watch you."

It was staggering to Kaye to realise that there might be another Kaye Fierch, the real Kaye Fierch, off somewhere in Faerie. "You said . . . glamoured. Does that mean I don't look like this?"

"It's a very powerful glamour. Someone put it on to stay." Spike nodded sagely.

"What do I really look like?"

"Well, you're a pixie, if that helps." Spike scratched his head. "It usually means green."

Kaye closed her eyes tightly, shaking her head. "How can I see me?"

"I don't advise it," Spike said. "Once you pull that thing off, no one we know can put it back on that good. Just let it be until Samhain – that's when the Tithe is. Someone might figure out what you are if you go messing with your face."

"Soon it'll be off for good and you won't have to pretend to be mortal any more if you don't want," Lutie chirped.

"If the glamour on me is so good, how did you know what I was?"

The Thistlewitch smiled. "Glamour is the stuff of illusion, but sometimes, if deftly woven, it can be more than a mere disguise. Fantastical pockets can actually hold baubles, an illusionary umbrella can protect one from the rain, and magical gold can remain gold, at least until the warmth of the magician's hand fades from the coins. The magic on you is the strongest I have seen, Kaye. It protects you even from the touch of iron, which burns faerie flesh. I know you to be a pixie because I saw you when you were very small and we lived in Seelie lands. The Queen herself asked us to look after you."

"But why?"

"Who can tell the whims of Queens?"

"What if I did want to remove the glamour?" Kaye insisted.

The Thistlewitch took a step towards her. "The ways of removing faerie magic are many. A four-leaf clover, rowan berries, looking at yourself through a rock with a natural hole. It is your decision to make."

Kaye took a deep breath. She needed to think. "I'm going to go back to bed."

"One more thing," the Thistlewitch said as Kaye rose from the bank and dusted off the backs of her thighs. "Heed the warning of your shattered eggshell. Where you go, chaos and discord will follow."

"What does that mean?"

The Thistlewitch smiled. "Time will tell. It always does."

* * *

　　　　　　　　　　HOLLY BLACK

Kaye stood on the lawn of her grandmother's house. It was dark except for the silvery moon, the moon that didn't seem anthropomorphic tonight, just a cold rock glowing with reflected light. It was the bare trees that looked alive, their twisted branches sharp arrows that might pierce her heart.

Still, she could not go inside the house. She sat in the dew-damp grass and ripped up clumps of it, tossing them in the air and feeling vaguely guilty about it. Some gnome ought to pop out of the tree and scold her for torturing the lawn.

A pixie. The word sounded so . . . so *frolicky*. It made her smile, though, to think of being magical, of having wings like Lutie, of having quick fingers like poor Gristle.

Her stomach clenched when she thought about her mother, though. Her mother, whose head she'd fished out of toilets, who dragged them from apartment to apartment and from bar to bar following some distant dream. Her mother, who once broke one of Kaye's favourite LPs because she was "sick of listening to that talentless whore." Her mother, who had never told her she was weird, had always encouraged her to think for herself, stood up for her, and never, ever told her that she was a liar.

What would her mother think if she realised that her daughter wasn't the girl she'd lived with for sixteen years? No, Ellen's baby had been boosted by quick-fingered elves.

It was just too fucked-up to dwell on.

And if she wasn't Kaye Fierch, freaky human girl, then what was she? She knew that they didn't want her to mess up the plan for Hallowe'en, but right now, she just wanted to see what she looked like.

There were patches of clover on the lawn.

Leaning into the patch of brown, half-dead clover, she spread her fingers out and searched. There were so many, even in autumn, there had to be one with four leaves.

It was slow going in the dark, and yet none of the clover she dug through had more or less than three leaves. She was getting desperate enough to tear one of the heart-shaped leaves down the middle and find out whether this magic stuff was more symbolic or literal. Still, it wasn't like she had to find it, she only had to touch it. . . .

Oh, that was too stupid. That could never work. Even if it did work it was still stupid.

Kaye spread herself out on the ground, hoping no cars were driving by at this hour. Then she rolled over the patch of clover. The ground was cold, the dew dusted with frost. She rolled dizzily, holding her arms above her head. She had to laugh as she did it – the whole thing was absurd and it was making her damp and really, really cold, but there was something in the smell of the earth and the touch of the

HOLLY BLACK

grass that enervated her. Her laughter spun up out of her mouth in warm gusts of breath.

She didn't feel changed, but she did feel better. She was grinning like a fool, anxiety put to rest by silliness.

Lying back, Kaye tried to imagine herself as a faerie, all sparkly with hair that was always blowing in the breeze. The only image she could summon up, however, was that of a pale green face she had thought she'd seen as she was leaving the diner toilets. She could remember it in such detail that it felt less real than a memory. Perhaps it was something from a movie.

Kaye rolled over to get up and go inside when she noticed that a piece of skin on her hand was loose. When she touched it with a tentative finger, it sloughed off like a sunburn, revealing tender green skin. Kaye licked her finger and tried to rub off the pigment. It didn't come off; the area only spread wider. Her hand tasted like dirt.

Kaye stopped moving. She was scared, scared, sick with scared, but calm too, calm as nothing. *Get a grip*, she told herself, *you wanted to see this.*

Her eyes itched, and she rubbed her knucklebones over them. Something came off against her fingers. It felt like a contact lens, but when she looked down, she saw that it was skin and that with the rubbing, even more skin had come off her hands.

As she looked up, it seemed that the whole world had grown brighter, shimmering with light. Colours danced along the grass. The brown of the trees was many-hued, the wrinkles of shadows deep as newly turned secrets, and beautiful.

She spread her arms as wide as they would go. She could smell the pungent green of the grass she stamped as she rose. She could smell the sharp chill of the air as she spun, full of car exhaust, of crumpled leaves, of smoke from some distant leafpile burning. She could smell the rot of desiccated wood, the spoilage of the hoards that ants piled away for winter. She could hear the churning of termites, the whine of electricity in the house, the wind rustling a thousand paper-dry leaves.

She could taste chemicals in the air – iron, smoke, other things she had no names for. They played over her tongue in dark harmony.

It was too much. It was overwhelming. There were so many sensations buffeting her, too many for her to filter out. She couldn't go inside the house like this, but right now she wanted to; she wanted to burrow under her blankets and wait for all-forgiving dawn. She wasn't ready for this – it had been a whim, her curiosity.

What did she really look like?

She should go back now, back to the swamp, confess all, and let the Thistlewitch explain what she'd just done to herself. Kaye forced herself to take a few quick breaths without thinking what they tasted like. She was fine, better than fine, she was fucking supernatural. All she had to do was walk back to the swamp and not touch any of her skin on the way.

But once she started, she knew she couldn't walk. She was running. Running through the backyards of houses, hearing dogs barking, and her legs wet from unmowed grass. Running, through a car park, mostly empty, where a boy pushing trolleys stopped to look at her, and into the yard behind, and the sweet reek of rubbish, where she stopped, panting, and held her sides. There it was, the thin disguise of trees and the small river that flowed through it.

"Spike! Lutie!" Kaye called, frightened by the breathless gasp of her own voice. "Please . . ."

Nothing answered her but silence.

Kaye staggered down the hill, her boots sinking in the mud. The eggshells were gone. There was only the stink of stagnant water. The shattered bottles shimmered like jagged jewels through her new eyes. She stopped, awed by the beauty.

"Please, Lutie, someone . . ."

No one answered.

Kaye sat down in the cold mud. She could wait. She would have to wait.

Kaye stretched and turned. The leaves over her shifted and blew with the morning wind. Drops of cold water tapped her cheek, then her arm, then the lid of her one eye. Kaye sat up. Her eyes felt hard and her lips were sore and swollen.

There was a green sheen to Kaye's skin when she turned her arm against the light. Her fingers seemed too long and curled fluidly with a new fourth joint, coiling like snails when she made a fist. She brought up her other hand, where the skin had come loose last night. Beneath it, her skin was a dusky emerald.

No one had come. Another droplet spattered her bare leg, and she jerked upright. Her nightgown was filthy, and she was shivering, even under her jumper.

Biting back tears, Kaye folded her arms around herself and started walking. She couldn't go home – not yet, not when she knew she wasn't the girl who belonged there – but she had to get out of the rain. At least Janet couldn't call her a liar this time.

She stopped in a car park and twisted the side mirror of a car towards her so that she could see her profile. Her hair was matted in a nimbus of twigs, wet with dew, and she saw that her skin was shadowed with the lush dark green of moss. Not a stain, but a tint, as though a veil of green lay over her. Her ear was longer, sticking up through her hair to the top of her head. Her cheek, sunken and sharp, and her eye, slanted and black, all shiny black, with a pinpoint of white pupil. Like a bird eye or a single bead.

She reached up and touched her face. The skin tore easily, revealing a strip of grass-green skin.

Her hand hit the mirror, spiderwebbing the glass, and surprising her. Ignoring the pain in her wrist and the damp burn of blood on her knuckles, she started to run.

Corny squinted. A girl in green makeup ran across the street and under the awning of the petrol station. She looked up, and he thought he recognised her, but when she got closer, he wasn't so sure.

"I was going to Janet's," she said, sounding just like Kaye. "But I just remembered she's at school."

Up close the girl didn't look anything like Kaye. She didn't look anything like anybody. Her upturned eyes were black as oil spills. She was too thin. Tall ears parted her tangled hair on either side of her head. Her skin seemed to be flaking, showing patches of green underneath.

"Kaye?" Corny asked.

The girl smiled at him, but her smile was too fierce. The skin tore on her lower lip.

He was frozen, staring at her.

She scooted past him into the office, stretching her twiglike fingers. He stifled a whimper, trying to keep his eyes focused on the credit-card unit, the dirty papers, the laminated nude air freshener, all familiar things. He could smell her, a weird combination of pine needles, moss, and leaf piles. It was making him dizzy.

She sat down on the floor on top of papers and fast-food boxes.

"What the hell happened to you?"

Kaye held out her hand and tilted it slightly in the light. "I'm sick," she said. "I'm really sick."

He crouched down and looked at her again. There was a luminescence to her skin, a kind of brightness about her that made her eyes glitter feverishly. There was something about her shape itself that was strange, a hunching of the shoulders, a slight bulge of the back.

He picked up a block of wood with a dangling key. "Let's go in the toilet. The light's better and you can wash more of this crap off."

She got up off the floor.

"I could take you over to the hospital," he said. She didn't reply, and he didn't pursue it. He knew this wasn't a hospital-type thing – he just felt like he ought to say it.

The toilet was grimy. Corny certainly couldn't recall anyone doing more than changing the toilet paper in all the time he had worked there. The once-white tiles were cracked and greyed. There was barely enough room for two people, but Kaye squeezed in obediently next to the toilet and stripped off her jumper.

"Take off the rest of it. There's something on your back."

She threw a considering look at him and seemed to decide either he didn't care or she didn't. She kicked off her boots, pulled off the jumper and then the nightdress until she was only in her knickers.

Bunching up her nightdress under the tap, he got it sopping wet. He used the cloth to scrub off what was left of her skin and the pigment of her hair. Her skin was thin as crepe on her back. As he rubbed the cloth over the bump between her shoulders, the skin cracked.

A thin whitish fluid leaked out between her shoulder blades.

"Uuughh!" Corny moved back from her.

Kaye looked back at him, and her face said that she just couldn't take any more weirdness. Of course it was hard to know whether he was reading her strange eyes right.

"Its okay," he said in as soothing a voice as he could. Outside he heard a car pull into the petrol station. He ignored it.

"What happened?" There was something moving under the surface of her back, something slick and iridescent.

"Hold on," he said. The thick fluid was wiping off, showing white-veined iridescence all the way down her back. Suddenly something flicked loose, rising so that it almost slapped Corny before it fell wetly against her back.

"Oh, God," Corny said. "You have wings."

The damp things moved feebly.

The sight of it sent a thrill through him, despite the fear. This was the real thing.

"C'mon," he said. "My house."

6

Kaye sat down gingerly at the edge of the couch, so that her new wings hung off the edge and wouldn't get crushed if she moved suddenly or leaned back.

She was wearing a pair of Corny's jeans, belted and rolled at the cuffs, and a black, hooded sweatshirt. Corny had taken a pair of scissors and cut a large section out of the back of it so that they could feed her wings through. Her skin was so sensitive that she imagined she could feel particles as they drifted through the air.

Corny poured himself a glass of Mountain Dew. "Can you drink this?"

"I think so," Kaye said. "I could before."

He poured some in a mug and handed it over to her. She didn't sip it – it was the same colour as her skin.

She could *smell* the drink, smell the green dyes and the chemical carbonation. She could smell Corny, the acid of his excited sweating and sourness of his breath. The air she breathed tasted of cigarettes and cats and plastic and iron in a way she had never noticed before – it nearly made her gag with each breath.

"It's starting to sink in," Corny said. "I can almost look at you without wanting to bang my head against the wall."

"I'm not sure how to explain. It started a long time ago. I'm not sure I remember important things."

"Recently, then." Corny sat down on the couch. He was staring at her with what looked like a combination of fascination and repulsion.

"I rolled in some clover." She gave a short laugh at the absurdity of it.

"Why?" Corny didn't laugh at all. He was totally serious.

"Because the Thistlewitch told me that that was one of the ways I could see myself the way I really am. See – I told you that it gets ridiculous."

"This is the way you really are, then?"

Kaye nodded carefully. "I guess so."

"And this thimble witch? Who is she?"

"Thistlewitch," Kaye corrected. And she told him. Told him how she'd known faeries for as long as she could remember, how Spike would perch on the footboard of her bed when she was small and tell her stories about goblins and giants while Lutie darted around the room like a manic nightlight. She told him how Gristle taught her how to make a piercing whistle with a blade of grass and described the Thistlewitch divining with eggshells.

All the while, Corny stared with greedy eyes.

"Who knew about these friends?"

Kaye shrugged. "My mum, my grand-mother – I guess I'm not really related to them at all . . ." She stopped suddenly. Her voice sounded unsteady, even to herself, and she took a deep breath. "Everyone in my first-grade class. You. Janet."

"Did any of these people see the faeries? Ever?"

Kaye shook her head.

Corny turned his gaze towards the wall, frowning in concentration. "And you can't call them?"

Kaye shook her head again. "They find me when they want to – that's the way it always was. Right now, that's the problem. I can't stay like this, and I don't know how to get reglam-oured."

"There isn't anywhere you can look?"

"No," Kaye said vehemently. "I already told you no. The swamp was the only place, and I was there all night."

"But you're a faerie too. Don't you have any abilities?"

"I don't know," Kaye said, thinking of Kenny. That was definitely not something she really wanted to discuss right now. Her head hurt enough already.

"Can you cast any spells?"

"I don't know, I don't know, I don't know! Can't you understand that I don't know anything at all?"

"Come on in the back. Let's go online."

They went into Corny's room, and he flicked on his computer. The screen went blue, and then his background picture loaded. It was a wizard hunched over a chess table while the two queen pieces battled, one all black and the other all white.

Kaye flopped onto the tangled sheets of his bed, stomach down, wings up.

Corny tapped a few keys, and his modem groaned.

"Okay. F-a-e-r-i-e. Let's see. Hmmm. Gay stuff – don't go there."

She sniggered anyway.

"Here we go. German changelings. Pictures. Yeats poetry."

"Apparently, I'm a pixie," Kaye supplied. "Click on the changeling thing, though."

"Interesting."

He scrolled through it, and she tried to read it from her slightly-too-distant vantage point. "What?"

"Says you throw 'em in the fire to get your

own kid back . . . that or stick a hot poker down their throats."

"Great. Next."

"Here we go. Pixie. Can detect good and evil, hate orcs, and are about one to two feet tall . . ." He started to laugh. "Makes pixie dust."

"Orcs?" Kaye inquired. She shifted her position, suddenly aware that it was hard to separate which muscles caused her wings to twitch. They seemed to move independently of her will and of each other, like two soft insects alighting on her back.

Corny couldn't stop laughing. "Pixie dust. Like angels make angel dust. International drug cartels grab seraphim and shake 'em. Priests who sweep up churches put that stuff in freezer bags."

She snorted. "You're an idiot, you know that?"

"I try," he said, still laughing.

"Well, try 'Unseelie Court.'"

A few clicks of his mouse and he said, "Looks like that's where all the bad guys hang out in Faeryland. What does this have to do with you?"

"There's this knight there who may or may not be wanting to kill me. My friends want me to pretend to be human because there's this thing called the Tithe . . . it's complicated."

Corny sat up again. "Why didn't you tell me?"

"I just told you the part that made sense."

"Okay." Corny nodded. "Now tell me the part that doesn't make sense."

"I don't understand it all exactly, but basically there are solitary faeries and court faeries. Roiben is one of the court faeries, and I met him in the woods after he got shot. He's from the Unseelie Court."

"Okay. I'm still with you, if barely."

"Spike and Lutie-loo sent me an acorn message to tell me that he was dangerous. He killed my other friend, Gristle."

"An acorn message?"

"The top came off. It was hollow."

"Right. Of course."

"Ha-ha. Look for 'Tithe' next, okay? As far as I know, it's this sacrifice that makes the faeries that aren't part of any court still do what the court people say. I have to pretend to be human so they can pretend to sacrifice me."

He typed in the keyword. "I'm just getting Jesus Crispy shit. Give-me-ten-percent-of-your-cash-to-me-so-I-can-buy-an-air-conditioned-doghouse kind of thing. This sacrifice – how safe is that? I mean, how well do you know these people?"

"I trust them absolutely . . ."

"But," Corny prompted.

She smiled ruefully. "But they never *told* me. They knew all this time, and nothing – not one hint." Kaye looked pensively at the joints of her fingers. Why should one extra joint make them horrifying? It did, though – flexing them bothered her.

Corny steepled his palms, cracking his knuckles like a villain. "Tell me the whole story again, slowly, and from the beginning."

Kaye woke up muzzily, not sure where she was. She shifted until she felt a solid shape that groaned and pushed at her. Corny. She squinted at him and rubbed at her eyes. It was dark in the room, the only streaks of light sneaking around the edges of the heavy brown curtains. She heard voices from somewhere in the trailer over the distant sound of canned television laughter.

She turned over again, trying to go back to sleep. The bedside table was in front of her line of vision. A book, *Vintage*, a bottle of ibuprofen, an alarm clock with flames on the clock face, and a black plastic chess knight.

"Corny," she said, shaking what she thought was the shoulder of the lump. "Wake up. I know what to do. I know what we can do."

He pushed the covers back from over his head. His eyes were slits of wet in the piles of duvet. "This better be good," he groaned.

"The kelpie. I know how to call the kelpie."

He pushed back the covers and sat up, suddenly awake. "Right. That's right." He slid out of bed, scratching his balls through once-white briefs, and sat down in front of the computer. The screensaver dispersed as he shook the mouse.

In the hallway, Kaye could hear Janet's voice distinctly, complaining to her mother about the fact that she wasn't going to get her licence if Corny didn't let her borrow his car.

"What time is it?" Kaye asked.

Corny looked at the clock on the screen. "After five."

"Can I use your phone?"

He nodded. "Do it now. You can't use it while I'm signed on. We only have the one line."

Corny's bedroom phone was a copy of the emergency bat-phone, bright red and sitting under a plastic dome on the floor. It even had a little bulb in it that she imagined might blink when a call came in. Kaye sat down cross-legged on the floor, took off the dome, and dialled her house.

"Hello?" Kaye's grandmother answered.

"Grandma?" She dragged her fingers over the synthetic loops of the rug she was sitting on. Her eyes fell on her long green toes with chipped red nail polish on the jagged, untrimmed toenails.

"Where are you?"

"I'm at Janet's," Kaye said, wiggling the toes, willing herself to realise they belonged to her. It was hard talking to her grandmother now. The only reason her grandmother put up with her and Ellen was because they were family and you always took care of family. "I just wanted to tell you where I am."

"Where were you this morning?"

"I got up early," Kaye said. "I had to meet some friends before school started." That was true enough, in a way.

"Well, when are you coming home then? Oh, and I have two messages for you. Joe from the Amoco called about some job – I hope you're not thinking of working at a petrol station – and some boy named Kenny called twice."

"Twice?" Kaye couldn't help the smile that was pushing up the corners of a mouth she was determined to keep grim.

"Yes. Are you coming home for dinner?"

"No, I'll eat here," Kaye said. "'Bye, Gram, I love you."

"I think your mother would like it if you came home for dinner. She wants to talk to you about New York."

"I've got to go. 'Bye, Gram."

Kaye hung up the phone before her grandmother could start another sentence. "You can sign on now," she said.

A few minutes later, Corny made a noise.

She looked up.

"Your plan has one little problem."

"Don't they all . . . no, tell me, what is it?"

"Kelpies basically like to drown people and then eat most of them – all but their guts. You're not supposed to get on their backs, yadda, yadda, yadda, they're fucking evil as hell, yadda, yadda, yadda, not to mention they shapeshift. Oh, yeah, you can tame them if you happen to manage to get a bridle on them. Fat chance of that."

"Oh."

"Did you ever wonder if some of these sites were designed by faeries? I wonder if I kept looking if I could find a newsgroup or a hub page or something."

"So, if we don't sit on its back, are we safe?"

"Huh? Oh . . . I don't know."

"Well, are there instances there where it drowns people without them getting on its back?"

"No, but then it's not all that comprehensive."

"I'm going to try it. I'm going to talk to it."

He looked up from the computer desk. "You're not going without me."

"Okay," Kaye said. "I just thought that it might be dangerous."

"This is the real thing," he said, voice dropping low, "and I don't want to miss even one little bit of it. Don't even think of running off."

She held up both hands in mock surrender. "I want you to go with me. Really, okay?"

HOLLY BLACK

"I don't want to wake up someplace with a screwed-up memory and nobody ever believing me. Do you understand?" Corny's face was flushed.

"C'mon, Corny, either your mum or Janet is going to hear you and come in here. I'm not leaving you."

Kaye watched as he calmed somewhat, thinking that she should stop trying to anticipate what was going to happen next. After all, when you were already in a slippery place, reality-wise, you couldn't afford to assume that things would be straightforward from here on in.

The metal of the car made her feel heavy and drowsy and sick, the way that carbon monoxide poisoning was supposed to make you feel before it killed you. Kaye rested her cheek against the cool glass of the window. Her throat was dry and her head was pounding. It had something to do with the air in the car, which seemed to scald her lungs as she breathed it. It was a short drive, and she was glad of it, practically tumbling out of the car when Corny opened the door for her.

In the daylight, it was easy to see rows of houses beyond the trees, and Kaye wondered how it could have seemed like a great woods when she had stumbled through here. The stream, when they found it, was thick with rubbish. Corny leaned down and smeared dirt off a brown bottle that didn't look like it was for beer. It looked like it should be holding some snake-oil salesman's hair tonic or something.

"Vaseline glass," he said. "Some of this stuff is really old. I bet you could sell some of these." He pushed another bottle with his toe. "So, how do we call this thing?"

Kaye picked up a brown leaf. "Do you have anything sharp?"

He reached into his back pocket and pulled out a penknife, flicking it open with a deft movement of his thumb. "Just remember what the site said – no getting on its back, no way, no day, no matter what."

"I saw the page, okay? You don't have to keep reminding me. Kelpie equals evil water horse that drowns people for fun. I get it."

"Well, just so you're sure."

He let her take the knife. She slid the tip of it into the pad of her thumb. A bright dot of blood welled up, and she smeared it on the leaf.

"Now what?" he asked, but for all that the words sounded cynical, he was barely breathing as he spoke them.

She dropped the leaf into the stream, blood side down, as she had done before. "I'm Kaye," she said, trying to remember the words. "I'm not from any court but I need your help. Please hear me."

There was a long moment of silence after

that when Corny let out his breath. She could see him start to believe that nothing was going to happen and she was torn between the desire to prove that she knew what she was doing and the fear of what was coming.

A moment later, there was no more doubt as a black horse rose from the water.

Either because it was day or with Kaye's new sight, the creature looked different. Its colour was not so much black, but an emerald so deep that it looked black. And the nacreous eyes were gleaming like pearls. Still, when it regarded Kaye, she was forced to think of the research Corny had done. That was chilling enough.

The kelpie strode onto the shore and shook its great mane, spraying her and Corny with glittering droplets of swamp water. Kaye held up her hands, but it hardly helped.

"What do you seek?" the horse spoke, its voice soft but deep.

Kaye took a deep breath. "I need to know how to glamour myself and I need to know how to control my magic. Can you teach me?"

"What will you give me, girl-child?"

"What do you want?"

"Perhaps that one would like to ride on my back. I would teach you if you let him ride with me."

"So that you can kill him? No way."

"I wonder about death, I who may never

know it. It looks much like ecstasy, the way they open their mouths as they drown, the way their fingers dig into your skin. Their eyes are wide and startled and they thrash in your hands as though with an excess of passion."

Kaye shook her head, horrified.

"You can hardly blame me. It is my nature. And it has been a very long time."

"I'm not going to help you kill people."

"There might be something else that would tempt me, but I can't think what. I'll give you the opportunity to think up something."

Kaye sighed.

"You know where to find me."

With that, the kelpie waded back into the water.

Corny was still sitting stunned on the bank. "That thing wanted to kill me."

Kaye nodded.

"Are you going to try to find something it wants?"

Kaye nodded again. "Yeah."

"I don't know how I feel about that."

"You read the site. You knew it would be like this."

"I guess. It's different to see it . . . to hear it."

"Do you want us to leave?"

"Hell, no."

"Any ideas what it might want that doesn't walk on two feet?"

"Well," he said, after a moment's consideration, "actually there are a whole lot of people I wouldn't mind feeding to that thing."

She laughed.

"No, really," he said.

"What do you mean?"

"I mean that there are a whole lot of people that I wouldn't mind seeing drowned. Really. I think that we should go for it."

Kaye looked up at him. He didn't look particularly fazed by what he had just proposed.

"No way," she said.

Corny shrugged. "Janet's boyfriend, for example. What a prick."

"Kenny?" Kaye squeaked.

"Look, it doesn't have to be him. I could think of a dozen people. The best thing is that they're all so dumb I'm sure I would have no problem convincing them to come down here and ride the horse. I'm thinking that stupidity should have consequences. C'mon, we can do a little weeding of the human race." He waggled his eyebrows.

"No," she said. "Think of something other than people we can give it."

"Oats?" he said vaguely. "A huge box of instant porridge? A subscription to *Equestrian's Digest*? Hay and lots of it?"

"We're not getting people killed, so just give it up, okay?"

She was getting sick of listening to Corny's sighs.

She bet that Roiben's name would be a fair price. After all, this thing was probably not part of any court, being tied to the stream here. She bet that he would be counted as a fair price indeed. And it wouldn't change the fact that she knew the name too.

It would be a fine revenge on him for killing Gristle.

But then, she imagined that the kelpie would just order him to bring people for it to drown. And he would do it.

What else was there to bargain with that a kelpie might like?

She thought about the dolls in her room, but all she could picture was a little girl following a trail of them to the shore of the stream. Ditto with any musical instrument. She had to think about something that the kelpie could enjoy alone . . . clothing? Food?

Then she thought of it . . . a companion. A companion that it could never drown. Something that it could talk to and admire. The merry-go-round horse.

"Oh, Corny," Kaye said, "I know just the thing."

Getting back in the car was the last thing that Kaye wanted to do, but she did, sliding into the backseat, pressing her shirt over her mouth as though the fabric could filter the iron out of the air.

"You know where you're going, right?" she asked, wondering if he could understand the words, muffled as they were by the cloth.

"Yeah."

She let her head slide down to the plastic seat, one wing twitched just out of her vision, sending scattered luminescent rainbows through the thin membrane to dance on her leg under each passed light. Everything narrowed to those rainbows. There was no Corny in the front seat, no scratchy radio song, no passing cars, no houses, no malls, no real things to protect her from the glittering patterns on her grass-green thighs.

There were no words for what she felt, no sounds, nothing. There was no word for what she was, no explanation that would keep back the numb, dumb dark. She felt the dizziness threaten to overwhelm her.

"Can you please open your window?" she asked. "I can't breathe."

"What's wrong with yours?"

She crouched on the edge of the seat and reached her hands into the front of the car, palms up like a supplicant. "Every time I touch the handle, it burns. Look." She held her hand out to him, and he could see that part of it was flushed. Her fingers wiggled. "That's from the door handle."

"Shit." Corny took a breath, but he could not seem to let it go. He rolled down his window.

The salt in the air cleaned her throat with each lungful from the open window, but it wasn't enough to battle the rising nausea. "I have to get out of this car."

"We're almost there." Corny stopped at the red light.

Corny parked the car outside the big building. It was strange to see it in the daytime. The overcast sky made the outside of the building look even dingier.

"Are you okay?" Corny asked, and turned his head to see her in the backseat.

Kaye shook her head. She was going to vomit, right there, right on top of the empty drinks cans and mashed fast-food boxes. She put her hand in the pocket of the sweatshirt and opened the door.

"Kaye! What are you doing?"

Kaye half fell, half crawled onto the asphalt of the car park and dragged herself to the edge of the grass before she started vomiting. There was little in her stomach, and most of what she coughed up was stomach acid and spittle.

"Jesus!" Corny crouched down next to her.

"I'm okay," Kaye said, rising dizzily to her feet. "It's all the metal."

He nodded, looking back at the car and then looking around sceptically. "Maybe we should forget about this."

Kaye took a deep breath. "No. Come on."

She ran around the back, following the

path she had walked with Janet. "Give me your jacket," she said. "There's glass."

Everything was different in daylight.

Up the stairs and there it was, dingier now that she got a good look at it, but still beautiful. The cream of its flanks was closer to a brown, and the gilt trim was mostly rubbed off. Its lips were carved in what she thought was a slight sneer, and Kaye grinned to see it.

Together, they dragged the horse over the floor towards the stairs. Leaning forward, the weight of it was resting on Corny as they eased it down step after step. It barely fitted.

Downstairs, Kaye climbed out through the window as Corny pushed it carefully through.

Outside, Corny started to panic. There was no way it was going to fit in the back of the car. Worse, the trunk was filled with boxes of used books and oddball tools.

"Someone is going to see us!"

"We've got to find a way to tie it to the roof."

"Fuck! Fuck! Fuck!" Corny dug around in the trunk of the car and came up with a single bungee cord, two plastic bags, and some twine.

"That string is very thin," Kaye said sceptically.

Corny twisted it around the wooden creature's neck and body and then through the inside of the car. "Get on the other side. Someone's going to see us. Hurry."

He tossed her the twine, and she looped it over the horse and threw it back to him. Corny knotted it.

"Okay. Good enough. We gotta go."

Corny hopped in on his side, and Kaye walked around and got in, wrapping Corny's jacket around her hand to close the door. He took off, stepping on the pedal so hard that the tyres screeched as they pulled out.

Kaye was sure that each car that pulled up behind them was going be the police or that the horse was going to fly off onto the road or hit another car. But they got back in one piece.

Pulling over, they hauled the merry-go-round horse down into the forest and to the stream.

"That thing better like this. I'm going to have splinters for a week."

"It will."

"And I'm going to have to pop the bonnet of the car back up in the centre."

"I know. I would help you if I could touch it, okay?"

"I'm just saying. That thing better like it."

"It will."

They set the legless horse down on the muddy bank, angling it so that it sat relatively upright without their holding it. Kaye looked around for another leaf, and Corny took the knife out of his pocket without being asked.

"'S okay. I'm just going to pick the scab."

He made a face but didn't say anything.

"Kelpie," Kaye said, dropping the leaf into the water, "I have something I think you might like."

The horse rose up from the deep and stared at the crippled merry-go-round horse.

Whinnying, it clopped up onto the shore. "It has no legs," the kelpie said.

"It's beautiful anyway," Kaye said.

The kelpie circled the wooden thing, snuffling appraisingly. "More, I think. Crippled things are always more beautiful. It's the flaw that brings out beauty."

Kaye grinned. She'd done it. She'd actually done it. "So you'll teach me?"

The creature looked at Kaye and *shifted*, and where it had been now stood a young man, nude and still dripping, hair tangled with rushes. It looked from Kaye to Corny. "She I will teach, but you must make it worth my while if you want me to teach you too. Come and sit near me."

"Nothing's worth that," Kaye said.

The kelpie-man smiled, but his eyes were on Corny as he traced a pattern on his chest. Corny's breathing went shallow.

"No," Corny said, so softly that it was hard to hear his voice.

Then the creature transformed again, sinuous energy coiling until Kaye was looking at herself.

"Are you ready to begin then?" the kelpie said in Kaye's voice with Kaye's mouth. And then the smile, not at all Kaye's, curled slyly. "I have much to teach you. And the boy would do well to listen. Magic is not the sole province of the fey."

"I thought you said he had to make it worth your while."

"His fear is worth something, for now. I am allowed so little consolation." The kelpie looked at her with her own black eyes, and she watched those lips, so like her own, whisper, "So long since I have known what it was to hunt."

"How come?" Kaye asked, despite herself.

"We, who are not the rulers, we must obey those that are. Mortals are a treat for the Gentry, and not for the likes of you and me. Unless, of course, they are willing."

Kaye nodded, pondering that.

"Do you know how it feels to build magical energy?" the kelpie asked. "It is a prickling feeling. Cup your hand and concentrate on building the energy in it. What does it feel like?"

Kaye cupped her hand and imagined the air in her hand thickening and shimmering with energy. After a moment, she looked up in surprise. "It feels like when your hand falls asleep and then you move it. Prickly, like you said, like little shocks of energy shooting through it. It hurts a little."

"Move it back and forth between your

hands. There you feel magic in its raw state, ready to become whatever you want it to be."

Kaye nodded, cradling the energy that was like a handful of nettles, letting some of it trickle through her open fingers. It was a feeling she remembered, sometimes coiling in her gut or pricking over her lips before some strange thing happened.

"Now, how did you accomplish raising the energy? What did you do?"

Kaye shook her head slightly. "I don't know . . . I just pictured it and stared at my hand."

"You pictured it. That is the easiest of the senses. Now you must learn to hear it, to smell it, to taste it. Only then will your magic become real. And be careful; sometimes a simple glamour can be seen through out of the corner of another's eye." The creature winked.

Kaye nodded.

"When you do magic, there are two stages: focus and surrender. Surrender is the part that so many do not understand.

"To do magic, you must focus on what it is you want to do, then let go of the energy and trust it to do your bidding.

"Close your eyes. Now picture the energy surrounding you. Imagine, for example, a ring on one of your fingers. Add detail to it. Imagine the gold of the band, then imagine the gem, its colour, its clarity, how it will reflect the light . . . that's right. Exactly like that."

Her eyes fluttered open as Corny gasped. "Kaye! There really is a ring on your finger. A real, imaginary ring. I can see it."

Kaye opened her eyes, and there it was, on her index finger, just as she had imagined it, the silver carved into the shape of a girl and the glittering emerald set in her open mouth. She turned it against the light, but even knowing that she had magicked it into being, the ring was as solid as a stone.

"What about undoing . . . things?" Kaye asked.

The kelpie threw back its head and laughed, white teeth shining even in the gloom. "What have you done?"

"Enchanted someone to . . . like me," Kaye said, in a low voice. Corny looked at her, surprised and a little annoyed. He wasn't going to be happy that there was another part of the story she'd left out.

The kelpie grinned and clucked its tongue. "You must remove the enchantment on him in the same way that you would take off a glamour. Feel the web of your magic, reach out and tear it. Practise with the ring."

Kaye concentrated, letting the energy swirl around her, feeling it run through her. It seemed to ebb and flow with each beat of her heart.

They were driving back when Kaye pointed to the hill. "Look at those lights. Wonder who's up there."

"I don't see anything." He looked at her sharply in the rearview mirror.

Cemetery Hill was a large sloping hill with a steep incline on the side that faced the highway. That side had neither graves nor tombs, and in the winter kids would blithely go sledding, piling spare mittens and scarves on the monuments. An abandoned, half-built mausoleum stood at the base of one gently sloping side. With two levels but no roof, the top was overgrown with smallish trees and vines. There were dozens upon dozens of monuments, tombs, and gravestones erected around it.

"Think that's where the Unseelie Court is?" she asked softly.

"I want to see it."

He drove into the graveyard.

They parked along the tumbled-stone path. She stared through the rear windshield at the darting lights as she waited for Corny to walk around and open her door.

"Those are definitely faeries," Kaye said.

"I can't see anything." There was an edge of panic in Corny's voice.

Kaye followed the lights, saw them dazzle and turn, keeping just enough ahead of her that she could not see them clearly. She sped up her pace, boots crunching the frost-stiffened grass. They were so close she could just snatch one out of the air. . .

"Kaye!" Corny called, and she turned. "Don't fucking leave me behind and make me have to wonder if I'm a goddamn nutcase for the rest of my life."

"I'm not leaving you! I'm trying to catch one of these things."

Suddenly there was an impossible explosion of fireflies, darting in and out of the trees. It must be well past midnight and too late in the season for fireflies anyway, the chill of autumn and recent rain stiffening the grass beneath their feet with frost. But the insects darted around them, each blinking for a long moment, then gone, then blinking again. Then she looked at them carefully. They were little winged creatures, even smaller than those she had snatched at. One flitted close to her and showed its teeth.

Kaye made a shrill sound.

"What?" Corny said.

"Not bugs . . . they're tiny, nasty faeries."

He dropped Kaye's hand and snatched at one, although it darted out of his grip. "I can't see anything. Are those the things . . . what you saw from the road?"

She shook her head. "No. Those lights were bigger."

He squatted down, his breath rising from his lips in puffs of white vapour. "Can you see them now?"

She shook her head. "Lutie said something about the opening being in a brown patch of grass, but practically the whole hill is covered with brown grass."

"Maybe the patch is bare by now."

Kaye knelt down next to Corny and cupped her ear to the ground. There was faint music. "Listen. You can hear it."

He moved to her side and pressed his ear to the ground as well. "Music," he said. "Sounds like pipes."

"It's beautiful," she said, the smile on her face before she remembered that this was not a good place they were trying to enter.

"Let's walk a circuit around the hill. We'll both look for any patch that seems weird." Corny stretched from his squat and waited for her to start walking.

The graveyard was unnaturally quiet. The moon was, if anything, fuller and fatter than it had been when she last saw it. It seemed unnatural; the thing looked bloated in the sky, and she thought again about the sun bleeding to death while the moon grew tumescent with devoured light.

The newer, granite gravestones were all polished to an unnatural mirror shine that reflected her and Corny as they passed. The older markers were a pale, milky marble, grass stains and dirt washed out by the moonlight. Pale as Roiben's hair.

"Hey, what about that?" Corny pointed to a patch of grass that did seem a different shade of brown.

Kneeling down beside it, Corny pulled back a corner as though it were the flap of a sod tent. Corny leaned in.

"No," Kaye said. "I have to go in there alone."

"I want this," Corny said. "You said you wouldn't leave me behind."

"It's probably not safe for *me* to go. I'll be back as soon as I can." Kaye shimmied into the entrance. "I promise."

The music seemed louder now, pipes and laughter swelling in the quiet night. Kaye heard Corny say "You get to have all the fun" as she followed the song inside.

HOLLY BLACK

7

"Listening to the prisoned cricket
Shake its terrible dissembling
Music in the granite hill"

— LOUISE BOGAN,
"Men Loved Wholly Beyond Wisdom"

She slipped inside the hollow hill.

The air itself seemed thick with sweetness, and breathing was disorienting.

Long, low tables were heaped with golden pears, chestnuts, bowls of bread soaking in buttery milk, pomegranates ripped in half and half again, violet petals on crystal plates, and all manner of strange delicacies. Wide silver goblets sat like toads on the tables, upright and overturned in equal proportion. Scarlet-clad faerie ladies brushed past men in torn rags, and courtiers danced with crones.

Revellers danced and sang, drank and swooned. The costumes were varied and completely unlike mediaeval clothes. They were more like some demented, organic couture. Collars rose like great fins. Outfits were composed entirely of petals or leaves. Ragged edges finished off lovely dresses. Ugly, strange, or lovely as the moon, none were plain.

"The Unseelie Court," she said aloud. She had expected something else, a cave, maybe, filled with gnawed human bones and faerie prisoners. Something simple. Looking out into the throng of revellers, she didn't know what to think.

The room itself was massive, so large that she wasn't sure what was on the other side. Far across the room, what looked like a giant, slouched near a dais. Each step seemed to push her in a new direction, full of splendours. A fiddler was playing an improbable instrument, with several necks and so many strings that the fiddler sawed his bow at them wildly. A long-nosed woman with freckles and ears like a jackal's juggled pinecones. Three men with red hair and double rows of shark teeth dipped their caps in a pile of carnage, soaking up the blood. A huge creature with bat wings and limbs like stilts sat atop a table and lapped at a beaten copper bowl of cream. It hissed at Kaye as she passed it.

Above them all, the domed ceiling was frescoed with dangling roots.

Kaye picked up a goblet off a table. It was ornate and very heavy, but it seemed clean. She poured a thin, reddish liquid from the silver carafe in the centre of the table. Small seeds floated at the top, but the drink smelled pleasant and not entirely strange, so she took a swallow of it. It was both sweet and bitter and went to her head so that, for a moment, she was obliged to hold the table for support.

She took a silvery apple from a pile of strange, thorny fruit, turned it over in her hand, and gingerly bit into it. It was crimson on the inside and tasted like watery honey. It was so good that she ate it core and all, till she was licking her hand for juice. The next was brown and rotten-looking as she bit into it, but the meat, though gritty, tasted of a fiery and sweet spirit.

She felt an infectious giddiness come over her. Here, nothing she did was strange. She could twirl and dance and sing.

All at once she was aware of how far into the crowd she had gone. She had been turned around so many times she no longer even knew which direction was the way back.

She deliberately tried to retrace her steps. Three woman walked past her, silver gowns trailing like fine mist. The low cut of the identical dresses showed off the women's hollow backs. She looked again, but their concave backs were as smooth and empty as bowls. She forced herself to keep moving. A short man – a dwarf? – with intricate silver bracelets and shoulder-length black curls leered at her as he bit into an apricot.

Every moment became more unreal.

A winged boy skipped up to her, grinning.

"You smell like iron," he said, and reached out a finger to poke her side.

Kaye scuttled away from his hand to a chorus of laughter. Her eyes focused on the pale grasshopper green of the insect wings attached to the boy's back.

She pushed through the crowd, weaving past dancers leaping in complex intertwining circles, past a clawed hand that snatched at her ankle from beneath the heavy scarlet cloth on one of the tables, past what looked like a debauched living chess game.

A satyr with a curly beard and ivory horns was hunched over, carefully ripping the wing off a small faerie trapped in his meaty fist. The thing screeched, beating its other wing hummingbird-swift against the fingers that held it. Pale green blood dribbled over the goat-man's hand. Kaye stopped, stunned and sickened to watch as the satyr tossed the little creature in the air. It flew in desperate circles, spiralling to the earthen floor.

Before Kaye could step close and snatch it, the man's boot stamped down, smearing the faerie into the dust.

Kaye reeled back, pushing folk aside in her haste to get away. Angling through the multitudes, she thought of her own foolishness in coming here. This was the Unseelie Court. This was the worst of Faeryland come to drink themselves sick.

Three men in shimmering green coattails, their arms and legs long and skinny as broomsticks, were pushing a doe-eyed boy with grasshopper legs between them. He crouched warily as if to spring, but each time was unprepared for a sudden grab or push.

"Let him alone," Kaye said, stepping up to them. The boy reminded her too much of Gristle for her to just watch.

The men turned to look at her, all of them identical. The boy tried to slip between them, but one of the skinny men locked his arm around the boy's neck.

"What's this?" a skinny man asked.

"I'll trade you something for him," Kaye said, scrambling for a plan.

One of the men sniggered, and the other drew a little knife with an ivory handle and a metal blade that stank of pure iron. The third threaded his hand through the boy's hair, tipping his head back.

"No!" Kaye yelled as the iron dagger stabbed into the boy's left eye. The orb popped like a grape, clear liquid and blood running down his face as he screamed. The flesh hissed where the iron touched it.

"So much better with an audience," one of the skinny men said.

Kaye stumbled back, reaching around on a nearby table, finding only a goblet. She hefted it like a small club, unsure of what she was going to do with it.

One skinny man drew the iron blade over the skin of the boy's cheek, down his neck as the boy trembled and squealed, his one good eye rolling weakly in his head. The iron left a thin red line where it passed, the skin bubbling to white welts.

"Going to save him, poppet?" another of the skinny men called to Kaye.

Kaye's hands were shaking, and the cup seemed nothing more than a heavy thing she held; certainly, it was no weapon.

"We're not going to kill him," the man who was holding the boy's hair said.

"Just softening him up a bit," the one with the knife put in.

Fury surged up in her. The cup flew from her hand, hitting the shoulder of the man with the knife, spotting his coat with droplets of the wine it had contained before falling ineffectually to the dirt floor, where it rolled in helpless circles.

One of the men laughed and another lunged for her. She ducked into the crowd, pushing aside a dainty woman and sidling through.

Then she came to a sudden halt. Half hidden by three toad-skinned creatures hunched over a game of dice, there was Corny.

He was wedged against an overturned

table, a goblet tipped in his hand. He was rocking back and forth with his eyes shut. A puddle of wine was soaking his trousers, but he didn't seem to care.

Revellers were packed in tightly around her, so she scuttled under the table.

"Corny?" Kaye said, breathing hard.

Corny was right in front of her, but didn't seem to see her.

She shook him.

He noticed that and finally glanced up. He looked drunk, or worse than drunk. Like he'd been drunk for years.

"I know you," Corny said thickly.

"It's me, Kaye."

"Kaye?"

"What are you doing here?"

"They said it wasn't for me."

"What wasn't for you?"

The hand with the goblet in it stirred slightly.

"The wine?"

"Not for me. So I drank it. I want everything that's not for me."

"What happened to you?"

"This," he said, and twitched his mouth into something that might have been a smile. "I saw him."

She looked quickly back into the throng. "Who?"

Corny pointed towards a raised dais where

tall, pale faeries spoke together and drank from silver cups. "Your boy. Robin of the white hair. At least I think it was."

"What was he doing?"

Corny shook his head. It hung limply from his neck.

"Are you going to be sick?" she said.

He looked up into her face and smiled. "I am sick."

He began singing "King of Pain," softly and off-key. His eyes focused on nothing, and he was smiling a little, one of his hands toying idly with a button on his shirt. It seemed as though he was trying to rebutton it. "'There's a king on a throne with his eyes torn out. There's a blind man looking for a shadow of doubt. Oh-oooh, king of pain, I will always be, king of pain.'"

"I'm going to find him," Kaye said.

She looked at Corny, who was muttering, wiping the inside of his goblet with a finger that he brought to his lips.

"Wait for me here, okay? Don't go anywhere."

He didn't make any reply, but she doubted that he could stand anyway. He looked well and truly wasted.

Kaye reentered the throng, weaving towards where Corny had pointed.

A woman with thick braids of crimson hair sat on a tall wooden throne with edges that came to worn peaks and spires. It was wormed through with termite holes, giving it the appearance of a lattice. At her feet, goblins gambolled.

Roiben walked up to the throne and went down to one knee.

Kaye had to get closer. She couldn't see. Then she noticed there was a small indentation in the wall where she could hide herself, close enough to observe what was going to happen. She would watch and she would find a way to make him sorry for what he had done.

Rath Roiben Rye walked through the crowd, past a table where a sprite was squirming in an ogre's embrace, perhaps with pleasure, perhaps in dread. His old self would have stopped, surely. His silver blade was at his hip, but his Lady awaited him and he had learned to be a good little slave and so he passed on.

Lady Nicnevin, Queen of the Unseelie Court, stood with her courtiers gathered around her. Claret hair blew around a white face inset with sapphire eyes, and he found himself halted once again by her cold beauty. Four goblins frolicked at her side. One tugged at her skirts like a toddler. Rath Roiben Rye dropped to his knees and bent his head so that his pewter hair puddled on the ground. He kissed the earth in front of her.

He didn't want to be here tonight. His chest still ached, and he wanted nothing more than to lie down and close his eyes. But when he did close his eyes, all he saw was the human girl's face, full of shock and horror as he threw her down on the dirty floor of a diner.

"You may rise," the Lady said. "Approach me. I have a task to set you to."

"I am yours," Rath Roiben Rye said, brushing the soil from his lips.

She smiled a little smile. "Are you? And do you serve me as well as you served my sister?"

He hesitated before answering. "Better, perhaps, for you try me harder."

The smile curled off her mouth. "You would jibe with me?"

"Your pardon, Lady. I mean no scorn. It is seldom merry work you set me to."

She laughed at that, silvery cold laughter that rose up out of her throat like crows going to wing. "You have no tongue for courtliness, knight. Yet I find you still please me. Why is that?"

"Sport, Lady?" he ventured.

Her eyes were hard and wet as blue beach glass, but her smile was beyond loveliness. "Certainly not wisdom. Rise. I understand that I have a mortal girl to thank for your presence here tonight."

His face was grave as he stood; he made sure of that. It would not do to let his surprise show. "I was careless."

"What a fine girl she must be. Do tell us about her." A few of the Unseelie Gentry that attended her smiled openly, watching this game as eagerly as they would a duel.

He was careful, so careful to keep the flinch from his face. His voice had to be easy; his words could not seem to be carefully measured. "She said that she was known to solitary fey. She had the Sight. A clever girl, and a kind one."

The Lady smiled at that. "Was it not the solitary fey that shot you, knight?"

He nodded and could not keep the ghost of a smile off his face. "I suppose they are not all so closely allied, my Lady."

Oh, she didn't like that. He could tell. "I have an idea, then," his Lady said, raising one delicate finger to her smiling lips. "Get us this girl. The Tithe to the solitary fey will cement their loyalty. A young girl gifted with the second sight would be an excellent candidate."

"No," he said. It was a sharp bark, a command, and courtiers' heads turned at the sound. He felt the bile rise in the back of his throat. Not clever, that. He was not being clever.

The Lady Nicnevin's smile bent her lips in triumph. "I might point out that if they do know her it will be just the thing to remind them not to break my toys," the Lady said. She did not mention his outburst.

There was a jibe in that meant for him, her toy, but he hardly heard it. He was already watching the girl die. Her lips were already cursing him with his true name.

"Let me find you another," he heard himself say. Once his Lady might have found it amusing for him to struggle with that, finding an innocent to take the place of another innocent.

"I think not. Bring me the girl two days hence. Perhaps after I see her, I will reconsider. Nephamael has just come from my sister's court with a message. Perhaps he could be persuaded to assist you in finding her."

His gaze flickered to the other knight, who appeared to be speaking to a goat-footed poetess and ignoring their conversation. It made Roiben queasy just to look at the iron circlet burning on his brow. It was said that even when he removed it, the searing scar ran deep and black in his flesh. He wore a cloak lined with thorns. What little revenge there was to be had on the Seelie Court, Roiben had it in the form of Nephamael. He had noticed how often the Seelie Queen sent her new knight back down to the Unseelie Court on some easy task or another.

He bowed low enough for his knee and brow to touch the earth, but her attention was already elsewhere.

He walked through the crowd, passing the table where he had seen the ogre. Nothing remained of the couple save three drops of cherry blood and the shimmery powder of the sprite's wings.

His oaths cut him like fine wire.

Kaye watched Roiben sweep off the dais, fighting down the feelings that seemed to be clawing their way up her throat. *A clever girl and a kind one.* Those simple words had sped her heart in a way she didn't like at all.

Did he know that his voice had softened when he'd spoken of her?

He is so unpredictable that even his Queen cannot trust him. He's as likely to be kind as to kill you.

But the memory of his lips on her skin would not fade. Even if she rubbed the spot. Even if she scratched at it.

Kaye rose as another knight approached the Queen and bowed low to press his lips to the hem of her dress.

"Rise, Nephamael," the Queen said. "I understand that you are here with a message for me." His slim figure rose with the same graceful, measured formality that Roiben had. This knight was wearing a band of metal on his brow; the skin around it was darkened, as though burned. There was something about his yellow eyes that Kaye thought was familiar.

"This is the message my Lady would have you hear." His smile emphasised his implication of disloyalty. "My Lady said that although there has been a truce in the matter of war, she wonders at the matter of mortal influence. She has some favourites that cross your borders and seeks a means of giving them safe passage through your lands. I am told to await your reply. She did not seem to think I need hurry back. I must confess that it is good to be home in time for the Tithe."

"Is that all she said?"

"Indeed, although one of the Queen's courtiers begged me to ask after her brother. It seems that she hasn't had any news from him since he joined your court. A sweet thing, that girl. Very long white hair – one could almost wind a leash of it if one was so inclined. She looks very like the knight you just spoke with." Another mischievous smile. "She wanted to know why you never use him as a messenger."

The Queen smiled too. "It is good to have you home, Nephamael. Perhaps you can help my knight acquire our sacrifice."

"It would be my honour. In fact, I think I have heard of a very suitable candidate indeed – she's already acquainted with a member of your court."

Kaye was suddenly caught by the arm and turned. She yelped.

"You shouldn't be here." Roiben's tone was icy, and his hand was tight on her arm.

Taking a breath, she met his eyes. "I just wanted to hear the Queen."

"If one of her other knights had noticed you spying here, they would have undoubtedly enjoyed making an example out of you. This is no game, pixie. It is too dangerous for you to be here."

Pixie? Then she remembered. He was seeing green skin, black eyes, folded wings. He didn't know her, or at least he didn't know that he knew her. She let go a breath she didn't even know she'd been holding.

"I'm no concern of yours," she said, twisting in his grip. Surely he would let her go, she told herself, but Spike's words echoed in her head. She saw Roiben on a black horse with glowing white eyes, face flecked with blood and dirt, eyes bright with frenzy, riding down poor Gristle as he hurtled through the brush.

"Indeed?" He did not release his hold on her and was, in fact, pulling her through the crowd. From this vantage point it was easy to see that people didn't just make way for him, they practically tripped over themselves to do so. "I am Nicnevin's sworn knight. Perhaps you should be more concerned about what I am going to do to you than what I might do for you."

She shuddered. "So what will you do?"

The knight sighed. "Nothing. Providing that you leave the brugh immediately."

Nothing? She was not sure what she expected to see in his face when she looked at him then, but it was not the weariness she saw there. No madness glittered in the depths of those pale eyes.

But she couldn't leave, and she couldn't tell him that her very human friend was sleeping it off on the other side of the hill. She had to play this out. "I'm not allowed here? It doesn't seem like there's a guest list."

Roiben's eyes darkened at that, and his voice dropped very low. "The Unseelie Court delights in guesting spies for the solitary fey. We so seldom have volunteers for our amusements."

Dangerous ground, now. The sadness was gone, and his features were carefully blank. Her stomach twisted. Delights . . . our amusements. The implication of his participation was not lost on her.

"You can leave through here," he said, showing her an earthen tunnel that was not the one she had come through. This one was hidden by a chair and seemed closer to the giant. "But you must do it quickly. Now. Before someone sees me speaking with you."

"Why?" Kaye asked.

"Because they might assume that I had taken a liking to you. Then they might assume that it would be amusing to see my face while I hurt you very badly." Roiben's tone was cold and flat. His words seemed to fall from his lips as though they meant nothing, just words dropping into darkness.

Her hands felt very cold as she remembered the diner. What would it be like to be a puppet? What would it be like to watch your own hands disobey you?

Fury rose up in her like a dark cloud. She didn't want to understand how he could have killed Gristle. She didn't want to forgive him. And most of all, she didn't want to want him.

"Now, pixie," he said, "go!"

"I don't know if I should believe you," she said. "Give me a kiss." If she couldn't stop thinking about his lips, maybe tasting them would get it out of her system. After all, if curiosity killed the cat, it was satisfaction that brought him back.

"There is no time for your snatched pixie pranks," he said.

"If you want me to leave quickly, you'd best be quick." She was surprised at her own words, wondering at the giddy viciousness of them.

She was more amazed when his lips brushed across hers. A sudden shock of feeling lanced through her before he pulled away.

"Go," he said, but he said it in a whisper, as though she had drained the breath from him. His eyes were shadowed.

Kaye ducked through the tunnel before she was forced to think about just what she had done. And certainly before she had time to wonder how it had anything to do with revenge.

Outside, it was cold and bright. It didn't seem possible, but the night was past. A breeze made the remaining leaves shudder on their branches, and Kaye crossed her arms to seal in whatever warmth she could as she jogged across the hill. She knew where the brown patch of grass had been. It was simply a matter of getting inside again. If she just stuck to the wall, she thought, probably no one would notice her. Corny would be there, and this time, she would pay better attention, mark the exit in some way.

The grass was no browner in one place than another. She remembered the location well enough. Next to the elm tree and by a grave marker that read ADELAIDE. She dropped to her knees and dug, frantically clawing at the half-frozen topsoil. It was dirt and more dirt, hard-packed, as though there had never been a passageway to an underground palace.

"Corny," she shouted, well aware that he would not be able to hear her deep beneath the earth.

8

"For beauty is nothing
but the beginning of terror we can just
*   barely endure,*
and we admire it so because it calmly disdains
to destroy us."

— RAINER MARIA RILKE,
"The First Elegy," *Duino Elegies*

Corny woke on the hillside to the sound of bells. He was shaking with cold. His teeth were chattering, his head felt thick and heavy, and just shifting his weight made his stomach lurch. His jacket was gone.

He was lying alone on a hill in a graveyard, and he had no idea how he had come to be there. He saw his car, hazard lights still dimly flashing where he had pulled off alongside the road. A wave of dizziness hit him. He rolled weakly to one side and retched.

The taste of the wine he vomited brought back a memory of a man's mouth on his, a man's hands stroking him. Shocked, he tried to form a face to go along with that mouth and those hands, but his head hurt too much to remember any more.

He pulled himself to his feet, trying to keep his queasiness under control as he stumbled down the hill toward his car. Despite the lights being on all night, when he turned the key, the engine turned over and roared to life. Corny flicked the heater on full blast and sat there, basking in the gush of hot air. His body shuddered with pleasure.

He knew that there was a bottle of aspirin under all the fast-food wrappers and discarded novels. He couldn't make himself move. He leaned his head back and waited for the warmth that was creeping through his limbs to relax him and chase away the nausea. Then he remembered Kaye in the backseat, and the beginning of the evening flooded back with disturbing intensity.

Kaye's skin cracked and peeling, the first flutter of wet wings, her strange new self stretched out in the car, the music . . . then alone on the hillside, tangled memories tripping over one another. He had heard stories like this – men and women waking on a hill, dreaming one night in Faery. The hill never opened for them again. Angrily, he wondered if Kaye was there still, dancing to distant flutes, forgetting that he'd ever tagged along.

His stomach clenched as he thought of another explanation for being alone on the hill.

It was a memory, really, Kaye hunched over him whispering, *I'm going to find him. Wait for me here.*

Because the more that he thought about it, the more he remembered the brutal parts. The distant scream he couldn't place, the sight of some of the revellers, teeth red with blood, and the man, the man with the cloak of thorns who had found him sitting drunk in the dirt and . . .

He shook his head. It was hard to remember the specifics, only that soft mouth and the scraping of those thorns. His hands fluttered to the sleeves of his shirt, rolling them back. Angry red wounds running up and down his arms were incontrovertible proof of how he'd spent the night.

Just touching them filled him with a longing so intense it made him sick.

Kaye stumbled in the backdoor. A quick look at the red digital numbers on the microwave told her that it was late morning.

Exhaustion settled over her as she strained to sense the wend and weft of magic in her fingers. She felt like a too-taut piece of string, fraying as it was pulled. She'd looked and looked, but there was no way back into the hill. Perhaps it opened only at dusk. She'd have to go back tonight, retrace the same path, and wait.

Her senses were overacute; the flimsy glamour she was wearing now was nothing like the one she had before. She could still feel the slight rustle of wings against her back, still smell the rubbish under the sink, even separate out smells – coffee grounds, eggshells, a bit of mouldy cheese, detergents, some thick syrupy poison used to bait cockroach traps. The air thrummed with energy she had previously ignored. If she opened up to it, she might be able to leave her fatigue behind.

But she didn't want to – she wanted to cling to the façade of humanity with both fists.

"Kaye? Is that you?" Kaye's grandmother came in from the other room. She was wearing a dressing gown and slippers, her thin grey hair pinned up in curlers. "Did you just get in?"

"Hi, Gram," Kaye said, yawning. She went over to the kitchen table, shifted a pile of newspapers and circulars out of her way, and put her head down in her hands. It was almost a relief to just let her grandmother yell at her, as if everything could be normal again.

"I called the school this morning."

Kaye forced herself not to groan.

"Did you know that you are not allowed to drop out of school without a parent's written permission? According to your transcripts you haven't been in school since you were fourteen!"

Kaye shook her head.

"What does that mean? Was that a no?"

"I *know* I haven't been in school," Kaye said, disgusted at how childish her own voice

HOLLY BLACK

sounded.

"Well, it's a good thing that you know, missy, but *I* want to know what it is you have been doing. Where are you sneaking off to?"

"Nowhere," Kaye said in a small voice. "I just didn't want you to know. I knew you'd be mad."

"Well, why didn't you hightail it back to school then? Do you want to be nothing your whole life?"

"I'll get my GED," Kaye said.

"Your GED? Like a drug dealer? Like a pregnant teenager? Do you want to wind up trailer trash like your little friend?"

"Shut up!" Kaye yelled, holding her head. "You think you know everything about everything, don't you? You think that the world is so easy to understand. You don't know me at all – you don't know one single thing about me! How can you possibly know anything about Janet when you don't know anything about me?"

"I will not have you shouting at me in my own house. You and your mother are just the same. You think that it's enough to want things. You think that if you just want and want then you're just going to magically get them."

Magically. Kaye felt her face twist with an expression somewhere between a wince and a smirk.

"Nothing but hard work gets anyone anywhere. Even then, people don't get what they want. People just suffer, and no one knows why they suffer. Talented people – like your mother – they don't make it, despite the talent, and what are you going to do then? You can't rely on luck. How do you know you're lucky?"

Kaye was surprised to hear that her grandmother thought that her mother had talent. "I'm not relying on luck," Kaye said numbly.

"Oh really? What are you doing then?"

"I don't know," Kaye said. She was tired, and she could feel a whine creep into her voice. She was afraid that she was going to cry, and if she started crying right now, she wasn't sure she could stop. Worse, she knew she sounded petulant, upset only that she was caught. It wasn't far from the truth. "We needed the money."

Her grandmother looked at her in horror. "What money?"

"Is that what you think? Don't even talk to me," Kaye said, burrowing her face in her folded arms. She mumbled into her own skin, "I was working at a fucking Chinese restaurant, okay? In the city. Full-time. We needed the money."

Her grandmother looked at her in confusion.

"I don't have a job yet here," she confessed, "but I thought I might go work over at the petrol station where Janet's brother works. I put in an application there."

"You are going to high school, young lady, and even if you weren't, a petrol station is no place for a girl to work. What kind of boy is going to go out with a girl like that?"

"Who cares about boys?" Kaye said. "Look, Mum will sign any form I need to get my GED."

"No, she will not!" Kaye's grandmother said. "Ellen!"

"What?" the annoyed shout came from above.

"Come down here and listen to your daughter! Do you know what she's planning to do? Do you know what she's been doing?"

A couple of minutes later, Kaye's mother was there too, hair pulled back with a red leather kerchief. She was wearing a black T-shirt and sweatpants. "What were you doing?"

"I wasn't doing anything," Kaye said. She should have known this fight was coming, but now she felt distant from it, as though she were watching from far, far away. "I *wasn't* going to school and I *wasn't* telling Grandma about it."

"Don't be smart," Kaye's grandmother said.

Ellen leaned against the doorway to the kitchen. "Look, it doesn't matter what she's been doing because we're going to be in New York the beginning of next week. I'm fronting Meow Factory."

Both Kaye and her grandmother graced Ellen with almost identical looks of horror. Ellen shrugged, moving past them to fill the coffeepot with water. "I was going to tell you last night, but you never showed up for dinner."

"I'm not going to New York," Kaye said, disgusted at how childish she sounded. This was the same girl who had insulted the Unseelie Queen's favourite knight? Who had talked down a kelpie?

"Ellen, you can't seriously mean that you don't care that your only daughter has not been attending high school?" Kaye's grandmother's lips were pressed in a thin line.

Ellen shrugged. "Kaye's a smart girl, mum. She can make those decisions for herself."

"You're her mother. It's your job to make sure that she makes the right decisions."

"Did that ever work with me? You tried to make all my decisions for me, and see where it got us both. I'm not going to make the same mistake with Kaye. So what if she doesn't want to go to high school? High school sucked when I had to go, and I can't imagine it's any better now. Kaye can read and write – that's more than plenty of high school seniors can say – she's probably read more books than most girls her age."

"Ellen, don't be stupid. What's she going to do for a living? What's in her future? Don't you want something better for Kaye than what you have?"

"I want her to have the future she wants."

Kaye slid out of the room. They would be arguing for long enough that they wouldn't notice or care for a while. She just wanted to sleep.

The phone rang close to her head, where she'd dropped it. Kaye groaned and pressed the on button.

"Hello," she said groggily. She hadn't managed more than a fitful sleep, tossing and turning. The blankets were too warm, but kicking them off had made her feel unsafe, exposed. Her dreams were too full of slit-eyed things poking her with clawed fingers.

"Fuck. You're there." She recognised the voice as belonging to Corny. He sounded astonished and very relieved.

"Corny! I got thrown out. I couldn't find a way back to you." She looked at the clock. It was one o'clock in the afternoon. "I thought maybe the hill was only open at night."

"I'm coming over."

She nodded and then, realising he couldn't see her, spoke the thought aloud. "Yeah. Definitely. Come over. Are you okay?"

The phone clicked off, and she scrubbed a hand restlessly through her hair before letting her head fall back onto the pillow.

"The glamour looks good," was the first thing that Corny said as he walked into her bedroom. Then he looked around. "Hey, you've got rats."

She blinked up at him. "How did you get out? I was going crazy looking for you. If the cops had seen me they would have thought I was some nutjob grave robber trying to dig up bodies with my bare hands."

"I woke up outside the hill this morning. I figured that you'd ditched me and I was going to do a Rip Van Winkle and find out that it was the year 2112 and no one had ever even heard of me." He grinned wryly.

"Roiben threw me out. I'm sorry. I didn't want to leave you, but I was afraid if I told him that he would figure out who I was."

Corny smiled. "He didn't know?"

She shook her head and shuddered. "So, what did you think of the Unseelie Court?"

A slow, wicked smile spread on his face. "Oh, Kaye," he breathed. "It was marvellous. It was perfect."

She narrowed her gaze. "I was joking. They were killing things, Corny. For fun. Things like us."

He didn't seem to hear her, his eyes looking

past her to the bright window. "There was this knight, not yours. He . . ." Corny shivered and seemed to abruptly change the direction of his sentence. "He had a cloak all lined with thorns."

"I saw him talking to the Queen," Kaye said.

Corny shrugged off his jacket. There were long scratches along his arms.

"What happened to you?"

Corny's smile widened, but his gaze was locked in some memory. He shifted it back to her. "Well, obviously I got inside the cloak."

She snorted. "What a euphemism. Did he hurt you?"

"No more than I wanted him to," Corny said.

She didn't like it, neither what he was saying nor the way he looked when he talked about it.

"How about you, Kaye? Did you revenge yourself on Robin of the White Hair?"

She couldn't help the blush that crept across her cheeks.

"What?" he demanded. And she told him, the blush growing hot as she did. It sounded even more pathetic out loud.

"So what you're telling me is that you got him to kiss you once on the lips and once on the ass."

Kaye glared at him, but she couldn't help

giggling.

"I don't know if I should call that slick or be really afraid what you are going to use that name of his for in the future. Can you just keep ordering him around indefinitely?"

Kaye aimed a mock-kick in his direction. "What about you and your knight? I mean, look at your arms; is that normal?"

"Makes me shiver when I touch them," Corny said reverently.

"At least we're scaring each other."

"Yeah, well, I better get back home. What's next on the faerie agenda?"

Kaye shrugged. "I get sacrificed, I guess."

"Great. When is that?"

Kaye shook her head. "Wish I knew. Samhain, that's Hallowe'en, right? Probably at night."

Corny looked at her incredulously. "Hallowe'en is in two days."

"I know," Kaye said. "But it's not like I have to *do* anything. I just have to yell and scream and pretend to be human for a while."

"What if they get pissed off that they were tricked?"

Kaye shrugged. "I don't know. It's not my problem, right? All I have to do is be a good victim."

"Yeah, hopefully not *too* good a victim."

"Spike and Lutie wouldn't ever put me in any real danger."

"Yeah, okay. Well, that's good."

"You think they would?"

"I think it sounds dangerous. I think we haven't seen too much so far that is part of Faery and isn't dangerous."

"True," Kaye said.

"Oh," Corny said. "Jimmy saw me when I went by the house. He said that if you want that job, you can start tonight at six. It's the shift before mine, so I guess I'm not fired after all."

She smiled. "So I guess I'll see you tonight. I'm glad you're okay."

"I would be even better if I was still there," Corny said, and all her worry returned in a flood.

"Corny . . ."

He smiled, that weird distant smile that he'd got under the hill, and she wanted to shake him by the shoulders. Something had to snap him out of it.

"See you tonight," he said, slipping on his jacket. He flinched as the lining brushed his arms, and, uncharitable as it was, she hoped that it was because the scratches hurt.

As Corny left, she looked at the pink sticky notes posted on the back of her door. They were the messages that her mother had taken for her. One was from Jimmy – probably about the job – and the others were all from Kenny.

Kaye settled on the mattress on the floor,

picked up the phone, and dialled the number on Kenny's first note. She could leave a message for him about where she was working tonight. It was a public place. If he came to visit her there, she could take off the enchantment, and then everything with Janet could go back to normal.

"Hey," a male voice answered. There was a vaguely metallic whirring and grating in the background.

"Oh. Hi," she stammered. "I thought you'd be at school."

"You called my mobile," Kenny said. "I'm in metalwork."

"This is Kaye." She felt stupid again, as though a few words from him were some kind of benediction of which she was unworthy.

"I know. Teacher is about to have a hernia, so we've got to talk fast. I want to see you. Tonight."

"I have to work. You could come by – "

"What time?" he said, interrupting her. She felt awkward, hyperaware of each word she spoke, waiting for him to start teasing her and absurdly grateful when he did not.

"Six."

"Meet me after school. You know which one my car is?"

"No. Why don't you just come by my job?" She tried to wrest back control of the conversation.

"By the entrance, then. The big one. I have

to see you."

She hesitated, but she had no real reason not to meet him there. After all, removing the enchantment would only take a moment. What happened after, well, maybe it would be better if she was somewhere she could leave. "Okay."

"Good." With that, the phone hung up, leaving her feeling as though she had drunk two-day-old coffee on an empty stomach. Her nerves were fried. When she lifted a hand, she was unsurprised to find it vibrating slightly, like a struck guitar string. She closed her eyes and took a deep breath, then shucked off Corny's butchered clothes and put on some of her own. They fitted over the illusion of a smooth back easily, but her dual senses could feel the soft cotton of the T-shirt against her wings.

It was weird to be standing outside a school that she should have been going to, but didn't. Some of the kids looked familiar, people she had known from grade school. Mostly they all just looked like the strangers they were.

Human, her mind whispered. *They're all human and you're not.*

She shook her head. She didn't like where those thoughts took her. It was alien enough that she hadn't been in a high school in years. Sometimes, like now, she missed it. She'd hated elementary school. She and Janet had been friends by default. Kids teased Janet for her secondhand clothes and Kaye for her stories. But in the city no one had known Kaye, and besides, there were lots of weird kids. But just when things in school had got better, she'd left.

"Hey," Kenny said. He was wearing sunglasses and a grey T-shirt under a heavy navy flannel shirt. He took off the glasses when he got close to her. Dark circles ringed his eyes. "Why didn't you call me yesterday? I left a million messages at your house. Your mother said that you were at Janet's, but I checked. You weren't there."

"I'm sorry," she said. "I was out." He looked so serious that there was something suddenly funny about it. The magic came easily now, rushing to her fingers and spiking along her tongue, but she made no move to lift the enchantment.

"Kaye, I . . . ," he started, then seemed to think better of whatever it was he was going to say. "I can't sleep. I can't eat. All I can do is think about you."

"I know," she said sweetly. Kids passing by them gave Kenny sidelong glances. She suddenly understood why she had let him kiss her in the diner, why she had wanted him at all.

She wanted to control him.

He was every arrogant boyfriend that had treated her mother badly. He was every boy that told her she was too freaky, who had laughed at her, or just wanted her to shut up and make out. He was a thousand times less real than Roiben.

Her face split in a wide grin. She had no desire to play pretend any more, no need to prove her worth by Kenny's regard, no desire to know how different the lips of a popular boy were from any other boy.

"Please, Kaye," he said, reaching for her wrist, holding it tightly, pulling her to him.

This time she pulled away abruptly, not letting him crush her to him, his lips nowhere near close enough to take another kiss. Instead, she twisted her hand out of his grip and sprung up onto the cement edge of the steps.

"Something you want?" Kaye taunted. Kids had stopped along the path, watching.

"You," Kenny said, reaching for her again, but she was far too quick. Dancing out of his grasp, she laughed.

"You can't have what you can't catch," she goaded, cocking her head to one side. Madness made the blood dance in her veins. How dare he make her feel awkward? How dare he make her measure her words?

He snatched for her hand, but she pulled it away easily, spinning along the cement wall.

"Kaye!" he said.

She squatted down, legs wide, chin thrust

towards him. "Do you adore me, Kenny?"

"Yes," he said frantically.

"Are you besotted with me? Would you die to have me?"

"Yes!" Kenny's eyes were dark with desire and fury. Behind him, students were laughing and whispering to one another.

Kaye laughed too. She didn't care in the least.

"Tell me again what you would do to have me."

"Anything," he said, without hesitation. "Give me a chance. Make me do something."

The laughter died in her throat. She tossed the magic off him, dispersing the threads of it with a sweep of her hand, as one would brush aside cobwebs.

"Never mind," she said, angry without being sure of why. Angry and suddenly ashamed.

Kenny looked around him, the school apparently coming into focus for the first time. She could see the blush creep up his tattooed neck. He looked at her with something like horror in his eyes.

"What the fuck did you do to me?"

"Tell Janet to call me," she said, not caring that that made no sense, not caring about anything except that she needed to get out of there, needed to get away before she careened totally out of control. She didn't even spare him a glance as she crossed the student car park, heading home.

Jimmy was waiting for her in the office of the petrol station. He handed her a blue jacket with an Amoco logo in the corner that Kaye had never seen Corny wear. She put it on dutifully while he explained what she had to do.

A few cars had come through, and she had handled the pump gingerly, careful of the metal.

Her head swam with the noxious fumes of the petrol and the terrible thoughts of what she had done. It had felt so good, so absolutely right to taunt Kenny as she had. And now, knowing what she could do, was it possible to unlearn it, or just a matter of time before she used it again?

There was a rustling sound nearby, and Kaye looked towards the woods warily. It was Mischief Night, and Jimmy had already warned her that kids might try to toilet-paper the place.

But the figure that emerged had hair as black as oil, and the cloak on his shoulders blew back to reveal thorns on the inside, set like a bed of nails. Other than the white of his skin, the only pale thing he wore was a single white stone swinging on a long chain.

"You?" she said. "You're the Seelie Spike told me about?" She'd seen him talking to Nicnevin at the ball. He had seemed loyal to the Queen. Was that part of the plan?

"You're in good hands now," Nephamael said.

"You made the marks on Corny's arms."

"Indeed I did. He is exquisite."

Up close his eyes were yellow. Looking into those eyes, she suddenly knew why they seemed familiar. She'd seen them in the bar the night that Lloyd had lost it.

"You," Kaye said. "You did something to Lloyd, didn't you?"

"We needed you to come home, Kaye."

The knight touched the stone around his neck, and Kaye felt magic sweep around her, settling on her body with an oppressive weight. She felt smothered for a moment as scents became vague and her vision dulled.

"Remember, we have to make it look real," he said as she choked.

"What are you doing to me?" Kaye managed to say. Everything felt numb and strange.

"That glamour you were wearing would fool no one. I am simply restoring the one you should have been wearing."

"But Hallowe'en isn't till tomorrow," Kaye protested. There was a strange prickling all along her arms. This time it didn't seem as though it came from inside her. Something was happening. Her heart sped, and she could feel . . . something, a strangeness. And then a dark shape hurtled out of the clouds.

Something roared over them.

Kaye threw her arms up over her face. She

tried to scream, but when she opened her mouth, it was filled with wind.

Hands clutched her shirt and legs and hair, lifting her and passing her up into a mass of creatures. She kicked and bit, tearing their long cornsilk hair and ripping their powdery wings. Pointed, catlike faces hissed, and fingers pinched her, but they flew on in a long train of monsters and she was with them.

9

*"You whom I could not save
Listen to me."*

— Czeslaw Milosz, "Dedication"

Kaye's throat was raw with screaming. Sharp claws bit into her wrists while bat and bird and insect wings moved with less noise than sheets drying on a line. They flew through the streets invisibly. She screamed, but it seemed that they moved between this world and the next because no one looked up and no one spoke and no one did more than shiver, maybe, or twitch a little as a horde of monsters vaulted through the skies above them. Kaye bit and scratched and squirmed and tore, till the feathery dander of her wings shimmered all over her captors. Not once did they loosen their hold. They were one sinuous being of which she was only a tiny, unwilling part, and all she could do was scream.

Then they swooped down, dropping through the sky so fast it stopped her breath. Cemetery Hill vaulted up to meet her. The air forced her screams back down her throat, and she swallowed them.

Her ankle twisted as she fell forward onto her hands and knees. For a moment she couldn't breathe. The monsters dropped easily around her, skittering and jumping on the ground. Every cut and bruise seemed to come alive, throbbing with vigour. Her bones felt loose in their sockets.

Black, shiny eyes like her own stared back from the dozen or so creatures that glanced at her. Something grabbed hold of Kaye's hair and pulled her head back so that she was staring up into gold-flecked owl eyes.

"Tasty mousie." The creature's thick, dark lips moved slowly over the words. Its voice was like dried leaves being crushed.

Kaye shut her mouth. Others were crowding in, their faces pressing too close. Their hungry heat dizzied her. She flailed her hands to keep them away. Little winged creatures flitted around and showed their teeth.

"Grab-snatch great fun," the owl-eyed woman said, jerking Kaye's hair hard enough to pull her whole body with it, "such a fine, fine treat." The creature let go of her, and she fell on already raw knees.

"Let her be," Nephamael said, jerking her to her feet.

It was as if something had sawed the hill off at the base and raised it on fat pillars. Mushrooms, corpse-pale and each the size of her fist, ringed the grounds. Beneath that earthen ceiling, marvellous folk feasted as though it were a tent.

Nephamael's fingers pressed into her shoulder as though determined to bruise. The thorns that capped each gloved finger scraped across her skin with each stumbling step.

He brought her to the raised earthen dais, and she had to take several deep breaths to keep back the terror that was threatening to overwhelm her. The Queen sat on her throne; twin boys with goat feet knelt on either side of her, one absently playing a flute. Roiben stood on her left side, his clothes all of a dark silver fabric that managed to look like cloth and metal at the same time. Jagged freshwater pearls circled his collar and cuffs, reminding her of teeth. He looked magnificent, shining like the moon herself.

He was as distant as the moon too, expressionless and grim.

On the Queen's right side, there were two more knights, one dressed in a red so dark it was almost brown and the other in smoky blue. Farther back on the dais, mostly hidden by the throne itself, a fox-faced creature wearing an oddly shaped skullcap paused, one claw holding a brush over a long curling sheet of

HOLLY BLACK

white birch bark that it was using as parchment.

Kaye was pushed roughly to her knees. She could feel Nephamael sinking down behind her.

The Queen of the Unseelie Court looked down on her, lips quirking into a smile. Her blood-red hair was pulled back into thick, jewelled braids, and the dusky grey of her dress made her skin all the more pale and creamy by comparison. She was inhumanly beautiful, but her smile held no fondness. Kaye was disturbed to find herself smiling back into those cruel blue eyes nonetheless, longing for them to light with approval.

The air was thick with a sweet-smelling pollen that made Kaye feel giddy and unfocused. It was hard to get a real breath. The Queen's eyes were too clear, too blue, Kaye thought. They looked fake. Then the vertigo hit.

"Kaye Fierch, the Unseelie Court would bestow a great honour on you." The Queen's words dropped into her mind, each one echoing separately, the words making no sense when put together. "Will you submit to it?"

Kaye knew she had been asked a question and that it was very important she answer it. She tried to gather her scattered thoughts. Blue eyes held hers. She wanted to close her eyes. She wanted to stop the chill that was unfolding inside her, spreading from her chest, filling her with trembling longing. The most she could do was blink slowly.

"Perhaps her silence is answer enough." Kaye heard Roiben's voice as from a great distance. There was some laughter after he spoke.

"Come closer, little mortal." The Queen leaned forward, stretching out one lily-white hand, and before Kaye had time to consider it further, she was crawling forward to touch it. The Queen ran her fingers through Kaye's hair, mussing and then smoothing it down again.

"You want to please us, do you not, little one?"

"Yes." She did. She had never wanted anything more.

Nicnevin smiled at that, a smile that curled up at the ends.

"In fact, your only desire is to please us, is it not?"

"Yes." She shivered with delight as the Queen's hand stroked her cheek.

"You will please us greatly, child, if you are obedient and merry and do not question those things that you find strange. Do you understand?"

"Yes."

"We ask that you honour us with your participation in the Tithe. Will you accept the burden of this honour?"

Something in the phrasing of the question

seemed strange, but Kaye knew what answer to give. "Yes."

The Queen's smile was dazzling. Out of the corner of her eye she saw Roiben scowl, and she wondered at that. Wasn't he pleased that his Lady was pleased?

"My knight will have you groomed and properly attired. You mustn't try too hard to please him. It's a hopeless task." The Queen gave an almost imperceptible nod.

Roiben was beside Kaye then, drawing her to her feet. He smelled of burning cloves.

Rath Roiben Rye stood on his Lady's left-hand side, in his place of honour, his fists clenched so tightly he could feel the half-moon incisions his nails made in his palms. The girl was answering fatally in her soft-as-ash voice. She had made no move to say his name, and now it was far too late for that.

He willed his hands to relax. He did not want his Queen to guess at the increasingly dangerous chances he took. Letting the girl ask his name – have absolute power over him – was unintended, but hardly an isolated case of foolishness. At first he had told himself that he was testing himself, but his reasons seemed more complex. He was becoming less clear to himself – a string of actions held together by nothing, with no sequence he could understand.

He let his gaze skim out over the crowd. He

knew the Unseelie Court, knew the factions and their plans, their squabbles with one another, their desires and their habits. He knew them as only an outsider could, and his Lady valued that. That value was balanced against her amusement at his pain.

Everything is balance. Everything is ritual. Everything is pain.

The solitary fey had gathered warily at the edges of the brugh. He knew that many among them had no wish to be tied to the Unseelie Court, and for a moment he wondered if they could somehow refuse the sacrifice. But he could see from where he stood that they were drinking the traditional wine pressed from nettles. They had come to accept their servitude. Indeed, servitude might offer them some protection that independence had not.

A soft sound brought his eyes back to Kaye. He noted the bruises and faint raised marks that looked like scratches. She was gazing at the Queen with an adoration that sickened him. Was that how he had once looked at the Seelie Queen when he had vowed himself to her? He remembered that when his Bright Lady had but glanced at one of her knights, it was as if the sun shone for that knight alone. His own oath to her had been so easy to say, all the promises he had wanted to make wrapped into those formalised phrases. And he was still doing her bidding now, wasn't he? He wondered again as he stared into Kaye's face, as she waited happily for him to betake her into the sunless caverns of the Unseelie palace and pretty her up for her murder, just what was worth the pain of this.

"Come," he said.

Roiben walked from the brugh down hallways that shone with mica, their ceilings tangled with roots. Lights were dim and infrequent, candles oozing wax down the side of the wall from the niches they were set into. He heard the dull thud of her heavy boots as she followed him and he wanted to look back, to give her the comfort of a smile at least as she tried to keep pace through these winding passageways, but a smile would be a lie, and how would that serve her?

They passed by orchards of trees, white as bone and heavy with purple fruit. They passed through caverns of quartz and opal. They passed through rows of doors, each with a different face carved on it. Above it all, the ceiling shimmered with a distant light.

"You may ask me what you will. The Queen's strictures are not my own." Roiben hoped that whatever enchantment the Queen had put on her was not irresistible.

"I'm sorry, you know," she said softly. Her eyes were drugged with enchantment, the lids half closed. One of her hands was running across the sparkling mica wall, stroking it as though it were the belly of some great animal.

"Sorry?" he echoed stupidly.

"The diner," she said, swaying slightly, the hand on the wall now holding her upright, "I didn't know what I was asking."

He flinched at that. Her power over him was greater than any oath – he was literally hers to command – and here she was apologising for her cleverness. But maybe that was the magic too, forcing her mind away from survival.

Her hand had stilled on the wall, and her eyes found the floor.

He took a deep breath. "It was well tricked. Perhaps you will find a way to make it serve you yet." Not wise, that advice. He didn't know why he had put her through all the trouble of drawing the arrow from his chest when he was apparently at such pains to get himself run through again.

Fey as one of his own Folk, she suddenly laughed. "Are we really going to get me a dress?"

He nodded. "There is a seamstress who can weave spiders back from silk. She will make sure you have a dress. . . ." He bit off the end of the phrase, not knowing how to finish it. This wasn't a ball gown – it was a shroud. "A fine dress," he finished badly, but there it was.

Kaye grinned with delight, turning delicately on one foot, improvising a staggering dance as she followed him down the shimmering hallway, repeating his words. "Spiders back from silk . . ."

Skillywidden's quarters were deep in the cavernous depths of the palace where Roiben seldom had reason to go. Bolts of satins glowing summer-warm and golden, silks that would easily pass through the eye of a needle, heavy brocades rich with strange moving animals were all scattered along the floor in the dim room. A long wooden table was covered with silver bowls of varying sizes holding pins, spools of thread, and trims – skins of mice, drops of shimmering dew, leaves that would never fade and other, less pleasant things.

The most fantastical things in the room were those that appeared the most ordinary, Roiben knew. The loom that could weave Folk into tapestries, binding them there till this or that term was met, looked like an old and much abused loom, nothing more. The spindle was much the same, rough wood and plain, but he knew that the long black thread it was wound with was human hair.

The seamstress herself was a small creature with spindly limbs, long and awkward. She was draped in sheer black cloth that hid half of her face and hunched so far over that her long arms almost touched the floor. Roiben bowed shallowly as shining black eyes regarded him.

Skillywidden hissed her greetings and shuffled over to lift Kaye's thin arms, measuring their width by squeezing them between her thumb and first finger. When Kaye's brown eyes caught his, he could see the glint of fear in them, although her body remained limp.

"Toothsome," Skillywidden rasped speculatively, "smooth skin. What shall I trade for her? I could make you a tunic with the scent of apple blossoms. That would remind you of home, no?"

Kaye shuddered.

"I am here for a gown, not to trade," Roiben said, repressing a shudder himself. "The Queen would like her better dressed for the revels seeing as she" – again, it was hard to find the right words, so as not to alarm the girl – "is a guest of honour."

Skillywidden chittered and began digging through her bolts of cloth. Kaye's drugged haze seemed to keep her from remembering that the seamstress scared her, and she was now stroking a fabric that shifted colour as she touched it.

"Stretch out your arms," the seamstress croaked, "wide as a bird. There."

Kaye held up her arms while Skillywidden draped her with fabrics and whispered incoherently. The little crone grasped Kaye's chin suddenly and jerked it downward, then shuffled over to her bowls, digging around in them.

There was nothing for Roiben to do but wait.

Apple blossoms no longer reminded Roiben of home, although the Seelie Court had reeked of them. No, now the scent of apple blossoms reminded him of a treewoman, whose brown face had been tranquil as dirt despite how far she was from her tree. She had been a prophet, but she would not prophesy for the Unseelie Queen. He had been ordered to persuade her.

What he remembered most now, however, were the treewoman's last words to him, spoken as mossy fingers scraped his cheek and thick sap ran from the many cuts in her body. "It is you who are dying," she had said.

You can break a thing, but you cannot always guide it afterwards into the shape you want.

"Knight?" Skillywidden said, holding up a skein of thin, white silk. "Is it meet?"

"Send the dress to my rooms," Roiben said, pulling himself from his thoughts. "The Queen desires her to be clad and back in the brugh tonight."

Skillywidden looked up from the collection she was assembling, blinked owlishly, and grunted. That was enough of a response for him; he had no need to urge further swiftness on the seamstress. Kaye was likely to benefit from any delays.

"Come," Roiben said, and Kaye followed him tractably. She looked drunken with magic.

Retracing their steps through the Palace of Termites, he at last brought them to a wooden door carved with a crude unicorn. He opened it with a silver key and let her go inside before him. He watched her stop to look at the books that covered a low table, running her hands over slim paperback volumes of Yeats and Milton, lingering as she touched a leather volume with silver clasps. It was a book of old songs, but there was no title on the dusty cover, and she did not unclasp it to look at the pages. On the wall, there was the old tapestry, the one he had slashed into shreds one night long ago. He wondered whether his room looked like a cell to her. It couldn't have been what she had expected after the marvellous things she had seen elsewhere.

Kaye was looking at the tapestry, studying what was left of it. "She's pretty. Who is she?"

"My Queen," he said. He wanted to correct himself, but he couldn't.

"Not the Unseelie Queen? The other one?" Kaye sat down on the drab coverlet of his bed, tilting her head, still looking at the figure. He didn't need to look to see the depiction, dark hair falling like a cape over the back of her emerald dress – beautiful, but only stitcheries. A mortal had woven it, a man who, having caught sight of the Seelie Queen, had spent the remainder of his short life weaving depictions of her. He had died of starvation, raw, red fingers staining the final tapestry. It was a long time that Roiben had envied him such perfect devotion.

"The other one," he agreed.

"I read that" – Kaye pointed to *Paradise Lost* – "Well, part of it."

"Horror and doubt distract his troubled thoughts and from the bottom stir the Hell within him, for within him Hell he brings, and round about him, nor from Hell one step more than from himself can fly by change of place," he quoted.

"It was in one of those huge anthology books, but we didn't actually talk about it in class. I kept the book after I dropped out – do you know what high school is?" Her voice sounded drowsy, he thought, but the conversation was relatively normal. While the enchantment lingered, it no longer seemed to overwhelm her. He allowed himself to see that as a positive sign.

"We know about your world, at least superficially. The solitary fey know more. They are the ones huddled around windows, watching television through the blinds. I've seen a stick of lipstick traded for an unseemly amount among dryads."

"Too bad they didn't let me bring my bag. I could have bribed my way out of here." Kaye sniggered, pulling herself all the way onto his bed.

She was drawn up against the headboard,

black jeans frayed at the ankles where they touched the scuffed boots. Just a girl. A girl who shouldn't have to be this brave. Around her wrist, a rubber band encircled the flesh, faded patterns drawn in blue ink still visible. No rings on those fingers. Nails bitten to the quick. Details. Things he should have noticed.

She looked tired, he realised. He knew little of what her life was like before he had made a mess of it. With a grimace he remembered the ripped shirt that she had ripped further to bind his wound. "At least we think we know something of your world. I do not, however, know near as much as I ought about you."

"I don't know much about the world," Kaye said. "I only know about the crappy town I grew up in and the even crappier city we moved to after that. I've never even been out of the country. My mum wants to be this singer, but mostly she just winds up getting drunk and screaming how other chick vocalists suck. God, that sounds depressing."

Roiben thought of what would happen if the sacrifice was not made, if by guile or chance or something else, Kaye escaped. The solitary fey would be free for seven years. He imagined the chaos that would ensue.

It very nearly pleased him.

"I don't think I've exactly been cheery myself, fair Kaye."

She sighed, smiling, and let her head fall

back, her ragged blonde hair spreading out in a halo over his pillows. He thought absently that he would like to braid that hair the way he had once braided his sister's.

"I went to high school for a while," she continued absently, "and then I got out of the habit. People usually think that I'm pretty weird, which is funny at the moment. Maybe funny is the wrong word."

He sat on the end of the bed, just listening.

"I thought weirdness was a good thing. I don't mean that defensively, either. I thought it was something to be cultivated. I spent a lot of time hanging around bars, setting up equipment, breaking it down, loading up vans, fishing my mum's head out of toilets – things other kids didn't do. And sometimes things just happened, magical things that I couldn't control. But still, all this – you – it's so hard to accept that you're really real." She said the last with a hushed reverence that was completely undeserved.

Still, she sounded so normal. Conversational. She even looked normal, if a touch too comfortable on a stranger's bed. "Do you still want to please me?"

Her smile was surprised, a little baffled. "Of course I do."

"It would be better if you did not," he said, hesitating, trying to find a way to reason her out of enchantment. He could do nothing for

her if she was like this when the actual cere-
mony took place. "It would be better if you
acted according to your own desires."

She sat up and looked at him intently. "Do
you? Don't you want to go home?"

"To the Seelie Court?" He allowed himself
to say it. For a long moment, he considered
what she asked and then he shook his head.
"Once, I wanted nothing more. Now, I think I
would not be welcome among them and, even
were I, it is unlikely we would suit."

"You're not the way everyone says you are,"
Kaye said, looking at him so fiercely that he
couldn't meet her gaze. "I know you're not."

"You know nothing of me," he said. He
wanted to punish her for the trust he saw on
her face, to raze it from her now so that he
would be spared the sight of her when that
trust was betrayed.

He wanted to tell her he found her impos-
sibly alluring, at least half enchanted, body
bruised and scratched, utterly unaware she
would not live past dawn. He wondered what
she would say in the face of that.

Instead, he forced a little laugh. "Let me
explain again. Of the Host of the Unseelie
Court are many unconcerned by blood and
death, save as amusement. But the Host is
more than a scourge. Nicnevin rules over
ancient secrets, buried in the bowels of warrens
and fens. The twilight holds as many truths as

the dawn, perhaps more, since they are less easily perceived. No, I do not think that I would be welcomed back, now that I can see that."

"But they –" Kaye began, and he held up a hand to forestall her objection.

"Smallish sects of beings, of which Faery is certainly one, require enemies to give them purpose. Think on Milton's angels. Was not his God wise in giving them a devil to fight?"

Kaye was quiet a moment. "Okay, you're saying that the Seelie Court needs to hate the Unseelie Court. But does that mean that you think that they're not all bad?"

"I can think of no insult too rich for the Unseelie Queen, but I have seen kindness in some of her court. More kindness and wisdom, surely, than I would have ever been given leave to expect."

"So what adversary does the Unseelie Court have?"

"Again, the parallels to your devils are amazing. They struggle with their own bore-dom. It is a struggle that often requires increas-ingly cruel diversions."

Kaye shuddered. "And you?"

Roiben shrugged. He had nearly forgotten what it felt like to just sit and talk with some-one. "I am some other thing, not of any court, nor truly solitary. There are too many posses-sors of my soul."

She moved to her knees, and reached for

both his hands. "Just so you know, I trust you."

"You shouldn't," he said automatically. Nevertheless, he found himself no longer wanting to punish her for her faith in him. Instead, he found himself wanting to be worthy of it. He wanted to be the knight he had once been. Just for a moment.

He watched her take a breath, steeling herself, perhaps, for the next turn of the conversation. He found that he could not bear it.

Roiben leaned forward before he might think to do otherwise and pressed a kiss to her dry lips. Her mouth opened with a rush of warm breath, and her arms ran over his shoulders to rest lightly, almost hesitantly, at the nape of his neck.

His tongue swept her mouth, searching for some escape from the chill inside him. It felt so good it made his teeth hurt.

Nor from hell one step more than from himself can fly. Charmed. He was kissing a charmed girl. He jerked his mouth back from hers. She looked a little dazed and ran her tongue over her lower lip, but said nothing.

He wondered what exactly she might think of it when her mind was better disposed towards the contemplation of such things. But then, his mind whispered, tomorrow would never come to her, would it? There was only now and if he wanted to kiss her, well, it was only kissing.

Kaye moved slightly back from him, folding her knees against her chest. "Would that piss her off?" Again, he didn't need to ask to whom she referred.

"No," he said, rubbing a hand over his face, giving a short laugh. "Hardly. It would doubtless amuse her."

"What about the other one – the other Lady?"

He closed his eyes reflexively, as if something had been thrown at him. He wondered why he was enamoured of a girl that could dissect him with the odd comment, throw him off balance with the idle, earnest question.

"You can kiss me, if you want," she said softly, roughly, before he found an answer. It seemed that the magic had burned out of her, because her eyes were as clear as they were bright. He could not tell whether the Queen's spell held her or what compulsions it put on her. "I should just stop asking you stupid questions."

He leaned forward, but there was a rapping on the door then, soft but insistent. For a moment, he didn't move. He wanted to say something about her eyes, to ask her perhaps a better question about her enchantment, or at least one that might produce a better answer.

Tell her that she could ask him anything she wanted. And he wanted to kiss her, wanted it so badly that he could barely pull himself to his feet, march to the door, and heave it open.

Skillywidden had somehow got a redcap to do her delivering for her. It stood in the doorway, stinking of congealed blood and rot. Pointed teeth showed as it smiled, looking beyond him to the girl on his bed.

Roiben snatched the white cloth out of its hands. "This better be clean."

"Lady wants to know if you're done with her yet." The leer on its face made it obvious how the Redcap interpreted those words.

Fury rose in him, choked him so unexpectedly that he feared he was trembling with it. He took a breath, then another. He trusted that the messenger would not notice. Redcaps were not much for details.

"You may tell her that I have not yet finished," he said, meeting that gaze with what he hoped was a small smile and a bow of his head as he shut the door, "but I expect to in short order."

When he turned back to her, Kaye's face was blank.

He swallowed the emotion he felt without even bothering to identify it.

"Put it on," he said harshly, not even trying to keep the anger out of his voice, letting her think it was directed at her. He tossed the gown towards Kaye, watched her flinch as the slippery silk slid over the edge of the bed, watched her lean down mutely to pick it up again.

She didn't trust him after all. Good.

"It is time," he said.

10

Corny sank lower in the warm, silty water as Nephamael swept into the room. The faerie women who had cut his hair and oiled his skin finished and left without being told to do so.

"They have made you quite lovely," Nephamael said, yellow eyes reflecting in the flickering candlelight.

Corny shifted self-consciously. The oil made his skin feel weird, even under the water. His neck itched where stray strands of cut hair stuck in the oil. "Making me look good is about as likely as turning lead into gold," he murmured, hoping he sounded witty.

"Are you hungry?" Nephamael asked in his rich-as-butter voice. Corny wanted to ask about Kaye, but it was so hard when the knight was walking towards him with slow, even strides.

Corny nodded. He didn't trust his voice. He still could only half believe that Nephamael had brought him from his ratty, ridiculous life, to this.

"In this country there are fruits that taste better than all the meat of your land." His wide lips twisted into a grin.

"And I'm allowed?"

"Very like, very like." Nephamael gestured to a pile of clothing. "Dress and I will show you."

Corny was both grateful and disappointed when Nephamael left him to dress on his own. Hurriedly pulling on the blue velvet tunic and tight pants, Corny ignored the dampness of his skin.

Nephamael was waiting in the hall. He ran his fingers through Corny's hair, smoothing it back into place. "A compliment would go amiss, I'm sure."

With those hands on him, he could hardly manage a reply.

"Come," Nephamael said, and Corny followed.

Candlewax dripped down the walls in an imitation of the stalactites above them. He could hear music and laughter as from far away. They walked through open doors of silver ivy to a garden where silver apples weighed the boughs of trees nearly to the ground. A slender path of white stones wound around the trees and back over itself throughout the garden. Above the orchard, the curved ceiling glowed as though it were day and they were no longer under the hill. Corny could smell fresh-turned earth, cut grass, and rotting fruit.

"Go ahead," Nephamael said, nodding toward the trees. "Eat whatever you desire."

Corny was no longer sure whether he was hungry. Still, to be polite and to avoid displeasing the knight, he went over and plucked an apple from one of the trees. It tumbled easily into his hand. The silver skin was warm to the touch, as though blood ran beneath the surface.

Corny looked up at Nephamael, who appeared to be studying a white bird perched in one of the trees. Corny took a cautious bite of the fruit.

It tasted of fullness, of longing and wishful thinking and want, so that one bite left him empty. Nephamael smirked as he watched Corny lick the broken fruit, devour the pulp, sink to his knees, sucking the pale centre pip.

Several of the Host gathered to watch him gorge, beautiful faces with upswept features and teardrop eyes turned towards him like flowers. They were laughing. All Corny could do was eat. He barely noticed Nephamael laughing uproariously. A woman with thin, curving horns tossed him a bruised plum. It burst in the dirt, and he hastened to lap up the pulp, soil and all. He licked the dirt after the fruit was gone, hoping for a darkened drop.

Black ants crawled over the sticky, fallen fruits and he ate those as well, blindly questing for any morsel.

After a time, Nephamael came forward, pressing a cracker to Corny's lips. He took it in his mouth thoughtlessly. It tasted like sawdust, but he swallowed it down.

It felt solid in his stomach, and the overwhelming empty hunger abated. It left him squatting under one of the trees, awake and aware. He looked at his filthy hands, the stained clothes, the laughing Folk, and he choked to keep from crying like a child for sheer helplessness.

"There, there," Nephamael said, patting Corny's shoulder.

Corny stood, fists clenched.

"Poor Corny. You look so fragile, I'm afraid your heart will break." There was amusement in the knight's tone.

Corny could feel himself reacting to that rich, smooth voice, could feel the shame and embarrassment receding until they seemed of only distant importance.

"Come here, my pet. You've made a mess of yourself." Nephamael raised his hand, beckoning.

One look into those yellow eyes and he

broke like a wishbone. Corny stepped into the circle of Nephamael's arms, basking in the feel of thorns.

Tonight the revels were quieter. No duelling fiddlers or raucous daisy-chain dances. There were no piles of fruit or honey cakes. Instead there were whispers and smothered laughter. The only light came from braziers throughout the brugh and the small faeries that flitted over the congregation.

It was hard to think. Kaye's feet were cold as they padded along the earthen floor. The haze of magic had lifted slowly, but the less she was enchanted, the more she was terrified.

She was going to die. It didn't matter if her feet were cold.

Roiben's back was to her, his pewter hair sliding like mercury over the shoulders of his coat as he led her through the crowd.

She wasn't going to die, she reminded herself. This was a game. Only a game.

One finger rose unconsciously to touch her mouth, which felt oddly soft and swollen. She remembered too well the pressure of his lips, their softness, and she remembered the expression on his face when he had pulled back from her – horror, perhaps, or disgust. She shook her head to clear it, but nothing would come clear.

Some of the eyes she passed sparkled with

greed, and she wondered how the solitary fey planned on dividing what was left of her.

Kaye took a deep breath of cold, autumn air, then another. Not funny.

Roiben's hand tightened on her upper arm, guiding her past beings both beautiful and grotesque. The dirt was damp under her bare feet, and she concentrated on that, steadying herself.

The Queen was standing at the centre of what looked to be a large, silver dance floor. It was composed of several pieces – each engraved with representations of bound humans and fey – fitted together like a puzzle. In the centre, Kaye could easily see ornate manacles attached to short, heavy chains. Unlike the base, the manacles and chains were unmistakably iron. She could smell it.

The layers of Nicnevin's diaphanous black robes blew in the breeze. The longest layer, the train, was held up at three points by goblin attendants. Her collar was stiff, rising like a translucent black fin behind her neck. Kaye trained her eyes on the collar, let her gaze stray to the looping mound of red braids piled on the Queen's head, let her gaze fall anywhere but into those deadly blue eyes.

Roiben dropped to one knee, and she did not need any prompting to follow.

"Do rise," the Queen said. Kaye and Roiben rose.

The Queen waved a dismissal at Roiben, an impatient gesture of her hand. He hesitated a moment, then approached the Queen, lowering himself to his knee again.

"I would give anything for her release," Roiben said in a voice so low Kaye was sure that only those very close could hear it. He stared downwards, whether at the earthen floor, or the Queen's slippered foot, Kaye could not say.

The sincerity in his voice frightened her. This was no safe thing, the way he was talking. Did he think he had to do this to repay some debt he thought he owed her? Did he think he had to do this because he'd kissed her?

Nicnevin's hand brushed over the crown of Roiben's head. Her voice was as soft as his, but her eyes sparkled with feral delight. She was looking beyond him and out into the blackness beyond the brugh. "Are you not already my servant in all things? Is there something of yours I do not already possess?"

He raised his head, then, looking up into the Unseelie Queen's blue eyes, and Kaye wanted to yell a warning, something, but the moment was frozen and she did not move.

"Perhaps I could offer my enthusiasm," he said. "You have oft complained of its lack."

The Queen's lips quirked at the edges, an almost smile, but she did not seem amused. "I think not. I find that I like you wilful."

"There must be something," Roiben insisted.

Nicnevin put her first finger against her carmine lips and tapped lightly. When she spoke, her voice was loud enough to carry in the natural amphitheatre of the hollow hill. "Tragedy is so compelling. I find myself moved to offer to play a game with you. Would you like that?"

"I am grateful, my Lady," Roiben said, his head still bowed.

She turned her gaze on Kaye. "Well, child, it seems that you pleased my knight after all. Answer a riddle, and the Unseelie Court will gift you to him."

There was a murmur in the crowd.

Kaye nodded her head, unsure of what constituted propriety in a faerie court.

There was true amusement in the Queen's voice as she spoke. "Cut me and I weep tears as red as my flesh, yet my heart is made of stone. Pray tell, mortal girl, what am I?"

You are yourself. Kaye bit her lip to keep back the hysterical laughter threatening to bubble up her throat again. Okay – red skin, stone centre – what matched that description? She thought she dimly remembered an old story about someone having their heart turned to stone and then restored by tears, but she wasn't sure where the memory came from. No, riddles usually had simple, commonsense, one-word answers. They always seemed obvious once you knew the answer.

Flesh. Maybe some kind of fruit? And the stone could be a pip? Oh – a cherry. Was that supposed to be funny?

Kaye bit her lip. If she answered the riddle correctly, she could walk out of here, something she desperately wanted to do. She cast her eyes to both sides of the Queen, looking for Spike or Lutie, but if they were in the crowd, her surreptitious glances did not find them. Walking out of here was not part of the plan. Right now she wasn't sure she cared much for what was part of the plan.

She bit her lip harder when she realised how far Roiben had already gone for her. Had Lutie and Spike realised that she might need protection while she was a prisoner in the Unseelie Court? If the various comments she had heard tonight were any indication, Roiben was being a prude – clearly a knight of the Host could do whatever he wanted with a human prisoner. Now, knowing all this, if Spike thought Roiben was such a scumbag, why convince her to go along with a plan that left her in his hands for the better part of a night?

No, she was going to answer the question before things got out of control. She was going to answer the question, tell Roiben everything – above all how sorry she was – and hope he understood. Then she was going to find Spike and get some real answers.

"A cherry," Kaye said as firmly as she could.

Roiben exhaled with a sharp hiss although he remained on his knees. She wondered how long he had been holding his breath.

"My Lady, you cannot . . . ," the fox-faced scribe began, but the Unseelie Queen quelled him with a gesture of her hand.

"Rise, my knight. You have chosen well. She is yours."

Roiben rose and turned slightly towards Kaye, an expression of unguarded relief on his face. Kaye reached out her hand towards him. She would explain everything as soon as they were dismissed. She would make him understand.

"Now, I order you to offer up your prize to be sacrificed for the Tithe," the Queen said.

There was laughter in the crowd.

She saw fury and shame coalesce into something horrible. She saw Roiben's hand drop, twitching over the hilt of his sword.

Then he seemed to regain control of himself, and he bowed to his Queen with a smile. Turning to Kaye, he pressed his lips against her neck, his hand holding her hip, speaking against the skin so that only she could hear him. "What belongs to you, yet others use it more than you do?"

His mouth moving against the skin of her neck made Kaye shiver. She opened her mouth to speak, but he shook his head, raising his hand to run his thumb over her jawline. "Think on it."

He let go of her and stepped primly to the side to join the other knights.

Three white-robed figures strapped Kaye down, their heavily gloved hands careful when handling the iron. First they shackled her ankles, then her wrists. The iron cuffs burned softly against her skin.

Four knights of the Unseelie Court stepped to the north, south, east, and west points. Roiben stepped to the south, below her feet. His eyes did not meet hers.

What belongs to you, yet others use it more than you do?

Four short, squat men carried braziers blazing with green fire to the four points around the circle where the knights stood. The little men went down on their knees, balancing the braziers on their backs like living stools.

The Queen's fox-faced scribe raised both his hands, and the brugh was entirely quiet. Eerily quiet. Kaye searched the crowd for some familiar face. For a moment she thought she saw Spike, but then she couldn't be sure. There were so many creatures.

More green flames flared around the edge of the brugh, casting strange shadows.

Somewhere, far outside the circle, a single drum began to beat.

The Unseelie Queen began speaking, her voice echoing in the near silence. "We gather on this sacred night to fulfil our sacred debt. Tonight, we who rule must kneel."

As one being, the Unseelie Court moved to their knees. Only the solitary fey remained standing. Even the Queen knelt, her gown puddling around her.

"We, the Unseelie Court, keepers of the earth's secrets, rulers of blood and bone, offer a willing sacrifice in return for the willing obedience of those who dwell in our lands."

Obviously, it didn't bother anyone that their willing sacrifice was in chains, Kaye thought. The slow beat of the drum was maddening. A calm contrast to her heart, which was beating itself to death against the cage of her ribs.

The Unseelie Queen went on speaking. "What is the sacrifice we offer?"

The Court spoke as one. "Mortal blood. Mortal spirit. Mortal passion."

Off to one side of the Queen, Kaye's eye finally settled on Corny, blankfaced beside Nephamael. His pale brown hair had been cut much shorter and combed towards his face. That and the absence of his glasses made his face look thin and vulnerable. He was dressed all in blue velvet, tricked out as though he was expected to perform Jacobean drama once the sacrifice was over.

Nephamael was watching her with his implacable yellow eyes. She hoped he was going to do something very soon.

Experimentally, she reached out her own magic to tug at the glamour that was over her. It did not budge, heavy as a wet sheet. She couldn't even feel her wings.

"What do we ask in return?" The Unseelie Queen's voice rang out, beautiful and terrible.

Again the Host spoke. "Obedience. Restraint. Submission."

Kaye's gaze shifted, and she met Roiben's eyes. On his knees, speaking the words of the ritual, his eyes blazed as he tried to communicate with her through the improbable channel of expression.

What belongs to you, yet others use it more than you do?

It was another riddle, obviously. What belongs to you? In the world of riddles, it's the basics – body, brain, spirit. She was pretty sure that she used all of those more than she let the next person use them.

"We ask: Do you understand the compact we offer?"

This time it was the solitary fey who spoke, their voices not as well timed, creating the effect of echoes. "We do understand."

She was looking at it backwards, she decided. He wanted her to do something. The riddle was about something she already knew.

She looked into his drawn face and understood so completely that it knocked the breath out of her.

What belongs to you, yet others use it more than you do?

Your name.

The Unseelie Queen's voice broke her concentration. She seemed to be speaking in time with the distant drum. "Do you accept this mortal as your sacrifice?"

"We do accept."

Kaye looked around, in a panic now. What the hell did he want her to use his name *for*? The brugh was huge and it was full. Did he really think he could somehow get her out of here?

"Do you so bind yourselves to us?"

The solitary fey spoke as one. "We do bind ourselves."

Kaye couldn't help the frantic pulling on her chain. Panic was spreading through Kaye like liquid, turning her blood to ice.

"What is the term of your service?"

Dawn was coming. Kaye saw the red glow out beyond the burning green flames.

"Seven years is the length of our binding."

The Queen raised her dagger. "Let the compact be sealed in blood."

No one was coming to save her. Kaye pulled hard on her chains, throwing her whole weight against them, but they were tight, and the heel of her palm could not slip through them. They burned even more as she shifted. The Unseelie Queen looked surprised. Dimly

Kaye realised that her calm and silence must have made her seem as though she were still enchanted.

She struggled to damp down her panic long enough to think.

She had to use his name. She had no idea what to command him to do.

A specific command . . . save me . . . stop this . . . get me out of here?

Roiben was glaring at her.

How could he want her to do this? It made no damn sense, but there was no more time to think.

"Rath Roiben Rye." Her voice was soft, the words running together in her panic. She realised what she was doing, and her throat almost closed up. "Cut my bonds."

Roiben drew his finger-slim sword, and the Unseelie Court seethed with noise. A moment of hesitation, and then he smiled. It was a dark, horrible smile, the most terrible expression she had ever seen.

Three knights were on him before he was even inside the circle. The green knight's heavy sword crashed against Roiben's at the same moment that a red-clad knight slashed at Roiben's back. He twisted, faster than she would have believed, and his blade sliced the red knight across the face. The faerie clutched at his eyes, staggering, his sword clattering into the circle.

Roiben tried to parry a blow from the third knight, a female wielding an axe, but he was too late. The blade bit into his right shoulder so hard that it probably hit bone.

Roiben staggered back, gasping with pain, sword drooping in his right hand, the tip dragging along the metal circle. It came up just in time to stab through the green knight's chest as he rushed forward. The knight fell on his side, completely still. There was only a small hole in his armour, but it was already welling with blood.

Roiben and the female knight circled each other, exchanging tentative blows. Their weapons were not suited for this kind of combat, his sword too slight and her axe too slow, but both combatants were dangerous enough to compensate. She lunged forward, swinging the axe towards his arm rather than his torso, hoping to catch him off guard. He sidestepped, dodging her blow but missing her with a wide sweep of his own blade.

Other Unseelie troops were surging forward, too many and varied for Kaye to count – trolls and hobmen and redcaps. The Queen was still, her lips pressed together in a thin line.

Kaye pulled at her chains, arching her body up hard. Nothing gave.

Blood had darkened the cloth at Roiben's shoulder in a disturbingly wide stain. Even as she saw him slash the other knight's side hard enough to throw the woman to her knees, there were ten more opponents surrounding him. There was a flurry of parry and lunge, his body spinning to slice at a clawed hand, to gut an exposed belly.

And still more came.

Kaye turned her head as far as it would go and spat at her hands, vainly trying to lubricate them enough to work them out of the manacles, muttering, "No, no, no."

The Queen was shouting now, but Kaye could not make out her words over the ring of blades and the shouts of onlookers.

A small form slid beside Kaye on the metal. Spike was scrabbling at her wrist cuffs with a small knife.

"It's all very bad," the little man said. "Oh, Kaye, it's all gone bad."

"He's going to die!" she yelled. Then it occurred to her, what she could do. As loud as she could, she shouted, "Rath Roiben Rye – run!"

The Unseelie Queen whirled at that, her face savage, advancing on Kaye. Her lips twitched over words, but Kaye still could not hear them.

Roiben slashed at another opponent, keeping his back towards Kaye. She wasn't sure whether he had even heard her command. Perhaps he had run as far as he could.

"Hurry, Spike," Kaye said, struggling to

HOLLY BLACK

keep her body from the wild, trapped animal thrashing that would prevent Spike from having any chance at popping the lock.

The little man's brows were narrowed in furious concentration, fingers burning where they touched the iron. Suddenly he was knocked aside as if by invisible hands.

"While you have been most diverting, I find this tiresome." The Queen of the Unseelie Court placed a slippered foot on Kaye's throat. Kaye rasped, the pressure cutting off her air, threatening to crack her neck.

Then the pressure was gone, and the Lady was falling. Droplets of blood spattered across Kaye's cheek before the body fell across her. There was a sickening hiss where the Queen's cheek hit the iron. She was dead.

Roiben looked down at her, but his eyes were unfocused and wild. There was a smear of blood across his mouth, but she didn't think it was his own. He raised his sword, and she only had a moment to scream before it came crashing down on the chains binding her ankles, hitting the metal so hard that it rang.

Spike was crawling close again, poking at the motionless body of the Unseelie Queen and muttering to himself. A hush had fallen over the court.

There was a sudden rippling in the air around Kaye. She could feel the magic swirling over her, making the iron cuffs that still clutched her wrists and ankles burn unbearably. Her skin was suddenly too tight, too hot, peeling back as it had done on her lawn, but this time it was not gentle. Her wings ripped free from the thin flesh that bound them just as Roiben slammed his sword against the chain binding her right hand.

His eyes went wide, and he stumbled back. He was so stunned he missed the parry as another redcap rushed him. He turned, almost too late, and the redcap's small curved blade cut his thigh.

Without the protection of the strange, strong glamour, the iron burned Kaye's wrists and ankles like hot brands. She howled in pain, struggling to get the things off, struggling to get out from under the weight of the Queen's body.

Spike seemed to recover himself enough to get work on the cuffs again, and this time he managed to pick the lock of the only one still attached to the chain. Her flesh was blistered where the iron had touched it.

"We have to go! Move!" Spike was pulling at her hand, his face blank with fear.

The court had erupted in chaos around them. She could not tell which of the creatures battling or running or hiding was a foe, or whether in fact she had any friends here except the hob who was urging her to her feet. And Roiben, whose sword was spinning in an arc, crashing against a spear held by a spotted creature with shining golden eyes.

Blood was running over his right hand; blood had soaked the left leg of his trousers. His movements were stiffening; she could see that.

Kaye tried not to concentrate on the pain of the iron, tried to focus on standing up. "We can't leave him here."

A volley of pinecones flew around them, bursting into flame where they fell.

"Oh, yes we can," Spike said, pulling her with renewed determination. "Better he not get a hold of you after you used his name like that."

"No, you don't understand," she said, but she knew it was she who had not understood. She, who had tried to pretend. Roiben had known all along that he was offering her his life.

You *idiot*, she wanted to scream.

"Rath Roiben Rye, I command you to get the fuck out of here with Spike and me, right now!" She screamed it, as loud as she could, sure that he was close enough to hear her this time.

Roiben turned, his eyes flashing fury. He seemed to channel that anger into his sword, because his next blow cut open the golden-eyed faerie's throat.

Kaye wobbled on her feet, trying to shore up her knees, trying not to fall into blackness.

Her ankles and wrist burned, and all she could taste or smell was iron.

Then Roiben was pulling her through the crowd with a blood-soaked hand. He tugged her into a run, and Spike was beside them, running too.

As they stepped outside the brugh, a figure stepped in front of them, but was cut down before she caught more than an impression of something awkwardly tall and pale grey in colour.

Then they were in the graveyard, running down the tumbled quartz path, past plastic flower grave markers, and flattened drink cans, stepping on cigarette butts, and they seemed like talismans that might actually keep the monsters at bay.

Until she realised that she was one of the monsters.

11

Kaye trod up the driveway, her mother's Pinto looking both familiar and strange, as though it was part of a painting that might suddenly be turned on its side and revealed as flat. The door to the back porch seemed like a portal between worlds, and, even close as she was, she wasn't sure she would be allowed to step through to the kitchen beyond.

More than tired, she felt numb.

Roiben leaned against an elm tree and closed his eyes, unsheathed sword dangling limply from one hand. His body was trembling lightly, and next to familiar things, the blood soaking his arm and thigh looked ghastly.

Right then, Lutie swooped down from one of the trees, circling Kaye twice before landing on her shoulder and scrabbling to press a kiss against the damp skin of her neck. It surprised Kaye, and she flinched back from the sudden touch.

"Scared, silly-scared, scared, scared, scared," Lutie chanted against her neck.

"Me too," Kaye said, pressing her hand against the buzz of the tiny body.

"There'll be a score of songs about you by nightfall," Spike said, eyes gleaming with pride.

"There would have been twice as many if I had died like you planned, wouldn't there?"

Spike's eyes widened. "We never . . ."

Kaye bit her lip, forcing herself to swallow the hysteria that threatened to bubble up her throat. "If Nephamael was going to take the glamour off me, he was going to take it off my corpse."

"Dismiss me, pixie," Roiben said. His eyes had a hollow look to them that made her stomach clench. "I was careless. I will hold no grudge against you or yours, but this foolishness ends *now*."

"I didn't plan this – your name. I never meant to use it for anything." Kaye reached out her hand to stroke the edge of his sleeve.

The effect was instantaneous. He circled her wrist with his hand, twisting it hard. Lutie squealed, springing from Kaye's shoulder into the air.

There was no anger in his voice, no sarcasm, no heat. It was as strangely hollow as his eyes. "If you wish me to endure your touch, you must order me to do so."

Then he dropped her hand so quickly it might have been made of iron. She was shaking, too scared to cry, too miserable to speak.

Spike looked at her wide-eyed, as though he was reasoning with a lunatic. "Well then, Kaye, tell him he can go. He says he won't hold a grudge – that's a generous offer."

"No," she said, louder than she intended. They all looked at her in surprise, although Roiben's gaze darkened.

She had to explain. She turned to him, careful not to touch him. "Come inside. You can clean up your cuts there. I just want to explain. You can leave tonight."

His eyes were dull no longer; they blazed with rage. For a moment, she thought he was going to kill her before she could manage to stammer out his name. Then she thought he might just walk away, daring her to stop him. But he did neither of these things.

"As you say, my mistress." The words curled off his tongue, cutting deeper than she had thought words could. "I would prefer no one else learned the calling of me."

Spike blinked up at the Unseelie knight, apparently unable to control a shudder. Lutie watched them from the crook of the elm tree.

"The Thistlewitch will need to know what

had happened tonight," Spike said slowly.

"Go ahead," she said. "We can talk about it later." Taking the spare key out from underneath a dusty bottle of bleach, she opened the door as quietly as she could. The house was silent.

Roiben followed Kaye into the kitchen, and the sight of him carefully closing the backdoor and filling what was probably a dirty glass with water from the tap was so incongruous, she had to stop and watch him. He drank, tipping back his head so that the column of his neck was thrown into profile. He must have seen her staring; as he finished the last of the water, he looked in her direction.

"Your pardon," he said.

"No, go ahead. I'm just going to make some coffee. Uh, the bathroom is there." She pointed.

"Do you have any salt?" he asked.

"Salt?"

"For my leg. I'm not sure what can be done about the arm."

"Oh." She rummaged around in her grandmother's spice drawer and came up with a canister of Morton's salt. "Wouldn't iodine or something be better?"

He just shook his head grimly and walked in the direction of the bathroom.

A few minutes later he returned in his more human glamour. As before, his hair was more white than silver, the bones of his face were slightly less jagged, and his ears were less prominent. He had discarded his shirt, and she was disconcerted to see the pattern of scars on his chest. He must have found some gauze; one thigh looked padded under the leg of his trousers.

She poured the coffee into two mugs, alarmed to see that her hands were shaking. Spooning sugar into one of the cups, she looked a query at Roiben. He nodded and nodded again when she offered milk.

"When I first met you, I didn't know I was a faerie," she said.

He raised an eyebrow. "I presume that you knew you were not human when you blackmailed a kiss from me."

Kaye felt her face flood with heat. She just nodded.

"The question, of course, is whether you aided me in the forest for the reward of my name."

She stammered, the queasy feeling in the pit of her stomach intensifying. If that was what he thought, no wonder he was furious.

"There was no way I could have known what you were going to offer me. I just wanted to piss you off in the diner . . . and . . . I knew faeries don't like to give out their real names."

"One day, someone is going to cut that clever tongue of yours right out of your head," he said.

She bit her lower lip, worrying it against her teeth as he spoke. What had she expected – a declaration of love because of one half-hearted kiss?

Kaye looked at the steaming cup in front of her. She was sure that if she took a sip of that coffee, she would throw it up.

She needed a cigarette. Ellen's jacket was draped over the back of the chair, and she fumbled through it for a cigarette and a lighter. Lighting it despite Roiben's look of surprise, she took a deep drag.

The smoke burned her lungs like fire. She found herself on her knees on the linoleum floor, choking, the cigarette burning the plastic tile where it had fallen.

Roiben put the cigarette out with a twist of his boot and leaned forward. "What were you doing?"

"I smoke," she said, sitting on the floor. Eyes already watery from coughing could no longer hold back tears. It seemed stupid that this was the thing that would set her off, but she sobbed, feeling more like puking with nothing in her stomach than any crying she'd done.

"They're poison," he said incredulously. "Even Ironsiders die from those."

"I know." She pressed her face against her knees, wiping her cheeks against the faerie gown, wishing she'd let him leave when he'd wanted to.

"You're tired," he said with a long sigh that might have been annoyance. "Where do you sleep? You might consider glamouring yourself as well." His face was impassive, emotionless.

She smeared the tears on her cheeks and nodded. "Are you tired?"

"Exhausted." He didn't exactly smile, but his face relaxed a little.

They went up the stairs quietly. Her new senses were distracting. She could hear the whistling snore of her mother and the lighter, muffled breaths of her grandmother. Up the stairs, she could smell the woodchips and excrement of her rats, smell the chemical soaps and sprays in the bathroom, could even smell the heavy coating of oily dust that covered most surfaces. Somehow, each odour was more vivid and distinct than she could remember it being.

Ignore it, she told herself; things had been the same way the last time she had the heavy glamour removed. Just a perk to make up for the fact she couldn't touch half the metal things in the house and one drag on a cigarette could make her almost pass out.

They went into her bedroom and she turned the old-fashioned key to lock the door. There was no way she was going to be able to explain Roiben to her grandmother, glamour or no.

"Well, I saw your room," she said. "Now

you get to see mine."

He waded through the mess to sit on the mattress on the floor. She dug through the rubbish bags and found a musty green duvet riddled with cigarette burns for herself. The pink one she usually slept with was already piled on the mattress, and she hoped that it didn't smell too much like her sweat.

Roiben pulled off his boots, looking around the room. She watched his eyes settle first on the rat cage, then on the drifts of clothing, books, and magazines lining the floor.

"Kind of a dump, I guess." She sat down on the boxspring that still graced the frame of the white bed.

She watched him, stretching out on her mattress, fascinated by the way the compact muscles moved beneath his skin. He looked dangerous, even tired and bandaged and wrapped in her pink duvet.

"What did you do with her?" He looked up through silver lashes of heavy-lidded eyes.

"What?"

"The girl this room really belongs to – what did you do with her?"

"Fuck you," she said, so angry that for a minute she didn't even care that she was supposed to be convincing him how sorry she was.

"Did you think I would credit the tears of a pixie?" he asked, turning so that his face was hidden from her.

Unspoken slurs hung on her tongue like thistles, hurting her throat with the effort of swallowing them. They were both tired. She was lucky – he was still talking to her.

As tired as she was, she couldn't sleep. She watched him instead, watched as he tossed and turned, tangling the blankets around him. Watched as his face relaxed into exhaustion, one hand curling tightly around the edge of the pillow.

He never had looked as real to her as he did in that moment, hair loose and messy, one bare foot hanging over the edge of the mattress, resting on a library book she'd always meant to return.

But she didn't want to think of him as real. She didn't want to think of him at all.

And then she was being shaken awake. She blinked in the unnatural darkness of drawn shades. Roiben was sitting next to her on the hard boxspring, hands gripping her shoulders so hard she was sure they would bruise.

"Tell me that you meant to tell me, Kaye," he said, eyes bright.

She struggled to be more fully awake. Nothing about this scene made sense, certainly not the anguish so plain on his face.

"You were going to tell me that you were a faerie," he insisted. "There was no time."

She nodded, still stunned by sleep. He

seemed huge; the whole room was swallowed up by his presence so that it was impossible to look anywhere but into his eyes.

"Tell me," he said, letting go of her shoulders, his hands moving to smooth the hair back from her face in a rough caress.

"I never meant . . . I wanted to," she stammered drowsily, the words hard to fit together.

His hands stilled. His voice was low this time. "Make me believe it."

"I can't," she said. She had to focus, to find the answer that would make everything right again. "You know I can't."

"Go back to sleep, Kaye," he said softly, no longer touching her, his hands fisted on his knees.

She levered herself up to her elbows, blearily realising that she had to stop him before he got up from the bed.

"Let me show you," she said, leaning forward to press her mouth to his. His lips parted with no resistance at all, letting her kiss him as though he could taste the truth on her tongue.

After a moment, he pulled back from her gently. "That wasn't what I meant," he said with a small rueful smile.

She flopped back, cheeks reddening, fully awake now and appalled at herself.

Roiben slid off the boxspring and onto the floor. He was looking away from her, at the sliver of light showing under the dirty plastic windowshade.

Rolling onto her side, she looked down at what she could see of his face. Her fingers chipped nervously at a drop of wax on the duvet. "I answered the riddle. I thought she would let me go and I answered it anyway."

He looked up at her abruptly, amazed. "You did at that. Why?"

Kaye wanted to explain it as best as she could. He was listening to her, at least for the moment. She made sure to keep her voice completely level, completely sincere. "Because it wasn't supposed to go like it did. I never even thought of using you like that . . . you were never supposed to – "

"Be glad I did," he said, but he said it gently. He reached up and ran three fingers down the side of her jaw. "It's strange to see you this way."

She shivered. "What way?"

"Green," he said, his eyes like mist, like smoke, like all insubstantial things.

She lost her nerve, looking into those eyes. He was too beautiful. He was a spell she was going to break by sheer accident.

His voice was very soft when he spoke again. "I have had a surfeit of killing, Kaye."

And whether that was meant as a prayer for the past or a plea for the future, she could not say.

This time, when he lay down on the mattress

and drew the duvet over his shoulders, she watched the cobwebs swing with each gust of air that crept through gaps in the old windows. Words echoed on the edges of her thoughts, phrases she had heard but not heard. She'd seen the scars that ran up and down his chest, dozens of marks, pale white stripes of skin edged in pink.

She imagined the Unseelie Court as she had seen it the night she'd sneaked in with Corny, except that now they were all looking at their new toy, a Seelie knight with silver hair and such pretty eyes.

"Roiben?" she whispered into the quiet of the room. "Are you still awake?"

But if he was, he didn't answer her.

The next time she woke, it was because someone was pounding on the door.

"Kaye, time for you to get up." Her mother's voice sounded strained.

Kaye groaned. She unfolded herself stiffly from her uncomfortable position on the little bed, feeling the impression of every metal coil along her back.

The banging didn't stop. "Your grandmother is going to kill me if I let you miss another day of school. Open this door."

Kaye lurched out of bed, stumbling over Roiben, and turned the key in the lock.

Roiben sat up, eyes slitted with sleep.

"Glamour," he said rustily.

"Shit." She had almost opened the door with massive wings attached to her back, and green.

She focused for a moment, drawing energy through her hands, feeling the thrum of it in her fingers. She concentrated on her features, her eyes, her skin, her hair, her wings. Her wrists and ankles were still sore, and she made sure to use the glamour to compensate for the discoloration of the skin where they'd been burned by the iron.

Then she opened the door.

Ellen looked at her and then looked beyond her at Roiben. "Kaye – "

"It's Hallowe'en, mum," Kaye said, pitching her voice in a low whine.

"Who's he?"

"Robin. We got too fucked up to drive anywhere. Don't look at me like that – we didn't even sleep in the same bed."

"Pleasure to make your acquaintance," Roiben said muzzily. In this context, his formality sounded like drunkenness, and Kaye felt an overwhelming urge to snigger.

Ellen raised her eyebrows. "Fine, sleep it off. Just don't make it a habit," she said finally. "And if either of you puke, you clean it up."

"Okay," Kaye yawned, closing the door. Considering the sheer volume of vomit she'd cleaned up over the last sixteen years – most of it belonging to her mother – she thought that was a pretty uncharitable comment, but she was too tired to dwell on it.

A few moments later, Kaye was curled up on the boxspring again, dropping easily back into sleep.

The third time that Kaye woke, it was dark outside the window. She stretched lazily, and her stomach tightened in knots. She reached out to the lamp on the end table and switched it on, bathing the room in dim yellow light.

Roiben was gone.

The pink duvet was crumpled at the foot of the mattress, two pillows beside it. The sheet covering the mattress was pulled off the corner, as though he had slept restlessly. Nothing to suggest where he'd gone; nothing to say goodbye.

She had only asked him to stay for the day. When darkness had come, he had been free to go.

Frantically, she pulled the faerie dress over her head, tossing it on the floor with all the other laundry, tugging on the first clothes she found – a plain white T-shirt and checked trousers with zips all down the sides. She unbraided her hair and hand-combed it roughly. She had to find him . . . she would find him. . .

Kaye stopped with one hand still dragging through tangled hair. He didn't want her to follow him. If he'd wanted anything more to do with her, he would have at least said good-bye. She'd apologised and he'd listened. He'd even forgiven her, sort of. That was that. There was no reason to go after him, unless you could count the odd, soft touch of his hand on her cheek or the gentle acceptance of yet another kiss. And what did those things mean anyway? Less than nothing.

But when she went down the stairs, Roiben was there, right there, sitting on her grand-mother's flowery couch, and Ellen was sitting beside him. Kaye's mother was wearing a red dress and had two sequin devil horns sticking out of her hair.

Kaye stopped on the stairwell, stunned as the utter impossibility of the scene crashed up against the utter normalcy of it. The television was on, and its flickering blue light sharpened Roiben's features until she couldn't tell whether he still wore his glamour.

He was drizzling pieces of plain, white bread with honey from the jar, thick amber puddles of it that he as much poured into his mouth as ate.

"Thank you," he said. "It's very good."

Kaye's mother snorted at his politeness. "I don't know how you can eat that. Ugh." Ellen made a face. "Too sweet."

"It's perfect." He grinned and licked his fingers. His smile was so honest and unguarded that it looked out of place on his face. She wondered if that was what he had looked like before he'd come to the Unseelie Court.

"You're one twisted young man," Ellen said, and that only made his grin widen. Kaye wondered whether he was smiling at the jibe or smiling because it was so true.

Kaye walked down a few more steps, and Ellen looked up. Roiben turned to her as well, but she could read nothing in those ashen eyes.

"'Morning," Roiben said, and his voice was as warm and slow as the honey he'd been eating.

"You still look like shit, kiddo," her mother said. "Drink some water and take an aspirin. Alcohol makes you dehydrated."

Kaye snorted and walked down the rest of the stairs.

On the television, a cartoon Batman chased the Joker through a spooky old warehouse. It reminded her of the old merry-go-round building.

"You guys are watching cartoons?"

"The news is on in ten minutes. I want to see the weather. I'm going up to New York for the parade. Oh, honey, when I saw Liz the other day, I told her how you were doing and everything. She said she had something for you."

"You saw Liz? I thought you were mad at her."

"Nah. Water under the bridge." Ellen was

always happier when she was in a band.

"So she sent me an album?"

"No. It's a bag of old clothes. She was going to get rid of them. She can't fit in any of that stuff any more. It's in the dining room. The grey bag."

Kaye opened the plastic bag. It was full of glittering fabrics, leather and shiny vinyl. And yes, there it was, as shimmeringly purple as in her memories, the catsuit. She pulled it out reverently.

"How come you didn't tell me the real reason you didn't want to move to New York?" Ellen glanced meaningfully in Roiben's direction.

Roiben's face was carefully expressionless.

Kaye could not seem to marshal her thoughts well enough to find a reply. "Do you guys want some coffee or something?"

Her mother shrugged. "There's some in the kitchen. I think it's left over from the morning – I could make some new."

"No, I'll get it," Kaye said.

She went out into the kitchen and poured some of the black stuff into a cup. Adding milk only turned it a dark, sickly grey. She added several liberal spoonfuls of sugar and drank it like penitence.

Roiben hadn't looked angry at all; to the contrary, he looked absurdly comfortable sprawled on the couch. She should have felt better, but instead it seemed as though the knots in her stomach were tightening.

It was evening already, and soon he would be gone. She wanted him, wanted him to want her more than she had any right or reason to expect from him, and that knowledge was as bitter as the day-old coffee.

"Kaye?" It was Roiben, a nearly empty jar of honey in one hand, leaning against the doorframe.

"Oh, hi," she said, stupidly, holding up the cup. "This is really bad. I'll make some new."

"I've been . . . I wanted to thank you."

"For what?"

"For explaining what happened. For making me stay here last night."

She took the old coffee and dumped it in the sink, hiding the embarrassed smile that was playing over her lips. She filled the pot with hot water and swirled a few times before dumping that too.

His voice was very quiet when he spoke again. "For not being afraid of me."

She snorted. "You've got to be kidding. I'm terrified of you."

He smiled at Kaye, one of his quicksilver smiles, dazzling and brief. "Thank you for hiding it, then. Quite realistic."

She grinned back at him. "No problem. I mean, if I'd known you liked it this much and all . . ."

He rolled his eyes, and it was so good to

stand there smiling shyly at each other. All the silly words she had wanted to say to him suddenly began clawing up her throat, desperate to be spoken.

"I'm just glad it's over," she said, breaking the spell while she turned to spoon coffee grounds into a filter.

He looked at her incredulously. "Over?"

She stopped in midmotion. "Yeah, over. We're here and safe and it's over."

"Not to distress you," he said, "but I very much doubt – "

"Kaye!" Ellen called from the other room. "Come and see this. There's a bear loose."

"Just a minute, Mum," Kaye called back. She turned to Roiben. "What do you mean not over?"

"Kaye, Faery is a place governed by a set of customs both severe and binding. What you have done has consequences."

"Everything has consequences," she said, "and the consequence of this is that the solitary fey are free again, you're free, and the bad Queen is dead. That seems pretty over to me."

"Kaye, it's going to be off by the time you get here," Ellen called.

Kaye took a deep breath and walked out into the other room.

Ellen was pointing to the screen "Will you look at this?"

On the screen, a reporter was standing in

the middle of Allaire State Park announcing that a man had been murdered and partially devoured. The announcer reported that, judging by the claw marks, authorities were speculating that it was a bear.

"Now I'm hungry," Kaye said.

The announcer went on, his salt-and-pepper hair slicked back so that it did not move, his voice overly dramatic. "The man's dog was found attached to the body by a wrist lead and was apparently unharmed. The dog has been taken into custody by the West Long Branch chapter of the SPCA, which is awaiting relatives to come and claim it."

"I wonder what kind of dog it was," Kaye said as Roiben came back into the living room.

Ellen made a face. "I'm going to finish my makeup. Can you just find out for me if it's going to rain? The weather should be on soon."

"Sure," Kaye said, sprawling on the couch.

On the television, the same announcer came back on, with another warning about the animal, reporting that there were several unconfirmed reports about missing infants and children. In some of the more unlikely reports, children were stolen from their beds, out of pushchairs, off swings in playgrounds. No one had seen anything, however, let alone a bear.

A Popcorn Park Zoo representative was speaking at a press conference. The white-haired man was polishing his glasses methodically, nearly in tears as he explained how it was difficult to tell what animal had escaped, since this morning all the animals had been found in the wrong cages. The tigers had eaten several of the llamas before they could be separated. The deer had been in a small bird enclosure, panicking in the enclosed space. He suspected PETA. He didn't understand how this could have happened in such a well-run, tidy zoo.

"In other news, a young girl on her way back from classes at Monmouth University was kidnapped this morning by an unidentified assailant. She was released tonight after a harrowing day in which she was forced to answer riddles to avoid torture. She is currently being held at Monmouth Medical Centre and is in stable condition."

Kaye sat bolt upright. "Riddles?!"

"This is your doing," Roiben said, looking at Kaye across the dim living room. "What do you think of the first day of the next seven years?"

Kaye shook her head, not understanding.

The screen showed men and women being strapped to stretchers in Thompson Park. They had been found naked, dancing in a circle, and had to be forcibly restrained by police to make them stop. Their clothes were found nearby, and the available identification showed no common link. They were being treated for dehydration and blistered feet.

Behind the cameras, Kaye could easily see

the fat toadstools growing in a thick circle.

Kaye rubbed a hand over her face. "But why? I don't understand."

Roiben spoke as he began to pace the room. "Everything is always easier when considered black and white, isn't it? Your friends, are, after all, good and wise, so all solitary fey must be good and wise. Your friends have some respect and fear and knowledge of humans, so all the solitary fey will follow in that example."

The phone rang, startling her. She got up and answered it. "Hello?"

It was Janet. She sounded subdued. "Hi, Kaye."

"Um, hi." Janet was the last person she expected to call.

"I was wondering if you wanted to hang out."

"What?" Kaye said.

"No, seriously. All of us guys are going to a rave tonight. You want to come?"

"Have you seen the news?"

"No, why?"

Kaye fumbled for an explanation. "There's supposed to be a bear on the loose."

"We're going to the Pier. Don't be weird. So are you coming?"

"No one should go. Janet, it really isn't safe."

"So don't go," Janet said. "By the way,

have you seen my brother?"

Kaye's insides suddenly turned to ice. "Corny's gone?"

"Yeah," Janet answered. "Since yesterday."

Kaye couldn't help wincing. Corny was under the damn hill. She knew it. She looked desperately at Roiben, but he regarded her blankly. He couldn't hear Janet. He'd never even met Corny.

"I'll see you, okay?" Kaye said.

"Sure. Whatever. 'Bye."

She hung up.

"Who was that?" Roiben asked.

"Janet's brother is still under the hill . . . with Nephamael."

Nephamael's name made Roiben stop in his place. "More secrets?"

She winced. "Corny. He was with me that night . . . when I was a pixie."

"You *are* a pixie."

"He was there that night – the one when you didn't know it was me – and when I left, he . . . met . . . Nephamael."

Roiben's eyebrows shot up at that.

"Corny was totally out of his head. Nephamael hurt him, and he . . . liked it. He wanted to go back."

"You left a friend – a mortal – under the hill . . . alone?" He sounded incredulous. "Are you completely heartless? You saw what you were leaving him to."

"You made me leave! I couldn't get back in.

I tried."

"I thought we were going to be honest with one another. What manner of honesty is this?"

She felt completely miserable.

"Do you know who Nephamael is?"

She shook her head, dread creeping over limbs, making her feel heavy, making her want to sink to the floor. "He . . . he's the one that put the enchantment on me and who took it off."

"He was once the best knight in the Unseelie Court – that is, before he was sent to the Seelie Court as part of the price for a truce. He was sent there, and I was sent to Nicnevin."

Kaye just stood, stunned, thinking about the conversation she had overheard between Nicnevin and Nephamael. Why hadn't she deduced that? What other meaning could there have been? "So Nephamael still serves Nicnevin?"

"Perhaps. It seems more likely that he serves only himself. Kaye, do you know who concocted the plan to sabotage the Tithe?"

"You think it was Nephamael?"

"I don't know. Tell me, how did your friends become aware you were a pixie when not even the Queen of the Unseelie Court could see through your glamour?"

"The Thistlewitch said she remembered when I got switched."

"Now, how is it that they know Nephamael?"

"I don't know."

"We lack some piece of information, Kaye."

"Why would Nephamael want to make trouble for Nicnevin?"

"Perhaps he sought revenge for being sent away. I doubt he found the Seelie Court to his taste."

She shook her head. "I don't know. I have to get Corny."

"Kaye, if what you say is true, you know that he may well no longer be alive."

She took a sharp, shallow breath. "He's fine," she said.

12

She'd only ever brought one other person to the Glass Swamp. The summer when she was nine and Janet had taken to constantly teasing her about her imaginary friends, Kaye had decided that she was going to prove they were real once and for all. Janet had stepped on a half moon of bottle glass, cutting through her trainer and jabbing into her foot on the way to the swamp. They'd never even made it down the ridge.

It had not occurred to her until now to suspect that Lutie or Spike or even poor, dead Gristle had something to do with that.

Darting lights were easily visible from the street, and shouts carried through the still air. She couldn't hear the voices well enough to discern whether they were about to stumble down into a bunch of kids drinking beer or into something else.

Roiben was all in black – jeans and T-shirt and long coat that all must have been conjured up from moonbeams and cobwebs because she was sure they didn't come from any of the wardrobes in her grandmother's house. He had pulled the top part of his hair back, but the shock of white somehow made him seem even more inhuman when he was dressed in modern clothes.

She wondered if she looked inhuman too. Was there something about her that warned people off? Kaye had always assumed that she was just weird, no more explanation necessary. Looking at him, she wondered.

He glanced towards her without turning his head and raised his eyebrows in a silent query.

"Just looking at you," she said.

"Looking at me?"

"I . . . I was wondering how you did that – the clothes."

"Oh." He looked down, as though he'd only then given a thought to what he was wearing. "It's glamour."

"So what are you really wearing?" The words left her mouth before she could consider them. She winced.

He didn't seem to mind; in fact, he flashed her one of his brief smiles. "And if I said nothing at all?"

"Then I would point out that sometimes, if you look at something out of the corner of your eye, you can see right through glamour," she returned.

That brought surprised laughter. "What a relief to us both then that I am actually wearing exactly what you saw me in this afternoon. Although one might point out that in that outfit, your last concern should be my modesty."

"You don't like it?" She looked down at the purple vinyl catsuit. There had been no reason for her not to put it on immediately. After all, it was still Hallowe'en.

"Now, that's the sort of question I begin to expect from you. One to which there is no good answer."

Kaye grinned, and she could tell that the grin was likely to stay on her face for a long time. They could do this. They could figure this out. Everything was going to be fine.

"Down here?" he asked, and she nodded.

"Indiscreet," was all he said before he hooked his boots in the muddy ledge and carefully walked down the ridge.

Kaye followed him, stumbling along at more or less her own pace.

Green women and men were half immersed in the deeper parts of the stream, androgynous forms rough with bark and shimmery lights.

A few of the creatures saw Roiben and

slithered into the pool or back up the bank. There was some whispering.

"Kaye," a voice rasped, and she spun around.

It was the Thistlewitch, sitting on a log. She patted the place beside her. "Things did not go well under the hill."

"No," Kaye said, sitting down. She wanted to put more anger in her voice, but she couldn't. "I almost died."

"Nicnevin's knight saved you, did he not?"

Kaye nodded, looking up to see him, half in shadows, his hands in the pockets of his coat, glowering impressively. It made her want to grin at him, although she was afraid he might grin back and ruin his furious demeanour.

"Why have you brought him among us?"

"If it wasn't for him, I'd be dead."

The Thistlewitch looked in the direction of the knight and then back at Kaye. "Do you know of the things he has done?"

"Don't you understand? She made him do them!"

"I have no desire to be welcome among you, old mother," Roiben said, kneeling down on one knee in the soft earth. "I only wanted to know whether you were aware of the price of your freedom. There are trolls and worse that are delighted to be without any master but their own desires."

"And if there are, what of it?" Spike asked,

coming up behind them. "Let the mortals suffer as we have suffered."

Kaye was astonished. She thought back to Lutie's disdain for mortal girls. They were only her friends because of what she was, and not for any better reason than that. Her fingers brushed over the purple plastic covering her legs, letting her nails cut little lines in the vinyl. She had wanted them to be better than people, but they weren't, and she didn't know what they were any more. She'd been flung back and forth through too many emotions over the past few days, she was hungover from adrenalin, she was worried about Corny and worried about Janet.

"So it's us against them now? I'm not talking about the Unseelie Court, here. Since when are mortals the enemies of the solitary fey?" Kaye said, anger bleeding into her voice, making it rough. She looked at Roiben again, drawing confidence from his proximity, and that worried her too. How had he gone from being someone she half despised to being the one person she was relying on, in the space of mere hours?

Roiben's hand touched her shoulder lightly, a comforting gesture. It amused her how wide Spike's eyes got. She wondered exactly what Spike imagined had passed between them.

"You think like a mortal," Spike said.

"Well, gosh, I did spend every week of my life except the last thinking I was one."

Spike's thick brows furrowed, and he tilted his head to the side, black eyes glittering. "You don't know anything about Faery. You don't know where your loyalties should be."

"If I don't understand, it's because you didn't tell me. You kept me in the dark, and you used me."

"You agreed to help us. You saw the importance of what we were doing."

"We have to tell the solitary fey that Nicnevin was innocent of the sacrifice. This has to stop, Spike."

"I won't go back to being a slave. Not for any mortal. Not for anything."

"But the Unseelie Queen is dead."

"It doesn't matter. There's always another, worse than the last. Don't you dare try to undo this. Don't you dare go around telling tales."

"Or you'll what?" Roiben said softly.

"It's not her place," Spike protested, twisting the long hairs of one eyebrow nervously between his fingers.

"The Tithe was not completed. The reason matters little. The result is the same. For seven years the solitary fey in Nicnevin's lands are free."

"Unless they enter into a new compact."

"Why would they do that?" Spike demanded. "Rumour has it that the Seelie Queen is coming down from the north, bringing practically the whole court, from what I hear."

Roiben froze at that. "Why is she coming?" he breathed.

Spike shrugged. "Probably to see what she can claim before the Unseelie Court gets on its feet again. Bad time to be making deals with anyone."

"Do you think Nephamael'll bring Corny to the Seelie Court?" Kaye asked Roiben.

He nodded once. "He'll have to if he intends to keep him." The assumption that if Nephamael didn't intend to keep Corny, he was already dead, went unspoken.

"Do you know where they're going to camp?" Kaye asked Spike.

"It's an orchard," Spike said. "A place where people pick their own apples. They should be there by tomorrow's dawn."

Kaye knew where that was. She'd gone there on a school trip and a couple of times with her grandmother. Delicious Orchards.

"Wait, I want to come with you," Lutie said, flying to Kaye's shoulder. Kaye felt a sharp tug on her hair as Lutie caught a strand.

"Sorry," the little faerie said contritely.

"Roiben, this is Lutie-loo. Lutie-loo, Roiben."

Kaye loved it when he grinned. She really did.

"It is my distinct pleasure to make your acquaintance," Roiben said, touching the tiny hand with two fingers.

* * *

Kaye walked down the boardwalk, as she had done not even a week before. Tonight, the moon was on the wane, distorted-looking, and the brine off the sea clung to her skin and hair in a fine mist. The tiny specks of silver glittered in the stretchy purple vinyl of Liz's catsuit as she moved.

Helplessness in the face of not knowing where Corny was had made her restless. She wanted to go everywhere, anywhere Nephamael might have taken him, but she didn't know where any of those places might be. Finally, she decided go to the rave after all. Kaye was worried about Corny, worried about Janet, so worried that she needed to *do* something, no matter whether it needed doing.

The pounding of music inside the abandoned building was loud enough that she could feel the bass beating through the wooden slats of the boardwalk. Once called Galaxia, the club sat half on the street and half on what remained of the pier. Several years ago part of the pier had burned down, wrecking game booths, a water slide, and a haunted house. The remaining blackened shell was used only to set off the city's annual fireworks. Galaxia had once been a typical Jersey Shore bar and dance club – the airbrushed sign still hung over the doorway, although it was greyed and the edges were abraded from wind-tossed sand.

Tonight she could see glow sticks and bright clothes pulsing with each flash of a strobe light through the window. Kaye wasn't sure if the place had been rented or just broken into. A large crowd was gathered around the door, some costumed for Hallowe'en in masks and face paint, others wearing their normal baggy jeans and T-shirts. A girl with her hair in hundreds of bright braids bounced in place, a teddy bear tethered to her belt loop with a fluorescent yellow cord.

Before they got too close, Roiben picked up two leaves from the gutter. In his hands they became crisp bills that he folded quickly into the pockets of his coat. Lutie peeked her head out and ducked back down.

"I have to work on this glamour thing, don't I?" Kaye said, but he only smiled.

At the entrance, a girl with a blue beehive wig, blue lipstick, and a blue lip ring gave him change.

"Nice outfit," the girl said to Kaye, her gaze flicking enviously over the catsuit. Kaye smiled her thanks, and then they were inside.

Bodies were pressed against one another, undulating like a great wave, dancers having room only to hop in place. A clown was dancing on the bar, his makeup done with neon paint that glowed under the black light. Two girls dressed as cats, both in white leotards with pin-on tails, danced beside him. The music was so loud that Kaye didn't even try to talk to Roiben; she just slipped her hand inside his and pulled him along through the crowd. He let her lead him towards the back where double doors opened onto the blackened boardwalk that was being used as an impromptu dance floor for those that couldn't fit inside the club.

It was as packed as inside, bodies jammed together so that even those that were sitting along the walls were touching.

"See anything?" she yelled.

He shook his head.

Two ends of a horse shouldered by them, holding water bottles. She thought she saw Doughboy in the crowd, not dressed as anything, but she wasn't sure.

"Kaye," Roiben yelled into her ear. "There. Look."

She followed the quick flick of his hand with her gaze, but she didn't see anything. She shrugged, knowing that would be easier to understand than speech.

"Look for your friends," he yelled. She nodded as he set off in the direction of a tall woman with thick lips and maroon hair. The woman stopped dancing and began shouting at him, arms waving wildly when he got close. Then the woman turned, as if to run, and he grabbed her arm.

Kaye left them still arguing and waded through the crowd. If there was just the one faerie and Roiben had already found her, then maybe there was nothing to be nervous about here. In the crush of bouncing dancers, it seemed impossible that there would be anything dangerous and unworldly. Kaye found herself relaxing.

Kenny was on the pier dancing with Fatima and Janet. Fatima had on three different layers of long skirts and a scarf over her head with big hoops in her ears, looking like a Gypsy or a pirate. Janet was wearing all black with whiskers drawn on her face in eyeliner. The whiskers reminded Kaye more of a mouse than a cat.

Kaye took a deep breath. "Hey."

Fatima raised her eyebrows, and Kenny stared at her as though she didn't have the glamour on at all.

"Hi," Janet said. Not for the first time, Kaye wondered why Janet had invited her. Was it to teach Kenny a lesson? From the way he'd paled when she came up to them, Kaye decided that it was probably working.

Kaye bounced with the music. There was little room to wave her arms unless they were directly above her head.

"Getting some water," Kenny shouted.

He walked off towards the inside of the building.

"I'll be right back," Kaye said to Janet, who tried to say something to her as she turned to follow Kenny.

She found him waiting in line for the men's bathroom.

"I'm sorry."

His eyes narrowed. He didn't answer.

She took a breath. Her mind was spinning from all the worry, and she found that she had nothing to say to him and nothing she needed to hear from him. It was enough that she knew he was all right, eyes clear and free of any enchantment.

"See you back over there," Kaye said, feeling foolish at having trailed him all the way across the club for nothing. She began to dance her way back to Janet and Fatima.

Then the music changed.

It was still the spacey, disjointed sound of trance music, but there were unusual instruments in the background, strange reedy sounds and whispers. *Dance.* Kaye's body complied unthinkingly, spinning her into the thick crush of bodies.

Everyone was dancing. People bobbed against one another, arms waving in the air, heads nodding with the music. No one sat against the wall. No one stood in line or smoked a cigarette along the water's edge. Everyone danced – sweaty bodies packed tight, drunk with sound.

At first, it was a gentle compulsion, slipping into Kaye's mind easily. Then she began to notice the fey.

A freckle-faced faerie with flame-red hair that rose up into a Dr Seuss curl was the first one that she saw. He was dancing like the others, but when he saw her stare, he winked. Looking quickly around, she noticed more, winged sprites with tiny silver hoops piercing the points of their ears, goblins the size of dogs drinking bottled water off the top of the bar, a green-skinned pixie boy with a blue glow stick lighting up the inside of his mouth. And other fey, dim shadows at the edges of the club, flashes of glittering scales, luring dancers into the empty bathrooms and out onto the pier.

Beside Janet danced a disturbingly familiar dark-skinned boy. Kaye pushed brutally through the crowd, knocking people aside with her elbows just in time to see Janet smile up at the kelpie and let him lead her off the edge of the pier.

"Janet!" Kaye screamed, pushing her way to the water.

But when she got there, there were only ribbons of red curls sinking below the waves. She stared for a moment, until desperation rose up in her and she jumped. Bone-cold black water closed over her head.

Her muscles clenched with shock as she went under once and then bobbed up, teeth chattering, spitting out briny water. Her flailing hands caught strands of hair and she pulled, cruelly, desperately. Her legs kicked automatically, treading water.

Her hand came up empty save for a clump of tangled red hair.

"Janet!" she cried as a wave broke almost on top of her, pushing her into the pilings beneath the pier. Taking a deep breath, she dived down, opening her eyes as she went, desperately hoping for a single flash of red hair, casting her hands like claws.

She bobbed up from the water again, out of breath and coughing. It had been too dark to see anything, and the reach of her arms had found nothing.

"Janet!" Kaye screamed, one hand slapping the top of the water, sending a spray of it showering down around her. She was treading water violently, raging at Janet, at herself, and especially at the frigid, black, unfeeling sea that swallowed Janet up.

Then, rising above the waves like a magnificent statue, there was the kelpie itself, nostrils flaring and clouds of hot breath rising from them.

"Where is Janet?" Kaye shouted.

"Oh no, now you are in my element. No demands."

"A deal then, please. Just let her go." It was hard to speak through chattering teeth. Her body was slowly adjusting, numbing to the temperature of the ocean.

Kaye looked into the softly glowing eyes, their whiteness reflecting in the black sea like distant moons. "Please."

"No need for deals and bargains. I am done. You may have the rest of it if you like."

A body bobbed to the surface beside the black horse, red hair tangled with seaweed, facedown, arms floating beneath the surface.

Kaye swam to her and tipped back her head, pushing aside hair to see the sightless eyes, smears of drawn whiskers still staining her cheeks, blue lips and open mouth, full to the teeth with water.

"She thrashed beautifully," the kelpie said.

"No, no, no, no." Kaye hugged the body to her, trying desperately to tip up the head. Water spilled out of Janet's mouth as though it were a decanter.

"Why so sad? She was only going to die anyway."

"Not tonight!" Kaye yelled, swallowing most of a wave she tried to bob above. "She wouldn't have died tonight."

"One day is much like another."

"Tell that to Nicnevin. Someday you're going to know how Janet felt. Everything dies, kelpie, and that includes me and you, faeries or not."

The kelpie looked strangely subdued. It let out a huff of warm air. Then it sank down, leaving her alone in the sea, treading water, holding Janet's body. Another swell came, pushing Janet's body towards the beach. Kaye took one of Janet's hands, no more chill than her own but frighteningly pliant, and scissored her legs towards the shore. As she swam closer, the waves grew larger and more violent, breaking over her. Janet's body was pulled from her grip and tossed up on the beach.

She saw Roiben running towards the edge of the waves. He bent to look at Janet while Kaye struggled to her feet in the shallow water, the pull of receding waves still strong enough to nearly knock her off her feet. She coughed and spat out a mixture of saliva and sand.

"Do you seek out peril? One would think that years of being a mortal would have made you more aware of mortality." He was shouting.

And that had too much of the echo of her previous conversation in it.

He opened his coat and closed it around her, heedless of the wet clothes that dampened his own. Sirens wailed, and she could see flashing lights.

"No." His hand cupped the back of her head before she could turn. "Don't look. We have to go."

Kaye pulled away. "I need to see her. To say goodbye."

Ten steps across the wet sand and she dropped to her knees beside the body, ignoring the edges of waves that sucked at the sand around her knees. Janet had washed up like a piece of rubbish, and her limbs were thrown at odd angles. Kaye smoothed them out so that Janet was lying on her back, arms at her side.

Kaye stroked back red hair, touching Janet's cold face with cold fingers. And in that moment it seemed that the whole world had gone cold and that she would never be warm again.

13

"For I have sworn thee fair, and thought
thee bright,
Who art as black as hell, as dark as night."
— WILLIAM SHAKESPEARE, Sonnet CXLVII

Kaye woke on the mattress in her bedroom, tangled in the covers, wearing only her underpants and the T-shirt that Roiben had borrowed the day before. Her head was pillowed on his bare chest, and for a moment she could not remember why her hair was stiff and her eyelashes were crusted together with a thin layer of salt. When she did remember, she pulled herself out of bed with a groan.

Janet was dead, drowned. Lungs filled with water. *Dead.* The word echoed in her head as though its repetition held some clue to its reversal.

Vague memories of the night before, of Roiben bringing her home, of him enchanting her grandmother to stop yelling as he led Kaye up the stairs. She'd screamed at him for doing that, screamed and cried and finally fell asleep.

Kaye padded to the mirror. She looked haggard. Her head felt heavy from crying, and her eyes were swollen with sleep. There were dark smudges the colour of bruises under her eyes, and even her lips looked pale and chapped. She licked them. They tasted like salt.

Janet was dead. All Kaye's fault. If only she hadn't followed Kenny. If only she hadn't made Janet jealous, she might never have gone off with the kelpie in the first place. If only.

And Corny was still gone.

Closing her eyes, she tore the glamour she was wearing and let it disperse into the air. What she saw was worse. Her hair was still stiff with salt, her lips were still chapped, and, if anything, the severe faerie features exaggerated how tired she looked.

In the mirror, she saw the reflection of the shirt she was wearing and blearily remembered being stripped down a few blocks from the boardwalk, when no amount of huddling under Roiben's coat could make her teeth stop chattering. The catsuit apparently hadn't been enough like a second skin, trapping water inside it. He'd helped her out of the outfit and then wrapped her in both his shirt and his coat.

Summoning magic to her fingers, she tried to lessen the darkness around her eyes and to shift her hair into magazine-smooth locks. It was easy, and a small, amazed smile tugged at the corner of her mouth when she applied eye-liner with a pass of her nail and dabbed her eyes to be a bright blue. She touched them again and they became a deep violet.

Looking down, she glamoured herself to be dressed in a ball gown and it appeared, ruby silk and puffy crinolines, the whole thing encrusted with gemstones. It looked oddly familiar, and then she realised where the image had come from – it was an illustration from "The Frog Prince" in an old storybook she had. Then, with a pass of her hand, she was wearing an emerald Renaissance frock coat over green fishnet stockings, a modified version of the prince in the same story.

Roiben shifted on the mattress, blinking up at her. He was unglamoured, his hair bright as a dime where the light hit it. Lutie was lying on the same pillow, wrapped in a silver tress as if it were a bedspread.

"I can't go downstairs," Kaye said. She couldn't face her grandmother, not after last night, and Kaye very much doubted that her mother had come home yet. Kaye's memories of the last time she'd gone to the New York Hallowe'en parade were a mass of feathers and glitter and men on stilts. That time, Ellen had drunk so much three-dollar champagne that she'd completely forgotten how to get where they were staying, and they had wound up sleeping the night in the subway.

"We could go out the window," Roiben said easily, and she wondered whether he was teasing her or whether he really had accepted her odd stricture so easily. She couldn't remember much of what she'd said the night before – maybe it had been so awful and irrational that more of the same didn't surprise him.

"How are we going to get to the orchard? It's in Colt's Neck."

He ran fingers through his hair, hand-combing it, and then turned towards Lutie. "You tied knots in my hair."

Lutie giggled in a way that sounded a little like panic.

Sighing, he looked back at Kaye. "There are ways," he said, "but you would mislike most of them."

Somehow, she didn't doubt that.

"Let's take Corny's car," she said.

Roiben raised both eyebrows.

"I know where it is and I know where his keys are."

Roiben got up off the mattress and sat on the boxspring as though it was the couch she had once hoped to make it into. "Cars are made entirely of steel. In case you'd forgotten."

Kaye stood a moment and began rummaging through the drifts of black rubbish bags. After a little searching, she held up a pair of orange gloves triumphantly, ignoring his look of disbelief.

"There's steel in my boots," she said, pushing her feet into them as she spoke, "but the leather keeps it from touching me . . . I can barely feel it."

"Would you like a cigarette to go with that?" Roiben asked drily.

"I think I liked you better before you acquired a sense of humour."

His voice was guarded. "And I thought you liked me not at all."

Kaye brushed back her now-silky hair and rubbed her temples. She should say something, do something, but she was sure that if she stopped to sort out the swirling thoughts in her head, she would fall apart. Was this about the night before? She could barely remember what she had yelled at him now; it was all a blur of grief and rage. But everything was different between them this morning, and she didn't know how to make it right again.

She reached her hand out, touching him lightly just below his collarbone, opening her mouth to speak . . . then closing it again. She shook her head slightly, hoping that somehow he'd understand that she was sorry, that she was grateful, that she liked him too much.

She shook her head again, harder, stepping back.

Corny first. All other things afterwards.

They went out the window, Roiben climbing down the tree easily, Lutie flying, and Kaye managing an ungainly cross between jumping and gliding. She stumbled when she landed.

"Flying!" Lutie said.

Kaye glared at her and put on the mittens. Looking down, she realised she was still glamoured in the frock coat. Roiben was wearing all black, head to foot, and mostly leather. Lutie's wings shimmered iridescent rainbows over them both as she looped in the air like a demented dragonfly.

"This way." Kaye directed them to the trailer park. The door to the car was locked, and Kaye didn't hesitate before she pounded one gloved hand against the glass. It spiderwebbed, and she battered at it again and again, until her knuckles were bleeding.

"Stop it," Roiben said, catching her hand when she drew back for another punch.

She stopped, dazed, looking at the window.

He took a knife from inside a boot. Had it always been there, or had he conjured it into existence?

"Use the handle," he said. His voice sounded very tired. "Or use a rock."

She managed to hack open the glass well enough to stick her hand inside and force up the lock. Looking around at the trailer park, she was amazed that no one had even come out to object to her breaking into a car in broad daylight.

Replacing the glove, she opened the door and got in, wincing as she took a breath of the stale, metallic air. She leaned over and popped the lock on the other side and winched down her window before getting the key down from where it was tucked in the sun visor. Roiben got in the passenger side warily, and Lutie flew in with him, wrinkling her nose at Kaye as she flittered around the backseat and then finally perched on the dusty dashboard.

Kaye put the key in the ignition and turned it, feeling the heat of the iron even through her gloves. It didn't feel unpleasant, not exactly, but there was a buzzing in her head that she knew would get worse.

Kaye pushed down on the accelerator. The engine wheezed, but the car did not move. Cursing under her breath, she slapped the hand brake down, threw the knob to Drive, and pushed on the accelerator. The car roared forward so fast that she had to slam on the brake to stop. Lutie tumbled into Kaye's lap.

Roiben looked over from where he was braced against the dash. "How many times have you driven?"

"Never," Kaye growled.

"Never?"

"I'm not old enough yet." She giggled at that, but it came out a little high-pitched, almost hysterical. She put her foot on the accelerator more gently, and the car responded better. Turning the wheel, she began to steer towards the street.

Lutie gave a tiny squeal and clawed her way up Kaye's frock coat.

The smell of iron was overwhelming.

Kaye took the ramp onto the highway, relieved that there would be no more turns, no more merging, and stop signs. All she had to do was stay in one lane until they were nearly there. She reminded herself that they had to get there before anything else happened to Corny. She pushed her foot down harder on the accelerator, willing the car to stay in the middle of the lane as she sped down the highway.

Kaye could feel her vision grow hazy as the iron made her head spin. Even the draughts of air blowing through the window were not enough. She shook her head, trying to throw off the feeling of weight that seemed to settle like a band across the temples of her skull.

"Kaye!" Lutie squeaked, just in time for Kaye to swerve violently to the right and clear of the car she had almost drifted into. The car hit the edge of the grass on the right side of the highway with one wheel before she got it back under control. Lutie's yelp was like the chirp of a sparrow. Roiben had made no sound at all, but she didn't want to take her eyes off the road long enough to see the expression on his face.

Finally, their exit was next and Kaye turned onto the off-ramp, navigating the turn at a

HOLLY BLACK

dangerous speed. She kept the car on the shoulder of the road since she couldn't find a way to gracefully merge into the regular lanes. It was only two traffic lights, and then she was able to pull into the orchard and park the car, one side hanging far over the yellow line in the parking space. She turned the key off with a sigh.

Roiben was out of the car nearly before it was fully stopped. Lutie clung to Kaye's coat, still trembling.

"Corny can drive back," Kaye said in a small voice.

"I have a new enthusiasm for our quest." Roiben's voice trembled slightly, despite his attempt at callousness.

The orchard was acres and acres of fruit trees and had a farmer's-market-type store that sold jam and milk and cinnamon cider that she remembered from a school trip. Today there were piles of pumpkins and gourds, marked down to dirt cheap, some of them looking bruised.

The parking lot was full of minibuses spilling out children, their mothers chasing and herding them. Kaye followed Roiben as he wove through the crowd and around a massive monument of hay and pumpkins. One of the mothers pulled her child abruptly to one side, out of their path. Kaye immediately checked her glamour, holding up a hand for inspection and turning it in the light to make sure it was still pink all over. Then she glanced at Roiben and realised that they looked freaky enough for that to be a normal mum-reaction.

She could feel the air change as they stepped into the grove of trees, and the sound of car engines and laughter faded away. She could no longer smell iron, and she took a deep breath, exhaling every exhaust fume. Like when she had stepped into the hill, she felt the odd fission that she was growing to associate with stepping over into Faerie.

White horses grazed in the meadow, the silver bells on their collars tinkling when they raised their heads. Knotted apple trees still hung heavy with a late-fall harvest of fruit. The air was warm and sweet with the promise of spring and new growth. Denizens of the Seelie Court were spread over the field, silken blankets spread out with Folk sitting or lying on them. As Kaye walked among them, she could smell fresh lavender and heather.

The Folk were as varied as in the Unseelie Court, although they were dressed in brighter colours. They passed a fox-faced man in a tattercoat of many fabrics, trailing ribbons. Another fey wore a golden sheath dress, bright as the sun. She whispered in the ear of a boy wearing a dress as well, his all in robin's-egg blue. A group of faeries were crouched over what looked like a game, one tossing shining

HOLLY BLACK

stones into the centre of a circle cut into the earth. She could not see what the object was, but the group would either sigh or cheer, depending, she guessed, on some pattern of how the stones fell.

Nearby, at the edges of the gathering, a treewoman with skin like bark and fingers that turned to leaves at the nails was whispering to a mute apple tree, every so often turning her head slowly to glare at seven little men who were standing on each other's shoulders. They formed a faerie ladder that wove back and forth from base to top, where one little man was grasping desperately for a fat apple.

A winged girl ran by with a very little boy toddling after her, his hair braided with flowers. A human boy. Kaye shuddered.

Looking around again, she noticed more human children, none older than perhaps six. They were being brushed and petted, their eyes half-lidded and dreamy. One sat with a blue-skinned woman, head on the faerie's knees. A group of three children, all crowned with daisies, clumsily danced with three little men in mushroom caps. Faerie ladies and gentlemen clapped.

Kaye sped up her pace, meaning to stop Roiben and ask him about the children. But then she saw where he was looking, and she forgot all her questions.

Next to trees thick with spring blossoms

even in fall, there was an auburn-haired faerie dressed in a deep emerald-green coat that flared like a gown. Kaye stopped walking when she saw the woman; she could scarcely remember to breathe. She was the most beautiful thing Kaye had ever seen. Her skin was flawless, her hair shone bright as copper in the sun under a woven circlet of ivy and dogwood blossoms, her eyes were as bright as the green apples that hung near them. Kaye could not just glance at the faerie woman; her eyes were drawn to look until the faerie took up the totality of her vision, rendering all else dull and faded.

Roiben did not need to tell her that this was the Queen of the Seelie Court.

Her women wore dresses in light fabrics of storm greys and morning roses. As they approached, one of the women inhaled so sharply it was almost a scream and covered her mouth with her hand. Roiben turned his head to regard her, and he smiled.

Kaye tensed. The smile seemed to sit incongruously on his lips, more like a twitch of the mouth than any expression of pleasure.

A knight suddenly interposed himself between them and the Queen. He was dressed in jointed green armour, and his hair was as the fine, pale gold of cornsilk. He held an interesting spear, so ornate with decoration that Kaye wondered if it could be used.

HOLLY BLACK

"Talathain," Roiben said, inclining his head for a brief nod.

"You are unwelcome here," the knight said.

Lutie clambered out of Kaye's hip pocket and peered at the new knight with unfeigned fascination.

"Announce me to the Queen," Roiben said. "If she does not wish to see me, then I will leave the grove immediately."

Kaye started to object, but Roiben laid a hand on her arm.

"My companions, will, of course be free to stay or go as they please," he continued.

Talathain's glance flickered to the Queen and then back to Roiben with something like jealousy writ in his expression. A motion of his gauntleted hand signalled several additional knights. A page came, listened to Talathain, then darted off to speak with the Queen.

After bending gracefully to listen to the little page, the Queen stepped away from her ladies and across the grass, towards them. She did not look at Kaye. Her eyes rested only on Roiben.

Kaye could see Roiben's face change as he looked at his Lady. There was a longing there that overwhelmed Kaye. It was the steady look of a dog, gone feral, but still hoping for the kind touch of his master's hand.

She thought of the tapestry on his wall and all the things he had said and had not said. And she knew then why he'd drawn back from her kisses – he must have cherished this love all that time, hoping for a chance to see his Queen again. Kaye had been blind, too full of her own wishful thinking to see what should have been apparent.

Kaye was grateful when Roiben knelt, so that she too could go to one knee and shield the pain on her face beneath a bowed head.

"So formal, my knight," the Queen said. Kaye stole a glance upward at the Queen's eyes. They were soft and wet and green as jewels. Kaye sighed. She felt very tired, suddenly, and very plain. Kaye wished Roiben would just ask about Corny so she could go home.

"Yours no longer," he said as though he regretted it.

"If not mine, then whose?" The conversation had too many undertones for Kaye to be sure that she was following it. Had they been lovers?

"No one's, Silarial," he said deferentially, a small smile on his face and wonder in his eyes. He spoke as one who was afraid to speak too loudly, lest some fragile thing – too dear to pay for – shatter. "Perhaps my own."

Her smile did not fade, did not change. It was a perfect smile – perfect curve of lips, perfect balance between joy and affection – it was so perfect that Kaye couldn't help getting lost in it, losing the thread of the conversation so that she was baffled when the Queen spoke again.

"And why do you come among us then, if not to come home?"

"I seek Nephamael. There is a young man with him that my companion would restore to Ironside."

Silarial shook her head. "He is not among my people any longer. When the Unseelie Queen died and the solitary fey went free . . ." Here she paused, looking at Roiben. Something about her face was unsettled. "He seized her throne and has set himself up as King upon it."

Kaye's neck snapped up. Wide-eyed, without thinking, she spoke. "Nephamael's the King of the Unseelie Court?" She bit her lip, but the Queen turned her gaze on her indulgently.

"Who have you brought to us?"

"Her name is Kaye. She is a changeling." He looked distracted.

The queen's auburn eyebrows rose. "You are aiding her in the recovery of the mortal boy Nephamael has spirited off?"

"I am," Roiben said.

"And what is the price of your service, Roiben who belongs only to himself?" Her hand came up and idly toyed with an amulet around her neck.

Kaye could not bear to look at the perfection of her face. Instead she looked at the

Queen's necklace. The stone was milky-pale and strung on a long chain. It seemed very familiar.

A rosy stain tinted Roiben's cheeks. Could he really be blushing? "There is no price."

Kaye did remember that necklace – Nephamael had worn one just like it. He had had it around his neck the night he'd come to take her for the Tithe.

The Queen leaned forward, almost conspiratorially, as though Kaye was long forgotten. "Once you told me that you would do anything to prove your love for me. Would you still?"

His blush grew deeper, if anything, but when he spoke, his voice was steely. "I would not."

What did that mean, Kaye wondered. It meant something, surely, something that had nothing to do with love and everything to do with the dead Queen. That was what this conversation was about, she realised. His Queen had treated him like a toy she had grown tired of and traded him, not caring whether his new owner would be careless with him, not even caring that his new owner might break him. Clearly, she had plans that included needing her toy back.

"And what if I told you that you had already proven it to my satisfaction? Come, tarry a time with us. There is honey wine and crisp, red apples. Sit by my side again."

Kaye bit her own lip, hard. The pain helped

HOLLY BLACK

her accept that he was not hers, would never be hers. And if it was much too late to pretend that didn't hurt, she could at least shove it down so deeply inside her that he would never know.

Roiben stared at Silarial with a mixture of longing and scorn. "You must forgive me," Roiben said, "but the smell of apples makes me want to retch."

The Queen looked shocked, then angry. Roiben seemed to watch those emotions flit across her face impassively.

"Then you had best make haste," the Queen said.

Roiben nodded and bowed. Kaye almost forgot to.

When they were a few paces away, the white-haired woman caught Roiben's arm, pulling him to face her, laughing.

"Roiben!" It was the woman who had gasped before. Her hair was to her knees, some of it swept up into heavy braids on her head. She wore the costume of one of the Queen's handmaidens.

"I was worried about you," she said, again, the smile wobbling on her face. "The things I had heard – "

"All true, no doubt," Roiben said, a touch lightly. He ran his fingers through the girl's hair, and Kaye shivered sympathetically, knowing how those long fingers felt. "Your hair is so long."

"I haven't cut it since you left." The woman turned to Kaye. "I heard my brother barely introduce you to the Queen. My question is – is Roiben trying to protect us from you or you from us?"

Kaye laughed, surprised.

"Ethine," Roiben said, nodding to one and then the other, "Kaye."

The woman's tinkling laughter was like breaking glass. "You've discarded your courtly airs."

"So I have been told," Roiben said.

Ethine reached up among the branches of the apple tree and broke off a single flower.

"All that matters is that you are now home," she said, tucking the flower behind his ear. Kaye noticed the slight flinch when Ethine touched him and wondered whether his reaction had hurt her.

"This is no longer my home," Roiben said.

"Of course it is. Where else would you go?" Her eyes travelled to Kaye, questioning for the first time. "She hurt you, I know that, but you will forgive her in time. You always forgive her."

"Desires change," he said.

"What did they do to you?" Ethine looked horrified.

"Whatever has been done to me, whatever I have done . . . as surely as blood soaks my hands, and it does, the stain of it touches even the hems of the Queen of Elfland."

"Don't speak so. You loved her once."

"I love her still, more's the pity."

Kaye turned away. She didn't want to hear any more. It had nothing to do with her.

She stalked off towards the car. One of the human children was on his toes, reaching for an apple just out of his grasp. He was wearing a green tunic, tied at his hips with a silk cord.

"Hello," Kaye said.

"Hi." The boy grinned up at her imploringly, and she plucked the fruit. It came free from the branch with a snap.

"Where's your mother?" Kaye asked, shining the apple on her coat.

He scowled at her, one lock of dark brown hair covering his eye. "Gimme."

"Did you always live with faeries?"

"Uh-huh," he said, eyes on the apple.

"For how long?" she asked.

He reached out one chubby hand, and she gave him the apple. He took a bite immediately. She waited while he chewed, but as soon as he had gulped down one bite, he started gnawing on it again. Then, as if he just remembered her, he looked up guiltily. He shrugged and mumbled through a full mouth. "Always."

"Thanks," Kaye said, ruffling the chestnut hair. There was no point in asking him anything. He knew about as much as she did. Then, she turned back to him. "Hey, do you know a little girl called Kaye?"

He wrinkled up his face in an exaggeration of thinking, then he pointed towards one of the blankets. "Uh-huh. Prolly over there."

As though all her blood rushed to her head, she felt a flush of heat and dizziness as if she'd been hanging upside down. Her fingers were like ice.

Leaving the boy to his apple, she walked among the cloth blankets, stopping each little girl she passed, no matter what they looked like. "Is your name Kaye, sweetie?"

But when she saw herself, she knew. The almond eyes sat oddly against the mop of blond hair, making the child look fey despite her chubby body and round ears. Oriental and blonde. Kaye could manage nothing more than staring as the girl – far, far too young to be Kaye in any reasonable world – picked a weed and, wrapping the stem carefully, flung the head in the direction of a pretty faerie lady who laughed.

All the questions Kaye wanted to ask choked her. She turned on her heel and stomped back to Roiben and Ethine, grabbing his arm hard.

"We have to go *now*," she shouted, furious and trembling. "Corny could be *dead*."

Ethine was wide-eyed as Roiben swallowed whatever he might have said and nodded. Kaye turned on her heel, stalking back to the car, leaving Roiben to follow her.

14

She didn't make it to the car.

"Kaye, stop. Just stop." Roiben's voice came from close behind her.

She paused, looking through the trees at the minibuses and the highway beyond. Anything to not look backwards at the Seelie Court and the ageless children and Roiben.

"You're shaking."

"I'm angry. You're screwing around while we have stuff to do." His calm was only making her angrier.

"Well, I'm sorry for that." He didn't sound sorry exactly, his voice hovering on the edge of sarcasm.

Her face was hot. "Why are you here?"

There was a pause. "Because you just wrested me from a conversation with a none-too-polite scolding."

"No . . . why are you still here? Why are you here at all?"

His voice was quiet. She could not see his face unless she turned and she would not turn. "Shall I go, then?"

Her eyes burned with unshed tears. She simply felt overloaded.

"Everything I do . . ." she started and her voice hitched. "Shit, we don't have time for this."

"Kaye – "

"No." She started pacing. "We have to go. Right now."

"If you cannot becalm yourself, you'll do Cornelius little good."

She stopped pacing and held up her hands, fingers splayed wide. "I can't! I'm not like you!"

He stopped her, placing his hand on her shoulder. She refused to meet his eyes, and abruptly he jerked her forward, pulling her body against his. Her muscles stiffened, but he tightened his hold wordlessly. After a moment, she subsided, her breath rushing from her in a long, shuddering sigh. Long fingers stroked her hair. He smelled of honey and sweat and the washing powder her grandmother used.

She rubbed her cheek against his chest, closing her eyes against the thoughts that were gibbering in her head, whispering bids for attention.

"I'm here because you are kind and lovely

and terribly, terribly brave," he said, voice pitched low. "And because I want to be."

She looked up at him through her lashes. He smiled and rested his chin on the top of her head, sliding his hand over her back.

"You want to be?"

He laughed. "Verily, I do. Do you doubt it?"

"Oh," she said, mind unable to catch up with the stunning joy that she felt. Joy, that was, for the moment, enough to push the other sorrows aside. Because it was true, somehow, he was here with her, and not with the Seelie Queen. "Oh."

His hands made long even strokes, from beneath the wings at her shoulder blades to the small of her back. "And that pleases you?"

"What?" She tilted her head up again, scowling. "Of course it does. Are you kidding?"

He drew back to look at her for a moment, searching her face. "Good," he sighed, and pressed her head once more to his chest, stroking her hair as he closed his eyes. "Good."

They stood like that for a long moment. Finally he pulled back from the embrace. "Thankfully," he said, "we don't need the car to get into the Unseelie Court. Walk with me."

The tree was gnarled and huge, its knobbed and gored trunk giving it the impression of sagging under its own weight. The bark was thin and chipped, flaking off like dry skin. At its base, there was a gaping hole where the roots split.

Lutie buzzed up from the hole. "No guards," she said, settling her small self in the tangle of Kaye's hair.

"And this leads where?" Kaye was trying to control her trembling, trying not to let on just how not ready for this she was.

"Through to the kitchens," Roiben replied, inching his body, feet first, through the gaps in the tree. Finally, his head disappeared into the dark, strands of silver catching on the splintered bark. She heard a clatter as he dropped down to the floor.

Kaye pushed her boots against the entrance, feeling some of the softer wood give way, chipping off as she slid them in and pushed, burying her legs to the knees. Then, on her back, wriggling forward like a snake, she pushed herself through. It was a long drop, and she bit back a yelp as she landed.

The tunnel was hot and cloudy with steam. Beads of moisture dotted Roiben's face, and his hair looked damp and heavy when he combed it back with one hand. He cocked his head to the left, and she moved ahead of him through the billowing steam.

The kitchen was a huge room with a firepit in the centre of it and no visible ventilation system. Faeries scuttled around in the smoke with large pots, piles of skinned rats, little cakes, baskets of silver apples, and rolled casks of wine. The reek of blood assailed her. Blood stained the walls and the floor, boiled in the pots and dripped over the plates of raw meat. Roiben walked behind Kaye, his hand on the small of her back, pushing when he wanted them to move and clutching her coat to signal her to stop.

They crept into the room, staying close to the wall. A withered old faerie sat on a nearby stool, skinny legs dangling off the side, tongue sticking out of his mouth in concentration as he painted black apples a shiny, nail-varnish red. His white hair stuck up in wild tufts, and he periodically adjusted his small spectacles as they slipped down his nose.

Next to the apple-painter, a huge green man with small horns on his bald head and fangs protruding over a fat upper lip wielded a cleaver over a collection of oddly shaped animal corpses, hacking them into stew-size chunks. Tattoos of roses and thorns ran up both of the man's beefy arms.

Kaye crept as quietly as any time she had snuck in late to the house, as any time she'd left a store with full pockets. She concentrated on her feet, bowing her head slightly and walking slowly and quietly through the doorway.

Soon the narrow hallway sloped down and opened into a larger passageway, this one floored with greyish marble and studded with huge, carved pillars. The ceiling dripped with stalactites. Kaye could hear people up ahead, shoes clicking like beetles on the stone floor.

Roiben pushed them both against the back of the pillar. He drew his sword from the sheath and was holding it against his chest. She found the dagger he'd given her earlier and clenched the handle desperately.

But the footfalls turned down another corridor. Kaye let out a breath she didn't realise she'd been holding.

They crept along like that until they came to a set of black double doors.

"What's in there?" Kaye asked.

"Wine and the ageing thereof," he whispered back.

The room was all stone, stinking of yeast, casks lining the walls and glass bottles filled with infusions of various flowers. There were rose petals, violet petals, whole heads of marigolds, nettles floating like organic space ships, and other herbs she could not identify.

"What are those?" she whispered. There was no one in the room.

"Wormwood, yarrow, cowslip, gillyflowers, agrimony, fennel – "

"I bet you drink a lot of herbal tea," she said.

He did not smile as he directed her towards the smaller of the two doors in the room. She wondered if he even realised it was a joke.

"Laundry," he said.

The next room was filled with as much or more steam than the kitchens. It wafted up through small vents in the ceiling. In the room were several large tubs filled with soapy water. One pale woman with dark eyes was wringing out a white cloth while another was stirring the contents of a tub with a long crooked stick. A man with long arms and a hunched back was adding some granules to the mix, making the water hiss.

It was a small space, and Kaye cast a glance at Roiben. There was no way they could get through the room without anyone seeing them.

"Maigret," Roiben said, grinning as he opened his arms wide.

One of the laundry women looked up, her grin showing she was missing a tooth. "Our knight!" She limped over and gave him a highly ordinary hug. Her feet were hidden beneath the long skirts of her dress, and Kaye could not glimpse to see if there was something actually wrong with them. Across the room, the man and woman looked up from their duties and smiled too. "You're one I thought sure never to see again."

"I'm looking for a boy," Roiben said. "Human. With your new King."

The woman made a disgusted sound. "That one . . . King indeed! Yes, there's a boy about, but I can't tell you more than that. I've learned better than to draw the eye of Gentry."

Roiben smiled wryly. "And I as well."

"They're looking for you, you know."

He nodded. "I made a rather spectacular end to my service here."

The old laundress cackled and bid them farewell. Roiben opened a small door and they emerged into a hallway of shimmering mica.

"How do you know they won't tell anyone they saw us?"

"Maigret thinks she owes me a debt." He shrugged.

"Is something wrong with her feet?"

"She disappointed one of the Unseelie Gentry. He had iron shoes heated red-hot before he made her dance in them."

Kaye shuddered. "Does that have something to do with the debt she thinks she owes you?"

"Perhaps," he allowed.

"What about through there?"

"There's the library, the music room, the conservatory, and the chess room."

"Chess room?"

"Yes, chess was well loved by the Queen. They gamble with it like mortals gamble with cards. She once used it to win a consort, as I recall."

"Corny loves chess – he was on the chess team in high school."

"We must go through the library to get there." He hesitated.

"What's the matter?"

"We've seen no guards. Not at the entrance and not even here."

"What if that means we're just doing really, really well?"

"Of a surety, it means something."

The door to the library was mammoth and elegant, clearly different from the plainer doors in the lower chambers. It was dark wood, banded with copper, carved with a language she could not read. Roiben pushed the door, and it opened.

Bookshelves were arranged in a maze, so tall that it was impossible to see across the room to whatever exit there was. The shelves themselves were intricately carved with faces of gargoyles and other strange beasts, and there was the overwhelming scent of turned earth. Whenever Kaye looked in one direction, something seemed to shift in the corner of her eye. The books themselves were in such varied sizes that she wondered who read them all. As they walked, she tried to scan the titles, but they were all in strange languages.

As they turned a corner, she saw a shape slide between the shadows. It was slender and vaguely human.

"Roiben," she whispered.

"The keepers of secrets," he said, not looking

back. "They will tell no one of our passing."

Kaye shuddered. She wondered what was written in the tomes that lined the shelves of the library if the idea was to keep secrets. Were the shapes custodians or guardians or scribes?

As they came to a crossroads in the bookshelves, she saw another dark shape, this one with long, pale hair that started too high on its forehead and large, glittering black eyes. It slipped into the shadows as easily and soundlessly as the first one.

Kaye was very glad when they came to a small, oval door that opened easily to Roiben's touch.

Heavy draperies hung on the wall of the chess room. The entire floor was inlaid with black-and-white tiles, and five-foot pieces loomed on the edges of the room. Corny was sleeping on the floor, his body overlapping two chess squares.

"Cornelius?" Roiben knelt down and shook Corny by his shoulder.

He looked up. His eyes were vague and unfocused and he was a mass of bruises, but even worse was the satiated smile he turned up at them. His face looked aged somehow, and there was a tuft of white in his hair.

"Hello," he slurred, "you're Kaye's Robin."

Kaye dropped to her knees. "You're okay now," she said, more to herself than to him,

HOLLY BLACK

reverently smoothing back damp strands of hair. "You're going to be okay."

"Kaye," Roiben said tonelessly.

She turned. Nephamael was stepping into the room, from behind the draperies on the far wall. His hand stroked the marble mane of the black knight chessman.

"Greetings," Nephamael said. "You will pardon my humour if I say that you have been the proverbial thorn in my side."

"I rather think you owe me," Roiben said. "It was I that got you the crown."

"From that point of view, it's a shame that life is so often unfair, Rath Roiben Rye."

"No!" Kaye gasped. It couldn't be. Roiben had been so far away from the others when she'd used his name. She had barely been able to hear herself. He'd killed all the knights close by, all the ones that could have heard.

"No one else knows it," Nephamael said as though reading her thoughts. "I killed the hob who thought to ingratiate himself with me by giving it over."

"Spike," Kaye breathed. It wasn't a question.

"Rath Roiben Rye, by the power of your true name, I order you to never harm me, and to obey me both immediately and implicitly."

Roiben's intake of breath was sharp enough to mimic a scream.

Nephamael threw back his head and

laughed, hand still stroking the chess piece. "I further order that you shall not do yourself any harm, unless I specifically ask you to. And now, my newly made knight, seize the pixie."

Roiben turned to Kaye as Lutie screamed from her pocket. Kaye sprinted for the door, but he was far too quick. He grabbed her hair in a clump, jerking her head back, then just as suddenly let her go. After an amazed moment, Kaye dashed through the door.

"You may be well versed in following orders, but you are a novice at giving them," she heard Roiben say as she ran back into the maze of the library.

Before, she had simply followed Roiben through the winding bookshelves – now, she had no idea where she was going. She turned and turned and turned again, relieved that she didn't see any of the strange secret-keepers. Then, careening past a podium with a small stack of books piled on it, she turned into a dead end.

Lutie crawled out of her pocket and was buzzing around her. "What's to do, Kaye? What's to do?"

"Shhh," Kaye said. "Try to listen."

Kaye could hear her own breathing, could hear pages fluttering somewhere in the room, could hear what sounded like cloth dragging across the floor. No sounds of footsteps. No pursuit.

She tried to draw glamour around her, to colour her skin to be like the wall behind her. She felt the ripple of magic roll through her and looked down at her wood-coloured hand.

What were they going to do? Guilt and misery threatened to overwhelm her. She put her head between her legs and took a couple of deep breaths.

She had to get them free.

Which was absurd. She was only one pixie girl. She barely knew how to use glamour, barely knew how to use her own wings.

Clever. The word taunted her, the sum of all the things she ought to be and was not.

Think, Kaye. Think.

She took a deep breath. She'd solved the riddles. She'd gotten Roiben out of the court. She'd even more or less figured out how to use her glamour. She could do this.

"Let's go. Please – let's go," Lutie said, settling on Kaye's knee.

Kaye shook her head. "Lutie, there has to be something. If I just think."

They were all faeries. Okay, then she had to think like a human girl. She had to consider things she knew how to do. Lighter tricks. Shoplifting. And she especially had to think about the things that faeries didn't like.

Iron.

Kaye looked back at Lutie. "What would happen if I swallowed iron?"

Lutie shrugged. "You'd burn your mouth. You might die."

"What if I *poisoned* someone with iron?"

Lutie shifted uncomfortably on Kaye's knee, looking incredulous. "But there's no iron here!"

Kaye took a deep breath and let it out slowly. Her mind was racing ahead too fast, she had to slow down, calm down. There might be iron in the Unseelie Court, part of weapons, certainly, although she had no idea where any of that would be kept. It was all over outside here, everywhere.

She looked down at her body. What did she have that was from Ironside? Her T-shirt, knickers, boots . . . the green frock coat was only glamour, after all.

Kaye unlaced her boots quickly. There was definitely iron in them, obscured from directly touching her skin, but there nonetheless. She pulled them off her feet and looked them over. There was iron in the steel grommets, she could feel the warmth, buried under the black plastic coating. There were steel plates buried in the toe of the boots too, although they would be much too big to use unless she could somehow file them down. Kaye took the knife Roiben had handed her out of her frock-coat pocket and began to pry the soles off the boots. There, as the soles were ripped up and off, were exposed shoe tacks, shiny steel nails so small that that they could be swallowed without anyone the wiser.

Kaye took the knife in one hand, a boot in the other, and began digging them out.

Corny was awash in new emotions. He sat on the dirt floor of a massive palace beneath the earth. Courtiers played instruments, and Nephamael fed him fat globes of cloak-dark grapes. Around Corny were creatures, small and large, slaking their thirst, gambling with riddles and a game that involved hurling somewhat round stones.

The world shrank to those grapes. Nothing was better than brushing his mouth over those fingers, nothing sweeter than the burst of each black jewel in his mouth.

"I think you have entirely too much dignity. I command that you dance," Nephamael said to his new prisoner.

Below the dais, a small crowd gathered apart from their regular activities to watch Roiben dance.

The knight's body was a bow string loosed. His silvery hair streamed like a pennant, but his eyes seemed apart from his body, darting like those of an animal that would tear off its leg to be free of a trap. He did not falter, but his movements were sudden, his spirals desperate.

Corny did not want to pity him, so he looked away. A grape fell from the King's hand, but Corny was no longer careful.

The knight danced on as the Unseelie Gentry laughed and japed.

"Too easy. It will take too long to tire him. Whip him as he dances."

Three goblins stepped forward to do as he asked. Red lines opened along his chest and back.

Corny was very glad that Kaye wasn't here now.

"What task shall I set him to for his redemption in my court? I want to keep him. He's been a lucky talisman so far."

"Let him find us a wingless bird that can still fly."

"Find us a goat whose teats are filled with wine instead of milk."

"Yes, bring us a sweet goat like that."

"Boring, boring, boring," Nephamael said and leaned back in the throne. Looking down at Corny, he smiled a smile that was like sinking your teeth into cake.

"You missed a few baubles," he said teasingly. "Pick them up . . . with your teeth."

Corny looked away from Roiben, not having realised that his eyes had strayed. He did as he was told.

It was hardly a plan, really. Kaye had glamoured herself to look like Skillywidden, the only person she remembered well from the Unseelie Court that she could guess wouldn't be beside the throne. She did impersonations of the crone quietly in the hall, but Lutie was no help at all, laughing so hard that the little faerie was barely able to control her flying.

Then with the thin iron nails burning the inside of her cupped palm, she went in search of the main hall. It wasn't hard to find. Past the chess room, there were other doors, but only one stairway that led up.

The hall of the Unseelie Court was much as she remembered it and nearly as full tonight as it had been the last time. This time, coming as she did, from the centre of the palace, she came directly behind the raised dais. Roiben was dancing there, raw red lines open on his back. Nephamael sat on the ornate, wooden throne, iron circlet burning on his brow. She saw him drop a hand to caress Corny's hair.

She took a deep breath and stepped onto the dais, walking straight up to the redcap who was acting as wine steward, holding a silver-and-lizard-skin carafe of wine ready for refilling the new King's goblet.

"Eh, seamstress?" the man queried, giving her a grin that revealed sharp, yellow, overlapping teeth.

And then Lutie did exactly what she was supposed to do, buzzing past the man's face so that he snatched for her with one hand and didn't notice Kaye dropping iron nails into the wine. Reverse shoplifting. Easy. Much easier than slipping rats into her pockets.

"Skillywidden." Kaye turned to see Nephamael was speaking to her. "Come here, seamstress."

Kaye looked around; Lutie had managed to flutter off, but Kaye couldn't see her. Even though Kaye knew that was the better thing, the safer thing, she couldn't keep from being worried. There were already so many people hurt because of her. Kaye took a deep breath and walked to Nephamael, curtsying in what she hoped was a fair approximation of the seamstress.

"Ah," he said, gesturing in the direction of Roiben. "My new plaything. Strong, as you can see. Lovely, even. I need a costume for him. I think that I would like something in green. Perhaps the livery of a Seelie page? I think I would like that."

Kaye nodded, and when he looked towards Roiben again, she began to back away.

"A moment more," Nephamael said. Her heart beat wildly in her chest. "Come closer."

She stepped obediently forward.

Grinning wickedly, Nephamael sprang from his chair and grabbed her by one spindly shoulder. His expression was near enough to glee to make Kaye's stomach twist in fear. Magic surrounded her, ripping at her glamour.

She felt like she was being clawed apart. She knew she was shrieking but she couldn't help it, couldn't do anything as her glamour was rent. She fell to her knees, now in the shirt and underwear she had woken in, hair still stiff with brine.

There were loud gasps and shouts.

"Gag her," he said, "then tie her hands behind her back and give me the leash." One of his people came forward to do so.

Settling back on his throne, he gestured for more wine. Kaye held her breath, but he merely took the goblet and did not drink.

"Now this is an unexpected treat. A prop for my little games. Come here, Roiben."

Roiben paused, his body trembling with the aftershocks of exertion and violence. The red welts across his chest and back, some still bleeding, were horrible to see. He came forward to stand in front of Nephamael.

"Kneel."

Roiben sank to his knees with a small gasp of pain.

Nephamael reached into the folds of his cloak and brought out a dagger. It had a golden blade, and the handle was made of horn. He tossed it in front of Roiben, where it landed with a clatter.

"My command is this: When I say 'begin,' take the knife and cut the pixie until she dies. The game is whether you will kill her slowly, making her suffer prettily for my amusement as you stall for time . . . or cut her throat in one easy swipe. That would be the considerate thing to do. Ah," he sighed dramatically, lifting the goblet high above his head, "if only you could stop hoping."

Roiben's face went blank with shock.

She shivered. It was hard to take breaths with the gag in her mouth, and there was no way she could speak.

"Begin," Nephamael said, saluting with the goblet.

Roiben turned, his eyes wet, his jaw trembling. He took a breath, looking at the knife in his hands and then at Kaye. He closed his eyes, and she saw him making some terrible peace with himself, coming to some terrible decision.

She wanted to close her eyes, but she couldn't. Instead, she tried to meet Roiben's eyes, tried to plead with her expression, but he wouldn't look at her.

As she waited for the knife to decide its angle, she saw Nephamael lift the goblet to his mouth, tipping it back for a deep draught. For a moment, there was no reaction; he only wiped the edge of his lips with two fingers. Then he coughed, looking startled, looking wildly around the brugh. His eyes met hers. Nephamael dropped to his knees, scratching at his throat. He opened his mouth, perhaps to speak, perhaps to scream, but there was no sound.

Then her vision was blocked by Roiben, taking a trembling breath, the golden knife still in his hand. She remembered that no counterorder had been given. Roiben was still bound to the command.

She thrashed, side to side.

And she felt tiny fingers working at the loops of the gag.

Roiben's face was a mask of shock and horror as he watched his own hand lower the golden blade towards her skin.

Kaye took a series of deep breaths, preparing herself. When she felt the gag loosen, she spat out the cloth and stepped *into* the knife, whispering, "Rath Roiben Rye, stop. . . I command you to stop. . . I command you to . . ." She felt the knife bite into her arm as she spoke, heard his sob, before the thing dropped from his hand.

Then she sprang up, beating her wings hard. She rose easily into the overturned bowl of the ceiling, hovering for a moment. Lutie rose up beside her, fumbling with the rope tying her hands.

Then from one of the entrances, there was the stomping of knights, the sound of armour, and of bells. The Seelie Court had arrived.

15

"Better to reign in Hell, then to serve in Heav'n."

          – MILTON, *Paradise Lost (Book I)*

The knights stepped into the room first, all of them costumed in deep green armour that resembled the carapaces of insects. Next came a dozen ladies, each one dressed in a different-colour gown. Kaye noted Ethine was in soft gold. After the courtiers came the Queen, resplendent in a moon-pale gown, very like the one in Roiben's tapestry. Over it she wore a peacock-blue cape that swept the floor as she walked calmly towards the dais.

"Roiben," the Queen said. A hissing came from the Unseelie Court. A large creature stumbled forward, only to be quelled by an iron look from one of the knights.

Nephamael writhed on the dais still, his fingers scrabbling at his neck and chest. He

          HOLLY BLACK

seemed completely unaware of the arrival of his mistress.

Roiben looked at the Seelie Queen, and his eyes closed with an exhalation of breath that was so evocative of relief, Kaye felt herself fill with dread. There was something wrong with all this.

Around the neck of the Seelie Queen, a white pendant swung on a silver chain. Kaye stared at it as though it could hypnotise her. The Queen's eyes were on the dais, watching the self-made King of the Unseelie Court squirm.

"Nephamael was serving *you*!" The revelation was so shocking that she spoke it aloud before she had thought it all through. She dropped down to stand beside Roiben.

It seemed as though everything stopped with those words. Even the Queen froze.

Kaye stumbled on, looking at Roiben, willing him to believe. "Roiben, you had to serve Nicnevin and Nephamael had to serve the Seelie Queen. You had to. He couldn't disobey any more than you could."

The Queen made a gentle smile. "The pixie is correct after a fashion. If I had commanded him to stay by my side for all time, he could not have left it. But I had given no such command. Once gone, he could no longer hear my commands and so, did not heed them. I come here today to put things to rights."

The words seemed so reasonable, spoken by those lips. Kaye wanted to be mistaken, but the amulet still swung heavily around the Queen's neck.

"But I saw the amulet. Nephamael was holding it when he glamoured me to look human. He seemed to be drawing his power from it."

"You are mistaken, pixie, and you will be silent. There are more pressing matters at hand." The Seelie Queen's voice was firm, and several of her knights moved toward Kaye.

"Kaye . . ." Roiben said, shaking his head. "The amulet is hers. It has always been so."

Kaye turned to him, eyes flashing. "I'm not wrong!"

The crowd murmured at that. Kaye was not sure what outcome the Unseelie Court would be most pleased with; probably the one with the greatest bloodshed. She could not doubt that they were at least glad someone was insulting the Seelie Queen.

Roiben held up his hand. "I will hear her." His pronouncement brought some measure of silence to the court. Kaye marvelled at that. He was leaning against the throne with blood streaking his clothes, unarmed, and yet he still commanded enough respect that the crowd quietened for him.

He nodded to Kaye. "Speak."

She took a deep breath and when she

spoke, she made sure that it was loud enough for everyone to hear. "I guess it's pretty obvious now that I'm a pixie, but I've been disguised as a human for . . . well . . . for sixteen years. I managed to find the human girl that I was switched with. She was still in Silarial's court." Roiben gave Kaye a sharp look, but she hurried on.

"So that means someone in the Seelie Court switched me, even though I was living in Unseelie territory very close to Nicnevin's court. When I was a little girl, I had three faeries that watched over me. They were also from the Seelie Court.

"I moved to Philadelphia where I lived for a couple of years until he" – Kaye pointed to Nephamael – "showed up at one of my mother's shows. He took the guy we were living with aside, and a couple of minutes later, the guy tried to kill my mum. The next day we moved back here. A couple of days after that, my old faerie friends contacted me and said they needed me to play along with their plan.

"But they weren't powerful enough to suggest me to Nicnevin for the Tithe. Nephamael was. He was the one in charge. So how did Nephamael wind up in the middle of a Seelie plot? Because she ordered him. It's the only thing that makes any sense. The only reason he benefited was because Roiben stepped in. If Nicnevin hadn't died, Nephamael wouldn't have benefited at all, only Silarial. Even as things stood with him being king, she would have ruled the Unseelie Court through him."

"I will hear no more!" the Seelie Queen announced.

"You will," Roiben said, his voice rising with impatience and then falling once more. "You are ageless, Silarial, so bide with us a time. I would hear the rest of her tale."

Kaye spoke quickly, words rushing together as she tried to get it all out. "The amulet around her neck. That's what made me realise what was going on. Nephamael had it the night he brought me to be sacrificed. He used it to put a heavy glamour on me. It was her necklace, her glamour. They were going to let me be sacrificed, then reveal the trick and blame Nicnevin. And today, when we got here, Nephamael was waiting for us, but no one knew we were coming to find Corny but Silarial and her Court." At the mention of Corny's name, Kaye couldn't keep her gaze from flickering towards Corny. What she saw froze her tongue.

He had crept forward to where Nephamael's body writhed. A lock of hair had fallen across his face. There was a bruise on his cheek the colour of his grape-stained mouth. That reminded Kaye entirely too much of Janet's cold lips.

As though he could feel the heat of her stare,

Corny looked up. His eyes were anguished.

"Corny," Kaye said, taking a half step forward.

Still looking at her, Corny picked up the golden knife Roiben had dropped. The beginnings of a smirk were on his lips as he lifted it.

"No!" Kaye screamed, running towards Corny, frantic to stop him from stabbing himself.

The blade plunged into Nephamael's chest. Again and again, Corny stuck the body of the faerie knight, the knife making a sickeningly liquid sound with each thrust. Blood soaked Corny's trousers. A keening sound came from deep in his throat.

The courtiers, Seelie and Unseelie alike, watched in rapt fascination. None made a move to help as Kaye grabbed Corny's wrists and tried to wrestle him away from the body.

He was shaking, but when Kaye pulled him forward to embrace him, she realised it was because he was laughing. Laughing so hard that he was nearly choking.

"Look what you've done," the Seelie Queen said. It took Kaye a moment to realise she was talking to Corny and not about him.

A Seelie knight stepped forward and reached beneath his cloak. Kaye watched in horror as he brought out a long branch and smoothed it into a sickeningly familiar arrow. It was pointed right at her.

"Roiben, end this or I will end it for you," the Seelie Queen said. "I have been patient enough. It is long past time for you to return home."

Roiben's voice was not loud but it carried through the brugh as he walked to where Kaye was standing. "I am home, Lady. Now tell your man to put down his weapon, and I will allow you to leave the Unseelie Court unharmed."

A hush settled over the court.

Kaye stood in stunned silence. Nicnevin had used Roiben well, far better perhaps than she realised. She had kept him close to her. She had used him against the rest of the Unseelie Court. Kaye remembered how they had drawn back from him when he escorted her through the crowd. He was not one of them, it was true, but he was remote as a king.

No one challenged him.

The Queen's slim, perfect eyebrows lifted. "You dare?"

Roiben's sister took a step forward, but said nothing. Her eyes were pleading.

He looked around the court, and Kaye could see him take a breath. Then he spoke. "Hear me and know the compact I offer. The solitary fey have gained seven years of freedom, but seven years will pass in the blink of an eye. Bind yourselves to me now, Unseelie and Solitary alike, and I will give you all of Samhain. Freedom from dusk until dawn forevermore."

Kaye saw several Unseelie creatures haul themselves up onto the dais. They did not advance on the Seelie party, but their toothy grins were all malice.

The Queen stiffened. "I think, my knight, that you will find claiming a kingdom far easier than keeping one." With that she turned, her long peacock cloak sweeping a circular pattern in the dust of the floor. Her knights and courtiers turned as well. Only Ethine hesitated.

Roiben shook his head.

Silarial looked back and, spotting Ethine, opened her cloak. Roiben's sister let herself be embraced and drawn away with the rest of the Seelie Court. She never saw the cruel smile that played on the lips of the Seelie Queen nor the way her eyes met Roiben's over his sister's bent head.

As the last Seelie left the hall, Roiben, self-declared King of the Unseelie Court, nearly fell into his throne. Kaye tried to smile at him, but he was not looking at her. He was staring out across the brugh with eyes the colour of falling ash.

Corny had not stopped laughing.

The funeral parlour itself was small and Victorian. The furniture was ornate and dark wood. Even the wallpaper was sombre, maroon fleurs de lis in a raised fuzzy velvet. There were people from school there, people Kaye only vaguely remembered. Kenny,

Doughboy, Marcus, and Fatima were all there, sitting in a huddle, whispering to one another constantly, even when the preacher was speaking.

Corny held Kaye's hand through the whole funeral service, his fingers cold and sweaty and clasping hers hard enough to hurt. He didn't cry, even when she did, but he looked pale and washed out in the black suit he wore. Each time she saw the bluish bruise on his cheek, it looked more obscene.

Kaye's mother had been terrified, thinking that Kaye had died too . . . so terrified that she'd resolved to commute into the city instead of moving there. Even Kaye's grandmother was being nice. Ellen had dropped Kaye off at the funeral parlour that night and promised to pick her up again when she called. It was strange and kind of nice, but Kaye didn't want to get used to it.

Janet was laid out like a painting, all red curls and red lips. She looked beautiful – Ophelia surrounded by bouquets of flowers that only Roiben could name. But Kaye could smell the chemicals they'd injected into her, could smell the rotting meat of what was left, and she almost gagged when they went close. She couldn't, however, keep her hand from straying to the cold, oddly firm flesh of Janet's arm. Kaye dropped the gift she'd brought – a tube of blue,

HOLLY BLACK

glittery nail polish – into the coffin.

Corny kept his death grip on her hand as he stared at the body of his sister.

Afterwards, Kaye and Corny stood outside, waiting for his mother to finish saying good night to the relatives.

"Oh, I almost forgot," Corny said, his voice very quiet, "my mum stopped by the store before we got here. I had to go in for cigarettes." He reached into the inner pocket of his leather jacket and pulled out several straws with different-coloured stripes circling down their packaging. "A bouquet of Pixy Stix."

Kaye smiled. "I should be trying to cheer you up."

"You already did your white charger bit," he said. "Check it out . . . rip this sucker open and you get genuine pixie dust. Tastes like sour sugar."

She sniggered and so did he, a weird, desperate laugh that spiralled up into the night sky.

"What are you going to do now?" Kaye asked.

"I don't know. Shit, I still have to digest what I've already done."

"I know what you mean . . . but, you know none of it's your fault, right?"

"Except the part at the end with the knife?"

"Even that part. Maybe especially that part."

"Next time . . ."Corny said, eyes alight in a way that Kaye was relieved to see until she heard the soft words that followed. "Kaye, I will never be powerless again. Whatever it takes. Whatever."

"What do you mean?"

He just squeezed her hand tighter. After a few moments, he said, "So how about you?"

She shrugged. "Did I ever mention that I know how to make leaves into money?"

"Yeah?" he said, eyebrows raised. His mother came over with a few relatives, and Corny finally let go of Kaye to get in the car. Her hand was damp and hot, and when the breeze hit it, it felt like she was wearing her insides on the outside.

The last people had left the funeral parlour and they were locking up, so Kaye crossed the street to use the pay phone in front of the supermarket. She called her mother and then sat down on the kerb in front of a plastic horse that rocked back and forth if you fed quarters into it. The fluorescent lights and the organic smell of rotting vegetables and the tumble of plastic bags across the parking lot seemed so utterly normal to her that she felt disconnected from the events of two days before.

She hadn't seen Roiben. It wasn't like anything happened badly between them, it was just that she'd needed to take Corny home and he'd needed to stay and do whatever it was that new monarchs did. She didn't even really feel bad that she hadn't seen him. It was more the feeling of relief that you have when you know that something painful is coming, but you can avoid it for the moment. If she saw him, then she'd have to listen to whatever he really thought about the two of them being together now that he was King.

Looking at the plastic horse, she summoned her magic. A moment later it shook out its mane and leaped down from the metal suspension it was held in. As she watched, it galloped away into the night, plastic hooves clattering over the asphalt.

"There is something of yours I would like to return to you." Roiben's voice made her jump. How had he managed to get so close without her hearing? Still, she couldn't help smiling vapidly any more than she could help scolding herself for doing so.

"What?"

He leaned across the distance between them and caught her mouth with his own. Her eyes fluttered closed and her lips parted easily as she felt the kiss sizzling through her nerves, rendering her thoughts to smoke.

"Um . . ." Kaye stepped back, a little unsteadily. "Why does that belong to me?"

"That was the kiss I stole from you when you were enchanted," he said patiently.

"Oh . . . well, what if I didn't want it?"

"You don't?"

"No," she said, letting a grin spread across her face, hoping her mother would take her time on the drive over. "I'd like you to take it back again, please."

"I am your servant," the King of the Unseelie Court said, his lips a moment from her own. "Consider it done."

Set in medieval times, *The Raging Quiet* by Sherryl Jordan tells the story of Marnie and Raver each set apart from the community around them: Marnie because she is a new-comer having been brought to the seaside village by her new - and much older - husband; and Raver because he is the village lunatic.

The villagers are suspicious of any newcomer, and they are especially wary of Marnie when her husband dies suddenly. She causes more consternation when she befriends Raver, but Marnie discovers that he is not mad: he is deaf. She develops a rudimentary sign language to communicate with the young man. This seals her fate: the villagers see Raver responding calmly to her hand gestures, and they try Marnie for witchcraft.

Reading Sherryl Jordan's *The Raging Quiet* is like getting lost in an oil painting by one of the old Flemish masters. The immediacy of the experience is unnerving. The reader is taken back in time to a place where ignorance, bigotry and self-righteousness rule. The plot devel-ops with ever-increasing suspense. The book's characters are so vivid they could live here and now.

And the central message - though embedded in a historical setting - has undiminished relevance today: Marnie and Raver are singled out because they are different.